G000164468

THE NUDER DETECTIVE

DEDICATION

In of the process of writing these books, I've learned that I am all initiation, character and story, and not grammar or polish. My long-suffering editor has taught me much and kept me focused, and in return I've taught her – or at least provided much opportunity to practice – patience. ***Anita Kuehnel-Atar****, I am so glad you stuck by me. Thank you – my readers don't know how lucky they ar.*

PS: I deliberately left off the last 'e' to emphasize that the last word on any editing argument is mine, therefore I am responsible for any remaining errors. Anita has been diligent, but I am not always obedient

Contents

HISTORY

York, England – February 1588

Jack put his weight against the sturdy oak door and carefully kicked the warped frame at its base. It made a soft groan, but it took a second, firmer kick to force the door fully closed. The damp cold of winter distorted the wood so badly that sometimes it jammed completely, and he had to let customers into his small bar through the back entrance. His toes hurt from the harsh contact with the wood and he wished for the thousandth time that he had had money for sturdy boots, or at least enough to hire a carpenter.

Jack hobbled towards the bar. As he passed the only two occupied tables, he asked if either of his patrons would take some more food or drink. Neither accepted. *Miserly buggers*, thought Jack. Nursing a couple of mugs of ale and a bit of goose pie for a whole evening. They were barely covering the cost of the coal for the fire – the warmth from which they were both happily soaking up – let alone what it cost to run the stove. But then he laughed to himself at the thought of the goose pie. Yesterday it was pheasant, and the day prior it was duck. As everyone knew, there hadn't been birds like that around since the middle of fall. The pie was rabbit, as it always was. It was his little joke. A different name for the same pie every night of the week. For rabbit pie. The laugh kicked off a racking cough. His wet-lung was worse this year by far and he wondered what would become of the Inn when he passed along. He had inherited it from his brother, who passed a decade ago. *Not too many more winters for me*, he thought.

At the bar stood Sam, the coach driver. Sam drove his coach up and down the King's Highway and could choose to direct his passengers to any one of several establishments lining the busy route. Jack always made sure that Sam got a few free mugs of ale. *An investment is what it was*, thought Jack. Sam also took advantage of the free lodging Jack offered in the small loft space above the small stable, nestled behind the inn. It cost nothing but brought in much needed trade to *The Barley Boy*. It was worth even some free pie. Sam was a tall, skinny lad of perhaps 23 years. Quiet, with a bit of a surly tone on occasion, if Jack was honest, but alright really. Kept to himself and caused no real trouble for Jack or the guard.

Jack refilled Sam's small tankard and was wiping the bar with a half-clean cloth when the door banged open. A whoosh of icy cold air carried in a little snow and a lot of dank fumes from the mine's slag heap situated across the pasture. Neil and Digger stomped in, stamping their boots and smashing their frozen hands together. Neil turned and quickly forced the door back into its hole, creating a sharp vacuum that drew a waft of coal smoke inward from the fireplace. A slight haze settled across things. The two town guards moved swiftly across and stood in front of the glowing embers to warm up. *A bit of luck,* thought Jack. Digger and Neil hadn't dropped in for a few nights, and Jack had worried they might have been lured down the road permanently. Davis the Bright, who ran the *Black Bear*, had a new girl — his cousin's daughter, apparently — who was serving the food wearing a low-cut blouse. Davis's morals had plunged with the neckline, and his revenues had increased at the expense of other establishments, including Sam's.

"Evening, Neil. Digger. Nippy out, is it?"

"Oh man! It's frostier than your old mother's tongue, Jack!" Digger was a wit and not at all wrong about Ma, thought Jack. Jack himself was considered old having seen 37 summers, but his Ma was a legend in these parts, having seen 14 more. Only Thackery the Elder had seen more than that, as far as anyone could remember. And then only two more.

"I've got some nice goose pie and a fresh barrel of ale open if you two are hungry. As usual, a half-penny for a bite and a tankard of the finest winter ale. You'll have to make do with looking at me, mind, not some young pretty like Davis has at *The Black Bear*."

"Hot pie is what we came in for, Jack. That and a break by the fire. Your ugly mug won't spoil our appetite none, eh, Digger?" Neil laughed at his own crack, and the two men shuffled over in a friendly enough fashion. Sam nodded respectfully to them and moved off, taking a seat in the back corner. Jack filled two mugs and put them in front of the guardsmen, then hustled off to get the pie.

In the small kitchen, Jack took two wooden plates off the wash rack and picked up a thick cloth, which he used to pull the hot metal pie tin off the stove. He carefully carried the tin and the plates out to the bar. As he took the lid off the tin, the gamey smell of rabbit filled the room. This was one of Jack's little tricks, hoping his other two stingy customers might be lured into a second slice by the aroma, but neither took the bait. Jack served a generous slice to each of the guardsmen and returned the tin to the kitchen. The leftovers would be his own dinner and breakfast as – aside from Sam – he had no overnight customers to feed, and it would spoil by the next night. Earlier this evening, Sam had brought a young girl and her uncle down the highway, but they had hustled off to The Nightingale. John, its proprietor, was apparently related to them both and money stays in the family, as it should. Jack sighed and nodded at the wisdom.

It was late, and Jack was considering the problem of the fire: You didn't want to waste costly coal feeding the fire if your customers weren't in a spending mood, but you didn't want to get a reputation of being inhospitable, either. The whole point was that customers should want to come in and feel welcome and warm, but Jack had money troubles to balance, too. He'd just decided he would add two more cups of coal, when the door burst open yet again and a terrified, sweaty face peered inside, out of breath and gaping – like a trout just tickled from the stream.

"Are the guardsmen here?" the newcomer wheezed, frantically looking about. He spotted them quickly. "Oh, thank goodness. There you are. This is the third place I've looked for you. You've no idea. Really." He rushed in and all but ran up to the bar. He left the door agape behind him, spilling more of Jack's precious heat into the cold, windy night.

"Slow down, mister! Slow down," commanded Neil. "You look like the devil's after you."

"I actually think it is," puffed the man. "The Brownwick Devil. It's here. I saw it. The cursed beast has struck again. Killed everyone at The Nightingale, including my Millie, it has." Saying this out loud seemed to bring home the enormity of the statement, and his head drooped, and his fists curled. He fell silent. Jack listened intently to all of this as he dragged his sore bones back over to the door as quickly as he could, before he would have to commit to a full scoop of coal. He shut out the cold once more with an annoyed thump. As he came back, he noticed that the stranger was covered in blood.

Digger was asking, "What is God's name is The Brownwick Devil and why are you all covered in blood? Is someone in trouble?"

"Is that you, Mr Gordon?" Sam came out from the corner of the bar where he had been sitting quietly, looking shocked. "I didn't rightly recognize you all flustered and bloodied like that. Who's dead? Your niece? Impossible. I just saw her a couple of hours ago, bright as summer." Sam crossed himself quickly as the man nodded, and his eye took on an involuntary tic. "The Devil has never been down this far south. Not that I've heard anyway," finished Sam. Jack then realized that this harried stranger was one of the two passengers Sam had ferried down from Doncaster earlier in the day.

"Jack, you keep Mr Gordon here, and don't let him leave. Digger, you and I are going up to the Nightingale to see what's what." They pulled their swords to the front of their bodies, ready to unsheathe at a moment's notice, and wrapped their cloaks tightly around themselves as protection from the cold – and perhaps from witches, devils or who knew what else. The snow had picked up, forming an opaque curtain across the exit, and the wind buffeted them as they headed back out into the night.

"Here, let me give you a shot of Kingsmead," said Jack, reaching behind the cupboard that stood at the far back of the bar, where no one could reach over to help themselves whenever he popped through to fetch food from the kitchen. He pulled out a small round bottle. Kingsmead was distilled from potatoes and pears and was potent as hell's breath. Jack had been nursing this last bottle since the tinker's last run through town and was unsure when he might see another. Looking at the terror in the eyes of the man in front of him, he felt he could give out one small dram. An act of charity.

A small voice with a slight Welsh motif asked, "What's The Brownwick Devil then?" One of the stingy customers crept over and put his tankard on the bar and signaled Jack for a refill. A good story in the offing was worth another drink. Jack jumped right to it and, with a gesture to the other miser, also talked him into one.

"I heard of the Devil f'years," offered Sam, crossing himself once more as he stepped back up to the bar. "I don't never talk about him. Well, at least not when its dark out, I don't."

"I only heard of him last night myself," said Mr Gordon, as he took a swig of the Kingsmead. His eyes bulged and he coughed and spluttered, but soon steadied, fortified by the alcohol. "Millie's my sister's girl and we share a house over near Doncaster. A small village called Pinkly Brow. Well, Millie's been mixing too friendly with the boys at Holt Farm and got diddled into the family way, if you get my drift. Anyway, my three sisters have all had awful luck with their young'ens. If I count correctly, they've lost four between them in the early weeks of carrying, and two more have been born as still as stone. Millie was the only baby to make it between the lot of them, but she has – *had* – the spirit of seven people. That's likely why she was with baby. We was worried Millie might have the same issue with bairns as our generation, so I said I would take her into Brownwick to see a real doctor. Not that we don't trust Martha Goodhands, our healer. We set off right early and it took most of the day to get to town. Millie on our old ass Nel, and me on foot.

"It was late when we walked into the Royal Oak Inn and the bar was full and noisy. Good, we thought, as there were plenty of people to ask where we could find ourselves a good physician. There was a group of professional-looking folk up near the gaming table and I made my way over and explained what we needed. It was the strangest thing: it was as if I had slapped the Queen herself. The room fell silent and people looked from me to Millie, and a space opened up around her. People muttered prayers and crossed themselves.

"When I asked what was wrong, no one would tell me – at least at first. Eventually we learned from an older gent — who used to be a minstrel by trade — that something had been preying on pregnant women for the past four or five years. Women were found dead. Mutilated. Their babies either taken or butchered at the scene and...not complete. Parts missing. Terrible business. Really, terrible business. After a few such deaths, people became protective and pregnant women were guarded, day and night. But it made no difference; the attacker seemed to be a ghost. Either slipping unnoticed past the guards — who didn't hear what must have been a loud and painful slaughter — or in a few cases, murdering the guards as well.

"At first, some whispered that it was some witch's doings, because of the missing body parts. It was thought the babies were taken for spell making and the like. But then sometimes the damage done to these poor wretches was not all with knives or cutting. There were bite marks on some, and so many thought the attacker was a vampire. And from what I saw tonight, that might be closer to the truth. But the name that eventually stuck was The Brownwick Devil, after the town where the murders are done."

Sam spoke up. "Nowadays, if someone gets knocked up, they quietly slip away to other towns, returning once their baby is a few months old. Anyone who hasn't fled to safety has been murdered within days or at most weeks of the knowledge about their state getting around."

Mr Gordon nodded along with Sam's words. "As you can imagine, we were part skeptical and part terrified. No one would let us stay in their Inn for fear of their own lives. Even the Guard turned us away. We spent a cold night hiding in a small stable on the town's outskirts. That's when young Sam here came through with his coach, and that's where we left our donkey behind. We've travelled as far and fast as we could, and I must admit that an hour ago, the whole episode seemed like a silly, silly dream. Millie and I even laughed about it." He took another swig but seemed lost in thought, his face severely pained.

"But what happened tonight?" prompted Jack.

"Well. The Nightingale was quiet, with no more than a dozen people including Millie, my brother, and me. My brother had often told me – bragged, really — about an old priest's hole — that's a hidden nook, by the way — in his Inn. It's hidden behind the fireplace and has been used by smugglers, criminals, and sometimes as a sanctuary over generations, if the stories are to be believed. Anyway, he took me back to the pantry to see where the hidden entrance is, and he showed me how to get inside. I climbed through a curtain of cobwebs into this dusty, hot space, but I could see through to the saloon right enough, as there is a crack in the chimney wall.

"My brother went back to serve a customer. I was watching, when I suddenly felt strange. I could see that the people in the room did, too. The sensation got worse, and it was as if we were in the thrall of some demon. Rooted to the spot. Alert but terrified of something. The door opened, and the Devil walked in. He wore a black hood, which masked his face, and his clothes were covered in a long, thick apron. The sort a butcher might wear. He was tall and skinny, and where his skin showed, pale and white. He walked about like he owned the place, stalking from person to person. In each case he stood in front of them and looked them directly in the eyes, demanding their attention. They stood and did nothing as, one by one, he slit their throats and they dropped where they'd stood.

"I couldn't move, either. Not because I was scared, which I was. Completely terrified, of course. But I would have run to save Millie and my brother had I been able, even at my own peril. I swear I would have. It was like I'd forgotten how to make my body move. I was stuck. I felt sure that if I could only move a little, then I would break free of whatever held me. But I just couldn't. Now they're all dead." He paused, and a tear melted out of his left eye and caught in the lashes before bursting onto his cheek.

"He saved Millie for last. That's how I know it was a vampire. It looked her in the eye, like the others. She was petrified. She knew it had come for her baby, even though it was only a month or two in the womb. It cut her throat and...drank from the cut. Like they say a vampire might. They say a vampire can hold you in its thrall and you can't resist. So, it must be a vampire. Right? What else could it be? Millie collapsed in a heap and it followed her down to the ground. It didn't gorge on her: It just wanted a taste. But then it used a short, curved knife on her tummy...." His face distorted in disgust, then resolved into sadness.

"It left quickly, when it had what it came for. It must have followed us down here and picked its moment. I couldn't move for a long time, but eventually I came back to my senses proper. I climbed out of the hole, and ran out to the saloon, but it was too late for Millie. Too late for all of them. The floor all coppery and slick with blood and mess. I ran and ran, looking for help. Looking for guardsmen. I saw no sign of the Devil. The vampire." He fell silent, weeping in full flood now. Events of the night coming back with the story and overwhelming him completely.

Jack put more coal on the fire and offered free rabbit pie to the room, but no one had an appetite. *Never mind,* thought Jack. Many will come here tomorrow to hear this story, and the news about the tales told at The Barley Boy would spread. *I'll bake fresh bread tomorrow*, thought Jack, guiltily.

It wasn't long before Neil returned, confirming the bizarre story. He took Mr Gordon away to answer questions from the Sheriff, who had been urgently raised from his bed. The remaining members of the stunned group reviewed the story in whispered voices – embellishments already creeping into this first retelling of the night's dark tale – before nervously stepping out into the dark, bitter night. Jack locked the doors and pushed a large table across each before dousing the lanterns. He didn't sleep a wink.

At dawn he came down, emptied the ashes from the grate, set a fire in the fireplace and the kitchen stove. The cold seemed more sinister today, and Jack hoped that the warmth of the fire would ward off any bad luck. Jack got the dough kneaded and into the oven before moving the tables away from the doors. There were no customers at that hour, of course. He methodically went around the room and collected up the plates and tankards from the night before, chastising himself for leaving them out overnight. *Rats and mice,* he thought. He fetched his broom and, starting from the front door, he swept the floor clean. When he reached the back corner, he saw something down beneath the seat. He bent over stiffly, picked up a cloth, and held it out to inspect it properly. It was black material, but sticky with dark red congealed blood. He held it up and upon seeing it was a black hood, threw it to the floor with a fright and stepped quickly away, his hand clutching feebly at his throat and his heart beating out of his chest. He calmed himself as best he could as he thought back to the previous night, and where the customers had sat. He saw each of their faces and remembered who had been sitting back here, in the dark corner. With a start, he turned at the sound of a soft footstep behind him in the kitchen doorway.

"I'd love some rabbit pie, Jack," smiled Sam. Sam had a small curved knife in his left hand.

PROLOGUE

Vancouver, Canada – September 2018

[ETHAN] — I was very glad that there was no breeze in the room. The tiny towel draped artistically across my lap — barely covering my embarrassingly perky manhood — didn't have a square inch to spare if it was going to protect my last molecules of dignity. Although, some might say that ship had long since sailed. Six female art students and their round-spectacled professor comprised seven-eighths of the neat semi-circle of people who sat studying me intently from behind their easels. My long-time crush, childhood sweetheart, and — for the last six weeks – girlfriend, Marcy, sat smugly in the eighth spot. They were all sketching the tiny towel — and my otherwise naked form — in charcoal.

Marcy and I had managed two quick dalliances years ago, but each was at the wrong time in our lives. When this third opportunity came up, the phrase we had both latched on to was that we were "all in." Total commitment. Marcy had quit her job as a Vancouver Police Department detective and joined me in our new life. This included using my largely inherited — but partly self-made — billions of dollars to help people in trouble. At the same time, we were throwing ourselves into a passionate exploration of each other emotionally, sexually and, occasionally, kinkily. I'll get back to that last part in a second.

Before she joined me, I had been a hobbyist private detective under the guise of the Ethan Booker (that's me) Detective Agency. Now that we have become a team, the agency needs a new name. Marcy lovingly called me 'The Nude Detective' because of the aforementioned kink, which is the reason I am sprawled here as an unwitting model for the fourth-year art class of our local university.

They say kinks are established when we are in our formative years, but recent studies are proving this is less true than researchers had previously thought. For the past two decades, academics and others fishing in the growing lake of data provided by the internet are catching some surprising facts. Some research confirms that many kinksters can trace back their first kinky memories to their early teens, but a growing percentage actually discovered it in their twenties, thirties, or even later. However, in my case, the stereotype was very true. In what I jokingly refer to now as "The Bremmer Case," at an innocent 12 years old, I ended up in a potentially very embarrassing situation. I was trying to get revenge on Bill Bremmer; a bully and Marcy's older brother. He had planted beer on me when his father was about to catch him in possession of it. I had been chastised in front of friends — including Marcy — but worse, my dad, who I still have on a pedestal as one was enjoying my torment to no end, this being our most daring game so far, and little E really wanted to 'level up' to higher and higher intensities.

The chime that came from a timer application on the professor's smart phone stopped my breath. For a second, I was emotionally transported back to that sandy beach and felt those exquisite tingles of fear and dread wrack my body. I snapped back to the present and quivered as Marcy dragged out the moment, a huge twinkle in her eye, memories of her abused childhood banished – for a while at least.

Marcy's Dad had been an alcoholic, abusive to the family in general, and to his wife in particular. As can tragically happen in such circumstances, Marcy's Mom bore the abuse in order to protect her children, but couldn't cope with it, in turn being hard on the three kids. Billy, the eldest and the object of my rage almost two decades earlier, had turned out to be a bad teen as a result. He grew into an angry — if somewhat more contained — human as a man. He was a bully first and foremost, and bullies are often scared of things that are more powerful than themselves, and he was afraid of the legal if not moral consequences of his own abusive nature. He had learned to rein it in, but it festered deep down.

By contrast, Max — the youngest — had become a hero. He joined the Canadian Forces to escape home and served his country with a tour in the Middle East. In a story too long to relay here, we had been told he had died in a roadside IED explosion in Afghanistan, and we had buried him with tearful honours. In reality, Max had secretly worked undercover for years against the evil of ISIL. He came back to us when, by a bizarre coincidence, he heard Marcy was in trouble with the aforementioned assassins. He had been my best friend and had returned from the dead. For Marcy, his resurrection was of course more emotional and magical still.

Marcy had escaped the home abuse to a different force, namely the Vancouver Police Department. She was driven and became notorious for her fierceness at resolving cases of abuse, which eventually set her in the path of the traffickers and their assassins.

When circumstances brought Marcy and me back together in the last month and a half, my secret kink came out, thanks to Gwen. Gwen is a wonderfully complex person and a newer, but great, friend. 'Gwen is my neighbour, renting the only other suite on my floor in the Booker building, which I own and use as my home and base of business operations. She is also a local business owner, namely of the best coffee shop in Yaletown — if not Vancouver — called The Crazy Bean. She is a retired sexual sciences professor and a qualified 'Kink Aware' counsellor. She is amazingly fun, and is our personal mentor in our kink-awakening. Her knowledge of the recently published data on BDSM, combined with her wisdom and sexual orientation, lead Marcy and me to nickname her "Lesbian Yoda." Before Marcy and I had reunited this third time, Gwen had discovered me naked, and had started this whole 'torture Ethan' rampage by trapping me into this game, which then Marcy had later inherited.

Marcy had been surprised to find out about my small kink and was very — almost overly — supportive. Hence my need to hold my breath for these long moments as she toyed with me. But she also had needed to untangle her own feelings towards abuse, and her kindling curiosity towards BDSM. Gwen had explained the primary differences between the two, and backed it up with data and research; this had truly resonated with Marcy. Education trumps stigma and allows us to make informed decisions for, or against, a controversial topic. In my opinion, she is still wrangling with and resolving these complex emotions, even if perhaps not at this tortuous moment. When I ask her which of the differences between abuse and BDSM resonated most in her own situation, Marcy repeated Gwen's explanation. The abused spend their time dreading the abuser's appearance, hate their time with them, and when the abuser leaves they are relieved but also terrified of the next occurrence. By comparison, in our few brief BDSM experiments, Marcy finds herself excited at the prospect, thrilled during the event, carries a little misplaced guilt she is now quick to get over — which is reducing each time — and is soon preoccupied with planning a repeat performance. I would point out that in our circumstances, she is the dominant and I am the 'submissive,' but that seems moot as I feel exactly the same as she does. We have a lot of awesome regular sex, and these additional kinky adventures add thrilling variety and a feeling of 'embracing the taboo'. We both feel we are 'getting one over on the world' in general, rather than feeling that Marcy is taking advantage of me.

She finished dangling me out in limbo land, and gave me my next, dreaded instruction.

"Ethan, could you stand up, and step away from the stool?" I nervously complied. *Still hold that breath, as well as the towel, firmly*.

"OK, I'm thinking a *Statue of David* pose. One hand up on your shoulder, the other to the side of your hip, hand forward." Gulp... this towel won't go around my waist, so it will drop to the floor. *Holy crap*!

"Oh, and I want to draw the muscles of your back and the curve of your hips. Would you mind facing away from us, towards the wall?" *Phew!*

*

Twenty minutes later, I was dressed and we were in the Aston Martin, happily yet vigorously reliving each step of this latest, risqué adventure. The soft leather scent of the car's interior enveloped us and was intoxicating as we laughed at my aroused embarrassment. Marcy fired up the engine with a roar, and then let the engine settle back to the purposeful burble of 450 horses, while we sat and let the oil warm and circulate properly.

I checked my email and saw some very sad news. Frank 'The Cap' had died. Frank is a Vancouver character figure, who is — or was, I guess — regularly found sipping coffee and reading the sports columns at The Bean. Frank had been ill for years, gradually losing his memory and other marbles and, sadly, he totally forgot to wake up yesterday morning. His daily help brought in his breakfast and found him still in his bed with Elvis — big eyed and sad — lying across his feet. Elvis is a lovable mutt who I have become very attached to over the years. Frank and I were never close; we were just acquainted through the love of good coffee and his pooch. I had no deep grieving to do over Frank's death but was nonetheless sad to see the passing of a man who no doubt had great stories from an adventurous life.

The sad message had come from Gwen who knows of my fondness for Elvis, and which she, too, shares. While, technically, the Booker Building has a 'no pet' policy, she was asking respectfully if we could make an exception and take in Elvis, rather than send him to the pound. No brainer. I said "yes" but replied that we were "co-parenting." Gwen would probably have ignored me had I said "no," and snuck Elvis in anyway. Thirty minutes later, Elvis was licking my face but there was a sadness about him. One of the benefits of having more money than you know what to do with is flying by private jet, so we called and delayed our impending departure to the Caribbean and hung out with the hound dog for an extra couple of hours.

Our trip was overdue and much needed. The battle for survival with the assassins left us emotionally and physically drained, on top of which, we had not had time to really be a 'normal' couple. The human traffickers — a morally corrupt family from Mississippi — were scary enough, but were mild compared to the assassins, who truly terrified us. They dispatched the Kingsman, whose attacks had narrowly missed us twice. Such escapes were virtually unheard of for this group of assassins. The shadowy group had later surrounded us in a hotel in Baton Rouge and were hours away from ending us, when their clients lost all of their money and, therefore, their ability to pay the contract on our heads. We learnt from a hacker acquaintance who called herself SkyLox — who had just drained the traffickers' coffers, thereby saving our asses — that the assassins were a group known only as *Chiyome*. Little was known about them, but in 15th century Japan, there had been a group of female and child ninjas led by a woman known as Chiyome, and it was thought that this group was inspired by that history. We really don't know if that is true.

We had promised ourselves that we would have a few weeks together when our hair-raising fight for safety was over, and so we were now flying off in our

Learjet to a private resort on a private island, as 'normal' couples do. Our bags were already packed and on the plane, so we eventually left Elvis with Gwen and had one of my team run us out to Vancouver airport's private terminal.

Vancouver isn't hot for many weeks of the year, but today it was. The sun beat off the tarmac and chased us across the ramp, and we skittered up the short steps, passing gratefully into air-conditioned splendor. The plane had six captain's chairs, a small bathroom at the rear, and boasted a full bar-cum-food-preparation area. A petite, pretty hostess waited dutifully. Her round face and Asian features were a picture of professionalism as she helped us politely into our seats and explained the pilot was just making a few last-minute checks. She handed Marcy a Prosecco — cool enough that water condensed down the outside — and a gin and tonic, in a tall glass, to me.

As she pulled up and closed the door, something struck me as being off; it took me a while to place it. Normally the door closes and peace descends because the door shuts out the noise of the engines, which are typically already spooled up when we board. Today the engines were silent. I was just processing why that might be as the hostess reached over the bar and pulled out a small pistol. Nothing *Dirty Harry* about it – in fact, it was almost cute – but as it could undoubtedly poke big enough holes in us to ruin our day, Marcy and I froze. At least physically. I could sense Marcy's brain doing the mental cop-gymnastics, looking for ways to control and defeat the impending situation.

Before we could speak, let alone make a move, the cockpit door opened and a slender Japanese woman emerged. She was dressed like a pilot, but I suspected she had no intention of flying us anywhere. Marcy and I were in the two seats facing forward, and the 'pilot' sat casually – as if she were part of our holiday party – in the rear-facing seat in front of me. The hostess stood behind the other chair, gun pointed at Marcy. We faced each other in silence. After a long pause, the newcomer spoke, in a flawless Canadian accent.

"Mr Booker. Ms Stone. My sincere apologies for this short delay to your trip. We can have you on your way shortly. I have a small favour to ask of you both, but first, I am sure you are wondering who I am. My name is Mochizuki Chiyome." My stomach turned to jelly. Chiyome is the name of the group of assassins that have done their best to kill Marcy and me for the past few weeks.

1: SELFLESS

[CHIYOME] — I sat in the silent cockpit, a space typically alive with lights and noise when occupied; but right now, it was stuffy, dark, and silent. The heat from the tarmac warmed through the skin of the aircraft, and without the engines, the external air-conditioning alone could not deal with the heat. Booker and Stone were late, which caused me complications. As a matter of course, the Kanbo automatically track my whereabouts in case I need assistance. I had arranged for Cho and I to be transiting through Vancouver at coincidently the same time as the resourceful private eye and his mate were due to take off from the city's private south terminal. I had planned to meet them in secret. My contact within Immigration Canada had kept the actual crew occupied until we notified them we were finished. Patience is essential in my life, but the clock had almost run out. I would have had to leave soon or explain my delay. I saw the pair walking across the ramp towards us, and signaled Cho to take position. I listened through the door as they came aboard, and when Cho had them at bay, I entered the main cabin.

As I sat opposite Booker, appraising him, I set my mental clock for ten minutes, by which time we would leave, with or without my answer. I was not at peace with this decision to approach them, but my options were severely limited.

Although I am the Sensei, the leader of the Kanbo – *The Group* – it is also my Mistress. The Kanbo has existed through successive generations for over three hundred years, and our rules have changed little. The Sensei is the undisputed ruler, until succeeded by one that she – and only she – names. She must choose one of the Jonin, our second rank. If we were a company, the five Jonin might be the executive committee, running the various aspects of the Kanbo; reporting to the Jonin are the Chunin, who would be middle management; and at the base of our pyramid are the Genin. The Genin are our soldiers, assassins, and spies. In other words, our workforce.

Although the Kanbo exist in layers like a company, the similarity ends abruptly. We are more military than corporate; more a secret sect than an army. The layers in the Kanbo are made up of strong horizontal communities, but the vertical connection between the layers barely exists at all. The people farther down in the pyramid never question orders from above, and those orders come down through a very small number of chosen leaders. Aside from the one vertical contact a subgroup might have, they would know no one else. The Genin are further broken up into cells of four women or, in some cases, women and children. Secrecy is paramount in all matters. However, despite the apparent disconnectedness, the information about our business of spying, espionage, sabotage, or assassination flows rapidly and freely, especially now in this world of high speed, encrypted communications and databases. And control is absolute. However, as much as I control the Kanbo, to use an old adage, the tail also wags the dog; I, too, am bound. Trapped by rigid protocols.

The Kanbo are led by me, but our strength comes from the ability of my five Jonin. All are powerful leaders in either government or businesses, but within our organization we take the names of animals. This has been a tradition for three hundred years, serving to remind us of the past, as well as to preserve secrecy. We never use real names in person or in correspondence, despite the heavy encryption we employ today.

To those of us raised in a western culture, where animals feature very little in our religion, it is difficult to understand the power the fox has in Japanese folklore. But westerners would recognize that animals have grown to personify a trait: As lazy as a pig; as wise as an owl; cunning as a fox. I have never met any of these animals, yet imbue them with those qualities. You might think the position of a fox might equate to our head of intelligence, due to the association of cunning, but remember this is a Japanese interpretation.

Kitsune, or the fox, was a servant or messenger from the god Inari, and Inari was prolific and had an association with rice. Three hundred years ago, rice was fundamental to society. Within the Kanbo, our fox is the head of both logistics and communication. Kitsune is responsible for ensuring anything we need is available where ever it is needed, and we can communicate securely and effectively.

In the west, we think of the butterfly – *choho* – as a pretty, dainty, 'flibbity' thing, but in Japan it is associated to souls of the living dead. Spirits of the dead take the shape of a butterfly on their journey to eternal life. In my Kanbo, Choho is the primary contact for our business of assassination. Butterflies run our front office. They are the people you talk to if you want to employ our services. If we agree to take you on as a customer, your enemy becomes the 'living dead' – dead, but they just don't know it yet.

Tatsu, the dragon, brings great power, success, and wisdom. In the Kanbo, Tatsu controls our finances, our overall business and investments, and is the primary advisor on how we grow our business. To be successful, we need to infiltrate key positions in government agencies for intelligence, access, forged documents, and so on.

Tanuki – or racoon dog – is mischievous and jolly; a master of disguise. Tanuki heads our network of assassins who succeed with their almost superhuman skill and get close enough to guarantee this success through stealth.

Kame, the turtle, is associated with wisdom and luck, but also protection and longevity. Kame leads our internal security, ensuring all of us are safe, our organization is not infiltrated or investigated, and that all behave appropriately to their respective roles.

I am the sensei but do not have an animal name. I am Chiyome Mochizuki, and *Chiyome* is our brand. If you live in a world where assassination is visible to you, to hear my name should fill you with dread.

My thoughts returned to the conversation we were about to have, which may achieve nothing or may start the most dangerous path of action I had been on since I ascended to Sensei. Booker was unreadable but, physically, he was like a coiled spring. Stone sat at ease, but her mind whirled like a propeller, perhaps fast enough to drive the plane. I took the step I had dreaded, onto the path of danger.

"Firstly, my sole intention today is to talk to you, not harm you in any way. Should you attack us, Cho will kill first you, Marcy, then you, Ethan. It would be so fast you would arrive at your maker's door for judgment together. If I had wanted to harm you, it could have happened many times from your time in Baton Rouge to the art class you attended a few hours ago. So, as I think it would be regrettable to harm either of you at this point, I ask you, as much as possible, to rest easy and relax. This can be short and simple.

"Secondly, as I said, I am going to ask a favour of you. I imagine that you are aware of what I am capable of, given my purpose in life. You may feel that what I am going to request from you seems more like an order, backed by the threat of death. I wish to assure you this is not the case. My request is personal to me – not a demand of my organization – and should you choose to help, it will be me that will be in your debt. The only person who knows we met is Cho, and she will not be party to the rest of our conversation." I reached out and laid two pairs of police-issue handcuffs on the small table between us. "If you agree to hear me out, I will ask you to handcuff yourselves to your chairs, then Cho will leave us to talk, all three of us unarmed. This is a precaution to protect you, not me. Should you decide to turn to violence, you will die needlessly, and that is something I would regret. However, should you choose not to hear me out, Cho and I will leave quickly, and you can be on your way. Now, time is short and again I apologize for the imposition, but I need an answer. What will it be?"

Ethan turned to Marcy and a look passed between them. She nodded, he reached over and passed her a pair of cuffs, and they both restrained themselves to a seat arm, tacitly indicating I should continue. Cho pocketed her gun, lowered the plane door, stepped out, and then closed it behind her.

"Thank you," I said, with more sincerity than they could realize. The first step accomplished.

"Ironically, I am about to trust you with my life and the safety of my organization. We can all think of reasons you would not be blamed for enjoying having me killed and my clan dismantled. I am gambling on your virtuous nature. As much as you believe that I represent a dishonourable profession, which from most perspectives is perfectly true, we see ourselves as following a code of honour and complex rules that have existed for four centuries."

"If you harm Marcy, I will do all in my power to kill you," interrupted Booker.

"I believe you would, and at the same time I think you appreciate how hard I am working to keep you both safe today. I am trusting everything I am that you will respect that effort, while I risk everything to get back the most important thing in my world. My daughter is missing, and I wish to hire you to get her back."

"We have witnessed your capabilities first-hand at locating people. Why would you need us?" Marcy was astute and not shy.

"My organization is powerful, yes, but constrained by an agreement. An alliance between guilds has existed since 1826, and to my knowledge has never been overtly breached. *Chiyome*, my guild, operate solely in North America. Other sister guilds occupy other geographies. To those who are aware of us at all, we are perceived as having intercontinental reach, but the truth is we collaborate as a collective and essentially contract out activities to each other. It is forbidden for one guild to operate in another's territory. Breaching that rule means war, with the guilds unifying against the trespasser and destroying them completely, replacing them with a new, if immature, organization. My personal code, which will be alien to you, is my organization comes before all else, including my daughter. At the same time, however, my daughter is everything to me. I am trapped between finding my daughter and destroying the people I lead by breaking my code, which would in turn lead to my daughter's demise. Out of rational, logical options, I have chosen to trust an enemy – you – in the distant hope I can resolve my personal conflict. By meeting with you without the knowledge of my Kanbo, my daughter and I are dead if you reveal that fact to the wrong person. By asking you to fly to London to find my daughter, I am essentially proposing operating in another's realm, which would sign the death warrant for my clan and my daughter.

"When I first spoke, I committed to leaving you a free choice. You will be thinking, I don't doubt, that if you refuse me now, then I will simply kill you to protect myself and my people. You will find I am a woman bound by rules and my word, admittedly except for the safety of my daughter, but you cannot know that yet. If you will take on this burden I ask of you, you will be putting yourself in harm's way, for me. For the sake of my daughter, and a personal favour to me. I could offer you money, and will pay it if you ask, but we both know money is irrelevant to us all." I took out a small box and laid it on the table with formal precision, as I would in a tea ceremony.

"This box has a timer and will open in five minutes. Inside is the key to the handcuffs and a note. The note contains simply a site on the dark web, which stores all of the information I can give you to find Moy Lei. Or destroy us all. I won't press you for an answer. I leave it to you to do what you feel is right for you. We are unlikely to see each other again. We part now, with no debt or allegiance, no obligation, and – on my part, at least – no ill will."

I was about to leave when Ethan stopped me with a question. "When? When did she go missing?"

"Three days ago," I answered truthfully. He said nothing but seemed to look deep into my soul, trying to solve some other question.

I stood and left the plane without another word. Had I spoken more, I would have begged. I crossed the tarmac and boarded a helicopter, which was already winding up its rotors. We lifted off before my seatbelt was locked, leaving all of my hope and my life in the hands of the two strangers below; two strangers I had tried to kill twice in recent weeks.

Irony is a bitch, and I pray her sister Karma has a sense of humour and a forgiving nature.

of the greatest men I know. Marcy is two years older than me, and back then I was already unknowingly in love with her. And in a little lust.

At any age, when we are duped into being someone else's patsy in a situation that is hideously unfair, we can be consumed by righteous indignation. At 12, I was overflowing with it, and so full of rage. I had been shamed and grounded, while the other teens took a boat out to a nearby island to party away from the grown-ups. Later that evening, I snuck away from my room and, leaving my clothes on the beach to keep them dry, skinny dipped my way over to the island to exact my righteous revenge.

I was hiding, naked and seconds away from discovery by two older girls who were oblivious to my presence, as they were in the middle of an experimental and very intimate act. Had they discovered me, they would have teased me mercilessly at best, and at worst, beaten the snot out of me. The lasting impact of this narrow escape is that I get aroused when I am trapped in a situation where I am naked and someone else has the power to expose me. So, the kinky game Marcy and I have begun to play in these precious last six weeks is that every time we solve some detective-type puzzle, I have to pay a forfeit. I have agreed to give Marcy control over me, to the extent that she can devise and place me in such a situation. She has proven incredibly creative and a terrific teaser, and today's art adventure would be a great example.

My current predicament was her creation. It followed our recent take-down of an international gang of human traffickers, while at the same time fending off a secretive group of global assassins. I should point out that my normal 'detecting' is typically limited to finding lost dogs or defeating small-time hoodlums. That last case got a little out of hand. Today, I had to give Marcy control, according to our game, and Marcy had ordered me to pose as a male model. Having made a generous donation to the professor's faculty, she was allowed to participate and choose the poses that I have to strike.

We were booked for an hour, and so far, we have changed the pose every 12 minutes. I had started off with a towel and tiny man-thong for the first two poses, and the latter was removed for the third pose. On the fourth pose, the small towel was exchanged for a tiny towel, and she positioned me reclining on a small stool, with my hands behind my head, so that I was left to pray to the gods of gravity, imploring them to be gentle and preserve my already whittled pride. I was counting the seconds until the fifth and final pose. Would she strip me off completely in front of seven strangers — who were oblivious to our kinky game — or would she let me off the hook? As always in such perilous situations, I was conflicted. Big Ethan, terribly embarrassed and blushing in a way that the blacks, greys, and whites of a charcoal sketch could never do justice; little Ethan, treacherously eager, aroused, and keen to take things further, seemed intent on dislodging the towel. My wonderful partner

2: THE SKITTLES SOLUTION

[MARCY] — "Well that was different!" Ethan looked as calm and casual as his comment, but his armour of bravado didn't fool me. I don't think he intended his forced relaxation to do anything other than calm my racing heart. It is really hard to sit opposite someone who had, by proxy, tried to kill you — and had succeeded in killing two RCMP officers of our acquaintance — without attempting to gouge out their eyes. Only Cho's gun had kept me in check before the application of the handcuffs. With my free hand, I pulled out my phone and one-handedly typed "we might be bugged" and showed this to Ethan, who nodded his agreement.

"So, to summarize," I continued, mimicking his fake-casual tone, "we can fly off to our holiday in the sun and forget this happened, or we can betray her, which will get those bastards all killed and maybe us, too; or, we can risk our lives and likely die attempting to save someone who may not want to be found, to please a monster who would then offer us a favour we would never want to collect. Is that about it?"

"I think you nailed it."

"I'm not sure I feel much for the daughter of a leader of a clan of assassins, who might be a cold-blooded killer herself. And I'm not sure I like the middle option at all: Even if we take Chiyome at her word and she would not attack if we betrayed her confidence, the whole war it would apparently trigger would inevitably blow back to us. And it won't make the world a better place, as the vacuum would fill quickly, and perhaps with people who didn't follow these apparent rules she talks about." At this point the box popped open, and I retrieved the key and released us. We both looked at the note, and it was as Chiyome had said.

"I agree totally," said Ethan, gingerly. I was beginning to know him well enough to know he was about to say something challenging.

"I'm leaning hard towards option one: we go to the beach and to hell with them all. But, let me just throw this out for giggles: in Baton Rouge, we both agree she could have killed us several times over, right?" He didn't wait for an answer. "Yet apparently, when SkyLox drained the Toussaints' accounts, and they were no longer in a position to pay for our assassination, she chose to kill Seth, and not us. That's been eating at me. Why do that?" The Toussaint brothers, Landon and Seth, and their witch of a mother, Destiny, were the traffickers who hired Chiyome to kill me when I busted up the Vancouver chapter of their human slavery operation.

"Maybe that is their business practice, or part of their bizarre rule set. Maybe she was planning to ask us this favour and spared us for her own purposes. Oh, that's why you asked about the date the daughter –Moy Lei was it? – went missing. Chiyome spared us and ditched the customer before the daughter was taken."

"Exactly. She could have been lying, but my gut says this time she wasn't. She doesn't seem to have much to gain by being untruthful in this situation. If we find out she is screwing with us, we can destroy her and her outfit."

I sighed heavily, my eyes rolling sarcastically to the ceiling. "Fuck it! the Stone-Booker Detective Agency is taking the case, isn't it? Shit, did I get dumber when I hitched up with you?"

"Hey, I think you mean the Booker-Stone Agency, honey..."

We spent ten minutes recounting and poking at what we knew, when the pilots arrived full of apologies. We said nothing of our adventure or the cause of their distraction, but we had them change the flight plans and fuel loading for London. In this plane, it meant a pitstop in Reykjavik, Iceland, for fuel, but that was better than delaying in order to switch to a longer-range aircraft. Ethan pulled out his laptop and let Kelsie Kobe know we had decided to holiday in London. He explained he had a call from an old friend who had asked him to look at something personal and sensitive, and he was treating it a little like a case. Kelsie was Ethan's — correction, I must get used to saying 'our' — head of operations at the agency. She is incredibly efficient and dedicated, and a whiz with logistics, planning, and operations; she is equally brilliant at leveraging the technology her tech-savant sister Darcy Fullerton creates for both us and various military organizations. I realized his story was the barest twist of the truth, which reminded me why I liked Ethan. Always as straightforward as he can be. Kelsie would automatically deploy people and technology resources in support of a case, and I could imagine the wheels were already turning before she even finished reading his encrypted email.

As the plane taxied out to take off, Ethan activated his TOR browser, which is like a regular browser but encrypted and masks the user's identity and location, making it ideal for dipping into the very dangerous world of the dark web. He typed in the address from the note in the box, a series of three-digit numbers separated by periods, and a white screen appeared, containing a single file and nothing more. Ethan copied it to his computer, into a special folder Darcy had designed for him that efficiently scanned the file with every known cyber-defence tool, and created a virtual container that would block any malicious attempt by the file to attack his laptop or anything connected to it.

When the folder bar had cycled from red to amber to green, signifying it was safe to proceed, Ethan opened the file, which turned out to be a two-page document. The document repeated what Chiyome had told us and contained a short biography on Moy Lei and included some photographs, her height, and other vital statistics including – bizarrely – her allergy to peanuts. Lastly, it contained details on her disappearance and reasons for thinking she may be in London.

There wasn't actually much on the disappearance; like Chiyome, Moy Lei was tracked everywhere. She had stepped into a limo — which was later found abandoned in a tunnel — to go to a party. A search found no trace of the occupants. On going to bed that evening, Chiyome found a note in her jewelry box that read, "Moy Lei is in London, and out of your reach. Do nothing if you wish her to stay alive." Not much of a clue, and questionable veracity. But to back it up, and probably another damning fact against Chiyome and her people if we chose to share it with the authorities, she indicated that a rule for one sect travelling to another sect's jurisdiction is that they must notify them in advance. They must check in within 24 hours of arrival with a member of the appropriate caste of the host region. And apparently Chiyome had learned through an 'illegal' spy that Moy Lei had in fact checked in and registered on arrival. The final paragraph was illuminating: It was a personal note from Chiyome to us. It explained, with some earnestness, that although Moy Lei was aware of her mother's 'business,' she was not considered to be involved. She was considered *setsudan sa reta shimai* – a 'disconnected sister; not an active participant, just guilty by association. It seems her mother went to pains to keep her daughter's hands as clean as possible. As far as we were concerned, they were still pretty bloody, but it explained why the European sect would accept her on their soil.

*

We conferenced with Kelsie from 42,000 feet. The subject was how to locate someone in London when all we know about them is that they are female, five feet six inches tall, 25-years old, Asian, and had a peanut allergy. And, their name. As a biproduct of the agency, Kelsie has a number of automated-database searches preset and ready for major countries and cities, including London and the rest of the UK: The Electoral Roll, which is the UK citizenship database; White and Yellow pages; 411; and all other public databases were searched in our first five minutes of the call. Kelsie could also access social media and a slew of private marketing databases that track and sell our online browsing and shopping activity. No joy.

Some of the gadgets we use at the agency are tiny cameras disguised as items you see on the typical street. Some can attach to lamp posts or road signs and monitor passing activity. You can preload them with images and they can do facial recognition on the fly, and signal home-base if they get a hit. We can and have blanketed many city blocks with discrete coverage when trying to locate individuals. Covering a city like London is another matter, and we don't have that scale of devices available. But the technology gave me an idea.

"Kelsie, am I right in recalling that London is saturated with cameras for traffic and crime control? Do we have a way to access them?" We all knew that this was illegal, and probably a line we would not cross.

"I don't have access to that today, but I could assign a team to locate a way in if you ask me too." *Willing, but signaling she would feel uncomfortable doing so,* I judged. She continued, "We know a hacker who I am sure could get us in there."

"Hmm, let's leave that on the back burner for now. What else?" said Ethan.

"I might be able to get us access," I said. "Not by hacking in but by going 'old-school'; I know a guy. Nigel Potter. He was seconded from the Metropolitan Police to the VPD and we did a couple of cases together in 2016. He owes me a favour. I could at least ask."

I called the number I had for Nigel while we were over Manchester, already in the descent to Gatwick Airport. The local time was 7.30 am. We didn't think calling earlier would win us any favours. Nigel's life partner Philip answered after a couple of rings, sounding distinctly groggy. I apologized for the early call, and he denied I had woken him — the way most people do — even though he had clearly not been awake long. Philip explained that Nigel had left on a job before 6 am, and never took his personal cell to work when undercover. He offered to text Nigel my number on his covert phone and I got the call back just 6000 feet lower now over Birmingham.

Nigel was working undercover at Kempton Park, a horse-racing track to the south-west of London. Normally Kempton hosted races around an oval track, but today a section of the venue was set aside for an international show-jumping tourney. We did the "hellos" and I was genuinely warmed to hear his voice. Nigel was pretty open about the fact he was investigating a betting scam. He was posing as a judge's assistant, a role that gave him access to pretty much anywhere he wanted. In turn, I was open about having left the force and that I was doing some freelance investigation; attempting to track down a probable criminal who had fled to London.

I asked him how he would feel about misusing the Met's computer network to aid our cause. He acknowledged the favour was owed and he would help us as much as he felt that he could, but he would be somewhat limited. He would not grant us direct access but, if I was prepared to join him at Kempton, he would do the searches himself from his laptop. Depending on what he found, he would consider how far he would go in breaching his code of ethics by sharing confidential data. In return, and to maintain his cover, he asked me to come alone and dressed as a trainer so that I would "blend in nicely."

We landed a short while later and Ethan and I split up; to divide and conquer, so to speak. He went to meet Ian Po and the small team he led that Kelsie had dispatched. I had spent a little time with Ian as part of our operation in Mississippi and he was a fantastically funny and likeable family man. We had already begun to become friends, which seems to be common with the people Ethan tends to employ. Ian and his team would land two hours later than us and set up a mobile-support centre in a rented truck. A drone capability would be installed; and anything we might want for field operations such as clothing, burner phones, transport, or fake identities could be produced from this mobile command post at short notice.

Last, but not least, one of the four protection teams we employed had flown in, and they would rent separate vehicles, bring or pick up surveillance equipment, acquire weapons, and always be close by in case we needed support. While Ethan was busy with all of that, I went in search of an equestrian store, as I had an outfit to acquire.

I rented a burnt-orange Range Rover *Evoke* convertible and set up my cell phone with Google Maps on the dashboard. I was en route to an exclusive equestrian store just to the north of Woking, Surrey, within 40 minutes of our brief customs and immigration inspection. This store didn't take me far from a direct route to Kempton. In light traffic it would have been a 45-minute drive, but with it being rush hour, the M25 motorway that circles London was a zoo, and it took me nearly twice that to make the trip.

Veniserum is a store which occupied a quarter acre of a small country estate and sold Italian Equestrian attire and tack to wealthy patrons. I'm comfortable on a horse and even had some time in the saddle riding English style instead of the Western style more common in Vancouver. What I was not as comfortable with was the staff's pleasant yet aloof – if not quite arrogant – mannerism. Few can out-aloof the British upper class, but throw in some Italian airs and you are pushing my barely ironed, blue-collar limits. I went in with the beginnings of a bad attitude, which I recognized at some level as based on my personal prejudices. At least it was the inappropriately mocking and amused kind of bad attitude, not the grumpy kind. It helped that, thanks to Ethan's wealth, I could buy the store 50 times over, but I still felt totally unsettled discussing my needs with the perfectly dressed, mid-fifties, bespectacled fellow who had graciously offered to help me in a way which felt like I was bothering him. Somehow, he managed to look down on me despite being nearly six inches shorter in stature.

I gazed around the Aladdin's cave of tack and equestrian garments. Racks of saddles, stirrups, bridles, halters, reins, bits, harnesses, martingales, and breastplates; boots, jodhpurs, jackets and hard hats. All polished and sparkling, the smell of leather filling the room. I could smell the polish from the rows of red oak cabinets and display cases, too. I felt like a little girl in a candy store for a second, but then I looked back at the haughty store assistant who succeeded in making me feel like a little girl in front of a slightly disappointed teacher.

I put my discomfort aside and soon emerged from the changing rooms with snug cream jodhpurs, riding boots that just crested my knee, a white blouse, and black jacket. Once approved, by me and the store assistant, the outfit was whisked away from me among a storm of tape measures and tailor's chalk to be fitted. I wasn't asked if I wanted this additional service; it was more about them wanting their brand to look perfect on the wearer. The first hat I tried sat nicely on my head once I'd tied my hair in a ponytail, and so I had 15 minutes to kill while the tailor did his thing. I browsed the shelves, recalling what most of the tack was for, lost in memories. I was interrupted by a polite cough and turned to find my personal assistant next to me.

"I assume Miss will be requiring a crop?" he asked politely, nodding at the stand in front of me that was bristling with riding crops. I had been day-dreaming of Ethan, tied tightly over a leather chair, his leg and arm muscles straining against ropes and his gorgeous naked butt pulled tight. I blushed and panicked.

"Err... yes. I do, but I haven't put much thought into it," I said truthfully, blushing like a lunatic.

"What sort of mount will Miss be riding?" he asked, genuinely and helpfully, and continued, "And what sort of activities did you have in mind?"

I squeezed my eyes shut, holding back the fit of giggles that threatened to burst out of my mouth. I thought about it. And thought about it. Trying to get serious, was I really ready to take a crop to that nice arse? A different flashback washed over me, one where Mom had used a belt on my little brother Max. My embarrassed panic was replaced by a gut-wrenching-panic reaching out to me from childhood. As I had done countless times back then, and many more times as a cop when a bad case triggered a near panic attack, I checked my breathing, and slowed down and practised a moment of mindfulness. *Be in the here and now, not in the painful 'then.'* I got my balance back and smiled; the past cannot hurt me anymore

"Actually, I'm not sure I am comfortable using a crop on my stallion. He's already very amenable and responsive to my commands. I was thinking something more for show. You know, to complete the outfit."

"I totally understand, Miss. Catherine Walters would be proud." At my puzzled look, he rushed to fill in the blanks and cover my embarrassment about my ignorance. "Ah, Catherine 'Skittles' Walters was said to have popularized the crop as an elegant riding accessory in the 1860s. Essentially, we can choose something that matches your style and feels comfortable. I recommend the 30-inch Darling in black, with a leather loop for your wrist and an expanded tress or popper at the tip. Stiff, stylish, and sharp. And at the same time, if your mount doesn't respond to your thigh and seat commands quickly enough, a quick flick on his hind quarters will bring him into line smartly." I lost it and cracked up in fits of giggles. Much to my helper's annoyance.

Eight minutes later, I left, dressed in flattering riding attire – which made me look totally hot, I might add – and a Darling crop for Ethan's training tucked into my right boot. Ethan's butt cheeks might sting from its use, but my cheeks were the sorest they have been for a decade from the giggling. I liked the 'Skittles Solution.' I wonder if Catherine 'Skittles' Walters also had a kinkier side. I found myself looking forward to teasing Ethan with it for show for now, and perhaps one day using it for more than a fashion accessory.

In no time, I was at Kempton, bumping across a grass field that doubled as a parking lot. I was ushered into a line of parked cars by a slightly pimply-faced youth in a luminous safety jacket. I left the top down and headed for the judge's entrance, but glanced back to check the car was parked and locked. I caught the youth appraising my outfit and quickly looking at his sneakers when he realized he was spotted. *Yes*, I thought, *Ethan would like this ensemble.*

Nigel had left a pass for me at the gate, which I collected simply by providing the fake name he had me using. The volunteer giving out the accreditation lanyards pointed me towards a row of trailers, specifically the seventh from the end. I inhaled the scents of hay, leather, and horses — both their pleasant aromas and the less pleasant waste smells — and enjoyed for a minute the sights of a busy venue getting ready for an under-eighteen gymkhana event. The PA system was being tested by a man with a heavy Cockney accent, reminding me of Sir Michael Caine. Crews were making final adjustments to the fences with the judges, measuring each carefully, and the concession stands were warming up and filling the air with sweet smells. Most of all, I savoured the faces of the teenage contenders readying themselves mentally, and admired their coaches' commitment to guiding them carefully towards the fulfilment of dreams.

I tapped firmly on the trailer door and it opened with a squeak. Nigel's smiling face appeared, followed quickly by the rest of him, and he drew me into a genuine hug. I couldn't say Nigel and I had become like a brother and sister during his short loan from the London police force to Vancouver's police department, but we had become firm friends. He fell into that category of person whom you have only known a short time, but it feels like you have many decades — if not lifetimes — of history. Old bones and all that. Nigel was one of those to me, as I was also to him. I know this because one night, while we were maudlin and drunk after failing to convict someone whom we had just hours earlier watched walk away while giving us the finger, we told each other. Several times. Drunkenly.

Nigel was a bear of a man, very tall, and a little overweight. Very little of the weight was flab; instead, he was encased in muscle, but not the gym-bunny 'defined' kind. I always thought of a rhino, and wondered why his parents called him Nigel instead of Goliath or Sasquatch. Not the perfect build for undercover work, as he was hard to forget, but he did surprisingly well nonetheless.

"God, you're a sight for sore eyes, Marce. Come in and have a cup of tea. I don't have long, but let's catch up while I do this search for you." I followed him into the cramped space, where his laptop was already set up and connected to the police network. He plugged the thumb drive I gave him into the slot and uploaded the few pictures we had of Moy Lei — who we had renamed 'Target One' to preserve her anonymity — and started a facial-recognition search. While the doughnut spun in circles on the screen, signifying the software was busy, Nigel brought me up to speed on Phil and his news, and I gave him an abridged version of my recent activities.

I told him about the death of the Toussaint gang, but not the full role we played, and said that we were following up on the gang of assassins they had sicked on us, mostly to see if we were still a target. I thought this would inspire him to help more than he already was. I positioned Moy Lei as someone who might have information about the assassins but was not a person of interest herself.

I talked rather glowingly about Ethan. I realized, with a bit of surprise, that Nigel was the first person I had told about him. I let a small part of the little girl in me surface as I babbled about him and enjoyed Nigel grinning back at me. I didn't mention our kinkier adventures or Ethan's billions, although the former was on my mind.

The computer let out a quiet but happy chime, indicating that it had completed the search and had some positive hits. Nigel pulled the computer around so he could pick through the findings. I had never noticed when Nigel was in Vancouver, but he bit his top lip when he concentrated. I fought down the urge to tease him about it, as I didn't want to distract him. He pushed numerous keys and, after five minutes, he printed out two pages and handed them to me.

"Here you go, love. Nothing about her at all in the system in terms of contact with authorities, tax records, or anything similar, but there are about 90 hits from facial recognition that have a high probability of being a match over the last two weeks. The system deletes anything older. There are many one-offs, but there are two sets of closely related hits. One group ranges from two weeks to three days ago and are clustered about The Hays Galleria and Tooley Street near London Bridge. The second cluster is more recent, including one this morning, in Durham in Northern England. I've printed the clusters out for you. Needless to say, if anyone finds these printouts, I am out of a job at best, and in jail at worst.

"Now, I have to get to work, but if you and Ethan are in town for a few days, Phil and I would love to cook for you. Or at least buy you a pint. I am intrigued to meet the man who can lock down Marcy Stone."

We hugged and I promised to get back in touch, and that we would be the one treating them, given his selfless supply of information. I called Ethan from my encrypted cell as I walked back to the car, and he answered after a couple of rings. I filled him in on our lead. I heard him tapping on a keyboard, and he confirmed he was looking at maps and travel options. We both wanted to get up to Durham while the trail was hot. As I waited, I heard the whine of a helicopter engine spooling up and noticed a small helipad set away from the horses, which was presumably used for VIP transport or medivac purposes. I told Ethan about it, and pretty quickly we had a plan to rent a helicopter and he would come and get me. I went back to the car and retrieved my bags from the 'boot' and went over to the parking volunteer who had checked out my wiggle on arrival. He blushed and preened a little when I asked him if he would hold my keys and give them to one of Ethan's team, who would come for the car in a couple of hours.

I spent an hour walking around the grounds and watching preparations, then made my way across to the helipad. A short while later, I heard a distant thumping, which grew into a dark blue Eurocopter that dropped low after clearing some taller trees at the far end of the course, eased down to the big white H on the ground, and settled lightly on its skids. I had almost dismissed this aircraft as Ethan's, but when the pilot took off his helmet it was him smiling, just like the parking volunteer had earlier. Ethan approved of my outfit, clearly. And I had totally forgotten Ethan was an accomplished pilot. I love my man. I hopped into the front seat, rubbed his thigh, kissed his lips hello, and then pulled on a helmet and seatbelt. Ethan got clearance and we were airborne minutes later heading northeast, keeping low to stay under Heathrow Airport's busy approach lanes.

"OK?" Ethan's voice came into my headset surrounded by the hum of the muted engine noise. "I like that outfit. I might be developing a new kink," – he winked at me. I pulled my Skittle crop from my boot and flicked his thigh lightly.

"Eyes on the road, mister. No distracted flying!" I commanded, in an awful imitation of a posh English accent. I was rewarded by Ethan unconsciously squirming in his seat.

3: BOKU-YŌKAI

[ETHAN] — Marcy looked great in her riding outfit, and her scent filled the cockpit. Neither of us had time to shower, and to her natural musk she had added the smell of leather and hay. Yummy. After the hasty take-off, she realized she was hot, so she had unbuckled for a moment to remove the riding jacket and sat next to me in a tightly fitted, white blouse. She gazed happily out of the window at the patchwork countryside flowing under us like a lazy river. Marcy takes care of her figure and is a dedicated exercise nut. She runs, swims, and does cross fit, plus a twice-weekly gym visit for unarmed combat. Her interests lately were box-fit and judo. She is taut in all the right places and has well defined, natural muscles as opposed to body-builder definition. I'm no expert on bra or cup sizes, but her slightly-smaller-than-medium breasts amply filled the slightly clingy blouse perfectly, especially as the seatbelt and jodhpurs combo pulled it tight across her flat tummy.

As a pilot, my licence is current for Eurocopter 130s, but I was not familiar with this exact configuration. Once we left the busy London airspace, I managed to get everything organized. I had the autopilot engaged and a route programmed in that would ease us around towns and villages and take us to Teeside Airport to refuel. The 130 cruises at about 150 mph, and the route was a shade less than three hundred miles, so flight time was a couple of hours. We actually had enough fuel to get us all the way to Durham, but we would arrive with virtually empty tanks, and we didn't know what we would need on arrival. Kelsie had sent along Ian Po, her second-in-command, to be our on-the-ground command-post leader. I left him and his team fitting out the truck, with a plan to follow us north as soon as possible. Ian was arranging landing permits in Durham, a car for us, and accommodation.

We touched down at Teeside 90 minutes later next to the fuel tender, and stepped out to stretch while the ground crew refuelled the aircraft. Marcy and I both visited the 'loo,' grabbed some coffee and snacks from the FBO lounge, then met back outside in the shade of a hanger. I put my coffee on a low wall and we hugged, and she wriggled in tight. I let my hands drop and check out the curves of her new pants, and in return got a playful kick in the shin from her shiny new boots. We broke apart and studied the printouts Nigel had supplied, as we finished our coffee. The pages contained dots on a map, each with an address, rather than the faces caught by the camera. Most of the recent sightings of Moy Lei, if it was her, were just north of the main area around the River Weir.

We called Ian from my phone and I put us on loudspeaker so that Marcy could hear. Before takeoff, Marcy had taken pictures of the printout with her phone and sent them to Kelsie for analysis, and Ian had been working on the data as he raced up in a car, ahead of the truck that would follow more slowly.

"The area where the sightings are clustered," he began, "are in one of the least busy areas of the city, but it still has two hotels, over thirty Airbnb accommodations, and who knows how many other places she might be staying within a half-mile radius. Durham is a university city, so housing is dense, and letting and subletting are plentiful. We brought forty of our street-cam detectors with us, and I have someone plotting where we can place them for best effect when they get up there in…" he paused, obviously consulting his watch, "four and a half hours. I'm a little ahead of them." The way he said that made me suspect a traffic law or two were being more than a little bent.

"We've booked you into a hotel, which is actually a six-hundred-year-old castle. It is a little out of town, but it has a landing pad, which they use for weddings and VIP visitors. Permits are filed and the hotel staff are expecting you within the hour. An Audi rental will be waiting for you, but you might want to take a taxi. Parking is apparently difficult in the area of the sightings."

"We'll grab the taxi. I brought fresh clothes along for us both, and we will shower and change, so can you have a taxi there for 90 minutes from now," I replied, wondering if I should add another 30 to explore Marcy's outfit further.

We took off and headed north. I had our 'castle' programmed into the GPS and it appeared to lie to the east of the city. Moy Lei's cluster of sightings were slightly north of the centre, and I had added that as a waypoint on our route, too. When Durham was in sight, I circled off slightly to the west so we could run in west to east, overfly the area to get oriented, and then drop onto the castle grounds to land.

The city was beautiful. Built on a series of steep hills, it boasted a Romanesque cathedral in the centre, adjacent to a Norman period Castle. As if this wasn't enough, a tall, arching, railway viaduct framed one side of the city, and the River Weir meandered in a lazy loop demanding several other bridge spans in a small space. I slowed us right down for the overflight, we took in as many details as we could, and we discussed if it could be possible Moy Lei was just 800 feet below us and how we could find her. Three minutes later, we touched down on a grass pad behind the castle, and staff came out to carry our cases as the engines spun down. We hopped out and I offered the porter our one bag containing our clothes and toiletries. He was dressed in period costume, as were all of the staff. We had been bound for sunnier climes than Durham so we had nothing really warm to wear with us. The weather seemed to sense our predicament and the heavens opened up as we walked to check in. We jogged the last hundred yards through the rain, twisting through stone archways and over rough stone paths.

We had a beautiful room on the third floor of the castle. Silk-papered walls, an embroidered comforter on a four-poster bed, an ancient claw-foot bathtub next to a modern two-person shower stall, and plumbing and electrical wiring dating back almost to the *Downton Abbey* period. A fire was already lit in the corner; we felt cozy and welcome and had no desire to head back out into the wind and rainstorm that was gathering outside. Our decision to freshen up before commencing our search quickly escalated from teeth brushing, to “just a quick shower,” to “can I help wash your back,” and ended with steamy, passionate sex on the elaborate canopied bed, which we barely made it to as we stumbled, dripping from the shower. After our long flights and this wonderful exertion, we set an alarm for 30 minutes, fearing we might drift off to sleep. Although we felt we were running against the clock, and that if we delayed our search we might lose the slim thread we had grasped, we agreed we needed some ‘us’ time, too. I pushed our worries about Chiyome and her complications out of my head and lost myself in thoughts of the wonderful woman at my side in bed – and life in general.

[Marcy] — I lay on my side with my cheek resting on Ethan’s rather well-defined chest and tossed a leg lazily over one of his muscular thighs. We both smelled of sex, and I nestled even closer to Ethan, enjoying the post-event bliss. I imagined his boy brain was vacant and at rest, as boy’s brains often are in the post-coital sprawl, but of course mine was whirring away. We were getting to know each other so well that I felt him stir as he sensed me working up to raising a sensitive topic. I had something on my mind, which I was nervous about letting out into the open. I recalled our discussion about such conversations being relatively high stakes because your partner is so important to you. If they react negatively to a taboo subject, it might loosen a bond, and such events are sometimes hard to recover from; a bell that can’t be un-rung. Silly, but real.

I decided to procrastinate a while, so I mentally reviewed some research I’d just found on why men are sleepy after sex. Studies using PET scans show that to achieve orgasm, a physiological requirement is to temporarily let go of all fear and anxiety. That step alone could help you sleep.

Another study mentioned the release of a cocktail of chemicals at orgasm, which include serotonin, oxytocin, and prolactin. Serotonin is apparently produced in the gut and the brain, and the latter helps us reduce stress. Baseball players who chew gum are stimulating its release to help relax before they go up to bat. Oxytocin and prolactin both are associated with causing sleepiness; the former is also intrinsic to the process of forming bonds. Men produce it during orgasm and, interestingly, women produce it during foreplay and the lead-up to release. I wondered if this difference related to women historically having way fewer orgasms than men. I made a mental note to ask Gwen, our sex-guru, when we saw her next. Oxytocin is also partly responsible for building the bond between mother and baby. There is a theory that because kinky sessions typically last much longer than regular sex, this elongated dousing in oxytocin is why kinky couples typically survey as having stronger relationships than non-kinky couples.

Prolactin is involved in regulating the recovery time between orgasms for men. It's an inhibitor, so lower producers recover faster. Ethan must have a very low supply, based on his performance. The other interesting factoid is that production of prolactin is four times greater from intercourse than from masturbation. I didn't know if men fell asleep faster after intercourse or masturbating. I considered asking Ethan that instead of the question I had in mind, then decided I didn't want to know, at which point I decided I should quit stalling and plunge ahead with my real question.

"Can I ask you something?" There. I got it out and it felt good to get started.

He filled his lungs, settled into the pillow in a very satisfied way, and played with my earlobe as he replied huskily, "Go ahead. What's on your mind?"

"I've been doing some research into your fun little kink, and I came across something similar, but a little different. It's interesting, and I wanted to know what you thought about it."

"You've been researching solo. Without Yoda?" he teased. "I approve. What did we find out?" He turned a little so I could slip deeper into the crook of his arm. I noticed I had absentmindedly dragged a finger over the sheet right above 'little Ethan,' who had immediately taken notice and had slowly begun to puff himself up. Again! See what I mean about low prolactin levels? I liked to get both Ethans' full attention for these little talks, and about half of the time I wasn't even conscious of doing so. The other half of the time I was definitely being a minx. Now that I had both of their attention, I continued.

"There's a kink called CFnm, which stands for *clothed female, nude – or naked – male*. I've seen the acronym spelled with the C and the F capitalized and the N and M in lower case, and I've seen it all capitalized, too. Sometimes it seems to be a practice to denote the bossy party by capitalizing their letters and reducing the submissive role with lower case. Simple, and I like it. Another example is D/s, for *dominant and submissive,* where the D is upper and the S lower case."

"Are you saying I am *lower case*, and you are *upper case*?" he asked teasingly, yet with something aggressive lurking in the sub-tone of his husky voice. He squeezed me playfully.

"CFnm is where the woman is fully clothed and the man is naked, which is a bit different to what you like, I know. You like the risk of being exposed. Almost a reluctant exhibitionist, right?"

"I'm not sure about the reluctant exhibitionist, but let's get back to that," he corrected. "I agree it is pretty sexy if I'm the only naked one at the party, though. Tell me more about this new thing."

I had a sudden thought, and it just popped out. "Does it matter if you are exposed to women or men?"

"Yes, I think so. It should be females. Does that seem disloyal?"

"Not really. I hadn't really thought about it, but I guess I had subliminally assumed it should be women." I elbowed him back. "So, for you, when we are playing, does it matter if I'm naked or in lingerie? Or is a full-on business suit preferred?" This time, it was definitely the minx in me that dragged her finger slowly along the length of him, making it harder for him to think. I rested my open hand on his testicles, and I felt them warm up and shrink a little through the sheet.

Ethen considered, then teased "I'm not sure, as I haven't considered it until now. We could be scientific. Try them all a few times and I could let you know?" I sensed he was grinning in the darkness.

"Think about it now!" I pressed, with a faux-stern voice. "Imagine me in a dark blue, pinstriped, power suit; sharp, white, tight shirt, all buttoned up; tanned, bare legs. You can use your own imagination as to what I am wearing underneath the suit. But you can see my high heel shoes. They're cream coloured and quite shiny. Got it?"

"Oh yes. Your hair is up in a tight bun, and your makeup is no-nonsense. Large librarian glasses. How am I doing?"

"You're getting it. What are you wearing?"

"To start with, I think an equally hot power-suit. I have a really well-cut black Hugo Boss I like, which I suspect won't be on me for too long. Try not to rip it."

"No, I won't. In fact, it is coming off right now. Imagine I've commanded you to strip for me. Slowly. I want to know what is going through your head as you undress in front of me, and as you stand there naked with me standing in front of you fully dressed. Why is it sexy?" I enjoyed setting this stage.

Ethan was quiet, thinking through a couple of scenarios, no doubt. His body was betraying how much he enjoyed them as he stretched out a little more on the bed.

"Being naked while you are dressed creates an immediate attitude adjustment on my part. A sudden and distinctive tone-setter. I imagine it is because we choose our clothes for an occasion, to make us feel confident in given situations. They are symbolic and make us feel secure, and we are safe behind the image they help create. Wear the wrong outfit and we feel out of place and, importantly in this context, vulnerable. If you and I get naked together, there is a sort of parity and we are sharing the risk. But if you are dressed in power clothing and able to see me without my cloth barrier, it would be very...err...what is the word? Polarizing? I'm laid bare before you, and you are masked from me. You can see any physical reaction I have. Am I blushing? Am I erect? Is my erection flagging? Are my muscles straining? Am I sweating? It's like I'm lit up in your spotlight, and you are behind the light in the shadows. I can see you, but nowhere near as intimately. It forces me into a mental, internal scramble to find cover, and that is very disorienting. Disorienting is good for this game.

"But it's more complicated than that, too: It's stripping away my tough persona along with my clothes. It puts me onto a mental path that gets harder and harder to deviate from once on it. It has its own gravity. When I'm naked, there is only really submission ahead. But you, by contrast, still have a greater number of options because you are still dressed. This inequity in choices emphasizes your control. Of course, I can stop at any moment, but that is not what I want to do.

"I think people who enjoy sexually submissive roles enjoy being made vulnerable initially because in the end, when things culminate in an intense, sexual high, the confidence and peacefulness resulting from the endorphin release is a strong counterpoint to that initial leap-of-faith sensation. It has *high psychodrama*, which inspires all sorts of physiological reactions."

"I'm really interested in unpacking psychodrama and comparing it to ritual," I broke in, caught up in his sensitive analysis. "Gwen talked about the power of psychodrama to catalyze the chemicals in our brains to increase their effect, and that really resonates. But BDSM can have a lot of rituals. What's the link?"

"I don't really know, but here is what I think: Ritual to me feels like the process or the steps, and psychodrama could be the resulting effect or state of mind. I helped track down a patient once for a client who was a psychologist and she talked about psychodrama in clinical terms as purposefully acting out a sequence of steps as part of treatment. Like acting out a play; to put yourself in the mind of a character; a way to reach or get access to a set of feelings you were unable or unwilling to connect with otherwise. Ritual, to me at least, is similar but more associated with a society. It could be a big ritual, like a wedding or a presidential inauguration; or a small ritual, such as shaking hands or going to a playoff game. What do you think, Marcy?"

"At cop school, we were taught that some rituals are transitional support processes: A potential gang member must complete a task to join the gang; a bride and groom must stand before witnesses and say words; cadets must go through a special parade and tests of endurance to become soldiers. When we change from one social role to another, we often mark it – or define and enable it – with a ritual. Rituals are very powerful forces in our psyche. Victor Turner defined it as three stages: Separation, transition, and aggregation. Separation is about stepping away from your old role, like changing clothes, leaving home, travelling to locations dedicated to the ritual such as a sport field or a church. Or, it could be like assuming a new name, such as Phoenix. And so on. In BDSM, you might step out of your suit and get naked or put on fetish clothing; or call me Mistress or be called Slave-Boy."

I clamped my hand down on his manhood and bit his nipple gently for emphasis on that last idea before continuing.

"During a transition, we step into the new space and new rules. We symbolize. Commonplace items take on heightened significance. A ring. A stripe for a uniform. A collar. Bread and wine become the body of Christ. There is a sense that the neophyte is stripped down to nothing, figuratively and sometimes literally, to show they have nothing, so that they are able to freely take on the trappings of their new status or enjoy the transitional stage without the baggage of normal responsibility. It is the people established in or guarding the future state who oversee the transition: The Platoon's commander; the senior students; the priest; or the Dominant. They have the power, and the neophyte has none."

I was becoming a little self-conscious about the long explanation but ploughed on bravely.

"Danger, real or represented, can be introduced or simulated, as it signals more strongly that change is taking place: Rites of passage; killing your first animal – or a protracted solo hunt to become a man; your first period to become a woman; gang initiation, which is often based on committing a risky crime; kids cutting themselves and mixing blood to seal deals or life-long bonds; stags and stagettes before a wedding. Often there is an effort to radically change a person's sensory perception during this phase. Dancing; drumming and marching; blindfolds in dorm hazing; drinking or doing drugs. This disassociation helps the ritual by enabling the creation of a virtual, societal box in which activities that are normally unacceptable can exist in a time and a place, to emphasize the change from the child to the man, or the university initiate to student. Spanking is all but outlawed in Canada, but with the temporary container we create that holds our mindset for a kinky session, it's almost expected. Anything that helps leave one set of rules behind and adopt the next, even temporarily, is how ritual helps grant us permission to change our status or behaviour.

"The aggregation phase is about moving on and being established in the new space or returning to the original state with renewed energy. Brides and grooms getting married is an example of the former, and the latter might be fans taking off their jerseys after a hockey game and then returning to a life where cheering enthusiastically when two men fight is not acceptable." I looked to Ethan to make sure he was following and had not dozed off at my lengthy response, but he seemed as fascinated with this stuff as I was.

He summarized back to me. “So, ritual in BDSM can help us transition from feeling awkward about being spanked, to enjoying it, and back again? I get it. I was thinking that ritualistic behaviours looked off-putting and embarrassing, but I see the other side, too: once you are into them, they actually assist with making it feel more acceptable, so you can relax into it.” I felt that Ethan’s enthusiasm was mounting. I took it up again.

“I think the point of ritual is to somewhat abruptly take us out of our safe routine structure to free the mind, then make us experience a highly emotional state, which will help us understand that society is more than just a bunch of rules. Then place us into our future place, or back to where they were before, in a better-informed position or state. Having you strip for me at the start of playtime, or what you called the ‘immediate attitude adjustment,’ really feels like the separation phase Turner talked about.” I decided it was time to return to the CFnm discussion.

“Is it better to be blindfolded? Surely that exaggerates that feeling even more. Helps you disassociate,” I asked.

“Yes and no.” he whispered, thoughtfully. “Both can be great, but apples and oranges. No. Closer than that, even. Perhaps lemons and limes. If I can’t see at all but know you can see me clearly, again, it is polarizing. It widens the gap between our powers, enhancing yours and reducing mine further. There’s the thrill that I don’t know what you are looking at. You might be reading a newspaper or inspecting me minutely; you might be about to touch or spank me.; or be checking your email and not back to me for a while; or taking a photo of me. Who knows? Sounds, smells, and touch get magnified and my world closes in, yet at the same time, my enhanced senses reach into the farthest corner of the room. But in a...what was it? Yes, in a CFnm moment without a blindfold, I would see exactly what you were doing. You are staring at my vulnerability. I don’t think I get the same expansion of my physical senses, but I would realize a further deepening of my submission. I’d be more conscious of my lowered status. A wider disparity between us; but a social status disparity only, not a social status *and* control difference. This is off the cuff – no pun intended – and I don’t think those words are quite right, but I hope you get the drift.”

“Yes, I think so. Do you have a preference?” I asked Ethan, somewhat shyly.

“Oh yes, I prefer all of it. Variety. Not knowing what is coming next.” I chuckled at his apparent appetite. “But what about you, how does it make you feel, being clothed with me naked?” he shot back. I hadn’t expected the question, but I didn’t need time to think about my answer.

“Powerful. It enhances my status, if that doesn’t sound silly. Unassailable. Even if I’m naked when we are not being kinky, I feel mildly embarrassed. So, if I am trying to be bossy, that embarrassment undermines my headspace. So, it helps me, especially at that moment. I really like being the bossy one and teasing you rotten, but I do have to work at being in character. One day, encouraging my dominant side might come totally naturally; but right now, it's a little frightening having to be so overtly controlling. When I first became a cop, I had to learn to control situations in an overt way, and it took practise. One of the things I'm enjoying about BDSM is its structure. There are trappings that reinforce the roles we both play. They help with clarity and remove assumptions and room for bumping heads. Being clothed when you are bare-assed is a strong reminder of my role, and your nakedness affirms you are playing submissive. That makes me feel more assertive and comfortable to put my bossy on. It's like when you make yourself smile, you actually feel happier, too, I guess."

"What do you see when you look at me when I'm submissive and naked?" Ethan asked, caution in his voice. I sensed he was worried about maintaining my respect. I took my time to capture in words the reassurance I genuinely felt.

"It's a bit like taking in a beautiful meal before you devour it. If our regular, awesome, but vanilla sex is like a burger or a hearty dinner you just launch yourself into, then this is more like constructed, nouvelle cuisine. You examine the artwork and the subtleties before swallowing everything and licking your plate clean. I stand there and tease you and really enjoy seeing your body react in its entirety. There's no hiding anything. It's so raw. Besides, you don't *feel* submissive; you choose to let me boss you about and you submit to my will. I can make you nervous, but you are not a weak submissive."

"I don't feel weak but do worry that one day it might make me look diminished in your eyes."

"Quite the opposite, Ethan." I reassured. "You look like who you always are — maybe stronger — being prepared to take such outrageous risks just for kicks. That takes balls. I'm not blowing smoke up your ass; you are a very intimidating man. You are always powerful, muscular, and confident. Even naked you project kick-ass and competence. And caretaker. You hand me this power over you and then challenge me at every step. I love it. You are a powerhouse and I want to take you down. Dominating a wimp wouldn't be sexy, for me. That sounds mean, sorry. Some people want to play the wimpy role – and good luck to them – but I get off on dominating my aggressive alpha. I want to have to work very hard to make you worship me. I want to earn the privilege to be your goddess."

I slid my hand up his rock-hard shaft and very lightly and slowly rubbed him back and forth through the sheet, then suddenly clamped my hand on his balls to punctuate my point. But his relief at not worrying about seeming weak made the alpha surge up within him, and despite my grip, he reared up and rolled above me, his muscular arms brushing the sheet aside and holding him up so that his chest brushed lightly on mine. Then he slowly drove his hips downwards, sinking his cock deep into me, and in an instant all of my articulate speaking abilities I had engaged in in the last five minutes evaporated, and all I could do was whisper, "You brat. Fuck me hard, Ethan. I need you now!"

*

[ETHAN] — Sixty minutes after arrival and smelling of sex again but at least dressed in clean jeans and t-shirts we were in the back of a taxi heading into town. The first stop was a store that sold hiking gear. Marcy bought a cream-coloured wool sweater, I bought a grey fleecy, and we both bought hooded rain jackets that reached down to our knees. As an afterthought, I added camping knives to our haul. Appropriately proofed against the elements, we ventured out into a steady rain and blustering winds.

Most of our time since taking off from Kempton had been spent devising search tactics. While we waited for the team, who were driving up, we wanted to get a head start with what we had at our disposal – which was basically our eyes and ingenuity. We decided we would split up, one walking the streets north of the Weir and the other walking along the south. I had mapped out a search grid and selected cafés, bars, and any place else we thought might we might bump into Moy Lei. We were pessimistic about finding the needle in the haystack, but quite pleased with ourselves for being so organized given that 24 hours ago, my only care was keeping my dignity in front of seven strangers in an art class. Little Ethan swelled anew at the thought. All of our cleverness was rendered moot, however.

Moy Lei found us.

We emerged from the hiking store into the old city centre's main market square to find our quarry standing below a statue of a nobleman dressed in a Hussar uniform, sitting on his prancing war horse. The gently sloping, grey flagstone market square was tightly flanked by light, sandy-brown buildings. At the lowest point of the piazza, the sharp-spired church of St. Nicolas and the statue of a nearly naked Neptune – I knew exactly how he felt – near the centre were green with age. Moy Lei appeared to have been searching for us and when we stepped out, she walked over briskly and grabbed Marcy's wrist with great urgency.

"Hurry up! This way! You have the worst timing. I am being hunted; it's here for me but if it thinks we are together, it might kill you, too. Follow quickly if you want to live to see tomorrow." She sounded desperate and frightened, rather than melodramatic. Her tone sent shivers down my spine. She referenced her pursuer as an 'it,' in a way we would talk about a 'he' or a 'she' but there was no time to ask, as with another urgent tug she broke contact and took off around the corner.

Marcy and I shrugged and jogged hastily in pursuit. Moy Lei was pulling away from us, so we picked up our speed over the slippery cobbles and began to close the gap. Durham, like Rome, is built on seven hills running up which soon had us breathing hard. She led us down a tight, shop-lined street which after 50 yards forked left and down, or up and right; we took the letter and soon emerged onto a large formal, grassy square across which sat an impressive cathedral. Moy Lei ignored the sidewalks and galloped diagonally across the lawn – to the annoyance of tourists patiently and politely circumnavigating the space – all the time glancing around anxiously. At one point, she seemed to sense some unseen threat from our left and spun off to the right, but then changed her mind and beelined across a large grassy square to a tall wooden doorway set in an ancient stone wall.

Once inside the cathedral proper, Moy Lei turned and ran down a wide stone corridor lined on the right with arched windows through which grey light painted matching, arched, shadows across the stone floor and up the opposite wall. We were within ten feet of her as we popped out onto the main cathedral floor. A vaulted, golden ceiling towered over us, deities and hundreds of years of history looked down on us; our drama a pin prick in its lifetime of dramas. Heads turned with surprise and annoyance at us running through the pews. It was like being a part of some Dan Brown novel. Moy Lei pulled up panting for breath at the main pulpit, then slumped onto a bench at its foot.

"We should be safe here," she gasped. "At least for now." Marcy and I were breathing hard, and clearly in better shape than Moy Lei, but both of us were overheating in our new clothes. We unzipped our coats, took them off, and settled next to Moy Lei — one on either side of her — and remained quiet while she recovered. She kept glancing around and appeared to be listening. Her nervousness made us equally concerned and our heads were on a swivel, too.

"Would you mind telling us who we are running from? And how do you know us?" asked Marcy.

"You would never understand if I told you. Just stay here until I tell you it's safe, then you can leave and go back to wherever you came from. I don't know anything about you, other than you were looking for me. Did Haha send you?"

"Haha?" I asked.

"Mother. Mochizuki Chiyome? Sorry, I'm flustered. Haha is Japanese for mother."

"Actually, yes. She did," I answered, not sure of which tack to take. She seemed under duress; on the run. From her kidnappers? Or had she fled from her mother? We were disadvantaged by not knowing her version of the facts.

"She seemed very concerned for your safety," I said, then I introduced us both, explaining that we work for a discrete and unique private detective agency.

"I fled to get away from danger. From the...the monster. And to keep her safe. But it nearly caught up with me in London, and it's found me again here."

"I didn't think your mother's...err...associates were welcome in this region." Moy Lei sat back at this. She was evaluating us. Trying to work out what we knew.

"Tell us how we can help. We have resources," cut in Marcy. Good tactic. Puts the onus of revealing information on Moy Lei. Cop training at work. Moy Lei looked at us both several times, then squeezed her eyes closed tightly. Almost painfully.

"I don't understand. You both have white souls. Why would mother involve you in this affair? Why would you do anything for her, if you know who she really is?"

"Why indeed," said Marcy, as puzzled as I was.

"Let's say she took a gamble on us, and because we are a little crazy, we said we would try to help," I added.

"Do you know anything about Boku-yōkai?" I looked at Marcy and got a head shake in return.

"That is a new term to us. What does it mean?" Moy Lei sat for a while, glancing around and appearing to listen to something that we couldn't hear. She was puzzling something out. Then, whatever it was, she seemed to come to a decision and, taking a deep breath, began to tell us her story.

"We have time. Its close by, but it won't come in here. We must stay for at least an hour, maybe more. Leaving before then probably will result in our deaths," she added cryptically.

"Let me explain how this will go: I will share information you won't believe. No one would blame you. It is unbelievable. When I am finished, you will be skeptical. You will think I am crazy. This is good, as you need to get away from me – for your own safety. I am on a path I must travel alone, and I cannot accept your help. But I am stuck, whatever I do. My problem will be Haha. Mother. You will return to her, and she will require an explanation. She will understand and believe what I am about to tell you, because she knows such things are real. But her reaction to my situation will result in her death. Once she is aware of my predicament she will be compelled to act, and she will bring down forces even she cannot outpace. I fled to keep this knowledge away from her. I had hoped she would just let me go, even if I broke her heart. Sending you after me tells me she cannot. I suspected this would happen, but had to make the attempt.

"But if I don't explain the situation to you, you will bumble around looking for answers, and you will cross the path of a dark soul. And then your death will be on my hands. I know what my mother does, and I don't condone it. She was put on her path by another, and she cannot leave it without sentencing me and her other loved ones to death. She has no choice, but I do. She has followed her path to provide me with a life – a choice – of my own, and I cannot betray that sacrifice. She did what her predecessor failed to do for her: She allowed me a white soul. I know, this is not making much sense, is it?"

Moy Lei stopped and looked at us, trying to think if there was a simpler way to explain her predicament.

"As I said, I had planned on mother letting me go," she continued, "but clearly she cannot. If I convince you to depart, so I don't have your death on my hands, she will just send someone else. So, I will tell you my situation. My story. Then you can relay it to Haha and then get as far away from our plight as you can. It seems to be my best option, as well as yours. In hindsight, I think now I should have found a way to tell Haha before I fled. It would have kept innocents like you safe."

In the silence that followed while we attempted to understand her cryptic explanation, Marcy tried to help.

"Don't worry too much about us, Moy Lei. We are harder to kill than we look. Your Haha tried to kill us twice and we are told she never misses." At this, Moy Lei burst out laughing. Us being assassinated seemed amusing?

"I'm sorry, but you can't call my mother Haha. One refers to one's own mother as Haha. If one refers to another's mother, we say Okaa, or Okaa-sama if we are close friends. Your saying, "Your Haha tried to kill me," to me, is a corruption of languages. I'm sharing too much, but I call my vagina my 'Haha.' My vagina has never tried to kill you, as far as I know. I am being silly, of course, and babbling. But that is why I laughed. I guess I am very scared.

"Brace yourselves for an incredible story. Remember, I don't expect you to believe it, just to listen to it. If you can, suspend your disbelief until I finish."

She gathered her thoughts and plunged in. We sat back enthralled.

"It might help if I explain why I am here in Durham. This story should include a crazy professor, and Dr Ellison has been called just that. Crazy. He retired here and helps out at Durham University when he is not doing research. He made a lifetime study of cults and religions, but also has a doctorate in quantum mechanics. An odd mix. Foremost he is recognized for explaining in current scientific terms how mystical powers and beliefs are, in fact, in practice, possible. He is basically the world's leading expert on explaining magic to scientists and lay-people.

"I think we are all familiar with the concept of how modern science, such as electricity and the workings of an airplane, would seem magical to someone from just as recent as a few centuries ago. His specialty is the opposite: He explains how, for thousands of years, people had been able to do things we consider magical today; that they had mastered a science we have yet to learn – or, at least, has been forgotten. This is not as absurd as it sounds. Think of the Roman Empire, which is coincidental given that the architecture we are standing in is in the Roman style. The Egyptians and Greeks built a vast knowledge base, which was added to by the Romans. When the Roman empire fell, most of the knowledge built from 20 thousand years was lost in a few decades. Here in England, the Romans built roads, viaducts, sewer systems, and other marvels. These achievements fell into decay for over a millennium because we didn't have the skills to maintain – let alone recreate – them. The Dark Ages were a colossal loss of intellectual momentum

"The premise is that *Homo Sapiens* have always been as smart as we are today. We have been since we came to be as a species 1.8 million years ago. In fact, Carl Linnaeus coined the phrase *Homo Sapiens* from the Latin for 'wise man' in 1758. The common misbelief today is that we are smarter than people from the past; but in truth, we are confusing recent advances in knowledge sharing, communication capabilities, teaching methods, and other cumulative achievements with actual raw brain power. Ellison's first point is that raw brain power has been consistent for 18000 years. So, what did we do with it since we could not put it to work on things we have today, which had not yet come to be?

"His second point is that modern science often trips over itself when it encounters things it doesn't understand. Look how much energy has gone into things like string theory. If we put as much money and energy into trying to work out if people can really bend spoons with their mind, perhaps we would solve magic. The spoon thing was a hoax, by the way. Silly example, sorry. But you get the idea.

"Also, these days we have far more rigorous ethics and rules than we had hundreds of years ago. Today, if someone has an idea that might cure cancer, there are years and millions of dollars of trials in petri dishes, then perhaps rats, and then possibly apes, before the test gets near a human. And the influences of 'big-pharma' should not be disregarded as they support, or suppress, ideas based on profit margins. But go back 2000 years, and none of these limitations existed. You had an idea, you just did it. Copernicus and a few like him might be an exception. He created a model which put the sun rather than the earth as the centre of the universe and created new math to explain the concept. He was a big thinker, but most people operated with a much less complex, nearer-term focus. What happens if I eat a chicken brain? What happens if I wrap certain leaves around it first? What happens if I chug a keg of beer and ski off a roof top? Much more experimentation and trial and error; much less worry or thinking.

‘‘I flip a switch and a light comes on. I don’t need to know how electricity works to find my socks in the morning. Random experimentation, which once in a blue moon turn up an amazingly useful result, doesn’t need to be explained to be used. It just needs to be recreated or repeated. When enough monkeys get enough typewriters, magic happens. Dr Ellison explains how those seemingly magical acts are supported by modern-day scientific principles.

“Boku-yōkai is a term that was coined in Japan roughly 200 years ago. It is a made-up word, used to describe a specific, sinister magician in the early 1800s. He was never named or documented, so to some he is a myth, but enough stories circulated about him to make others speculate that such a person existed in history, even if they can’t explain his apparent powers. Many just think he was a master illusionist, or con-man. Yōkai are a class of supernatural monsters in our folklore, to whom legend attributes unaccountable powers. Boku is a corrupted word: in one sense, in Japanese, it is one of our first-person pronouns, like the word ‘I’ in English. But it is also part of Haitian voodoo, a sort of priest. *Boku-yōkai* has the meaning ‘I, the monster’. The abilities of such a person wielding these lost arts could appear to be magical by our modern standards. The term implies one who is an ‘Adept’ in supernatural powers. Sometimes there are referred to simply as Adepts.

“What Ellison would have told you is that fables and myths are often founded on quite repeatable – if sometimes accidental – experiments or events that have given apparently super-human powers to a few people. If we properly understood the factors surrounding each scenario, we could reproduce the results, and so it is not ‘magic.’

In most cases, such things happen in very discrete circumstances. Think of First Nations ‘vision walkers’: Perhaps a person learns that eating a certain combination of herbs and inhaling smoke from burning a certain type of plant engages a dormant part of their brain, which helps them see remote places over impossible distances. It might be a one-time experience that they dismiss as a dream, or, they might find they can recreate it and become a ‘vision walker.’ A legend is born. But when they die, their ability and secret dies with them if not taught to others who are able to also synthesize the herbs and smoke in the same manner. Part of Ellison’s theory is that in most of these cases, one must be compatible with the increased ability. For example, one in a million might have the genes associated with enabling the ability to be a seer by eating those herbs and smelling that smoke. Others just get a headache; i.e. they are not compatible. So effectively the ability either won’t be passed on due to genetics, or in a small number of cases, it can in fact pass through blood lines.

"He thought that, in a very few cases, secretive groups have recorded and amassed data on these combinations of genetic or chemical triggers which activate the unusual abilities that are associated with them and have passed down this knowledge within their bloodline or their 'cult' for generations. Some individuals with this knowledge, and the right genes, become Boku-yōkai. Magical Adepts."

"You warned us this would be far-fetched, and I admit I am struggling to believe any of this. Give me a current example," prompted Marcy.

"OK, let's go back to how I knew you were coming and how I sought you out. I simply felt you looking for me. Crazy, right? Now, I would not call myself Boku-yōkai. I know very little of how I do this, which is why I sought out Dr Ellison. To me, I am flipping a light switch and the light gets brighter. I can partly explain my talent in the same way as I could tell you the light in my bedroom comes on because someone at the power station created electricity, and electrons flow down the wires and overload the bulb filament to make it glow, but I really don't know what I am talking about in either case. But here is what I *do* know.

"Firstly, Haha's Kanbo dates back to the early 1500s to an all-female ninja clan, some of whom allegedly did feats which could not be explained and are considered myths today. I share their DNA – I've proven that much through DNA-based, family-tree analysis services – so might have inherited some of their inexplicable abilities. I have also isolated part of my triggering or ability-activation mechanism. Ellison believed there is a strong connection between Boku-yōkai, and the modern developments around stem cell technology. I'll come back to this, but simply stem cells are most common in embryo-state life. They are cells that have the potential to multiply to become anything. A brain cell, or a foot, or an ear. It's our raw material, which is influenced by enzymes, body chemicals, electrical pulses, and so on, to build our bodies from that initial set of cells in the zygote. Once we are built, we lose this potential, which is why we can't regrow a foot if it gets amputated.

Modern stem-cell technology is very controversial, because in many cases it relies on harvesting stem cells from an embryo that could otherwise have the potential to be a person, and then experimenting with those cells before disposing of them. Shades of Joseph Mengele to some. For others, these embryos are byproducts of invitro fertilization treatments, which are independently controversial for other reasons. Some of the viable embryo go on to be implanted into the mother, some put aside in case the first set is not successful, and the remainder would be disposed of in any case. To some of this group, who feel they are creating life where it wouldn't have otherwise existed, they are being less wasteful by using the harvested stem cells to improve quality of life. I'm not proposing we debate ethics here or take a side. Enough people are doing that already. To my knowledge, I've never consumed stem cells produced by others, but Dr Ellison believed that they would be an important component to stabilizing a body exercising these unusual abilities. I don't know why he believes this, but he was actively pursuing this theory, so I have accepted it is relevant to the science.

"I also know that my few unusual talents grow significantly when I eat peanut derivatives. Ellison recited several similar cases. My allergy is real. If I consume more than a gram or two at any point I break out in hives, get incredibly asthmatic, and get a topical reaction where the peanuts touch, such as on my lips or in my throat. I've been maintaining my powers with some special cookies containing minute amounts of peanut oil, plus some strong, non-drowsy antihistamine.

"You can partially thank Albert Einstein and Erwin Schrödinger for this next piece of my personal jigsaw: Entanglement theory. This falls into the category I mentioned earlier, whereby science is spending heavily to comprehend something it can observe enough to believe that something is going on but can't explain or harness it. If they ever do, it has huge potential for telecommunications, encryption, and many other areas. We are talking quantum mechanics; atoms, electrons, and the sub-atomic particles that they consist of, which we barely understand. Anyway, if you create certain pairs or groups of these sub-atomic particles together, at the same time, and then cause the attributes of one of the particles in the group to change, it changes the other particles in the group, too, even if the particles are separated by great distances. Even more interestingly, the change to the counterpart occurs faster than the speed of light can convey the information, and we are not supposed to have things go faster than the speed of light. The entangled particles are proving to be connected through dimensions we don't understand. It is magical to us, but we can repeat it through experimentation, so it is becoming a science. So, the rough theory I have developed is that my DNA, in conjunction with some chemical or similar I put into my system when eating a very small amount peanuts, triggers some dormant ability of my brain that no one understands, which through entangled particles lets me sense certain connections to others that we can't explain with today's science. When this happens, I appear to be magical."

"I find it much easier to believe your mother tracked us here and phoned you and said to stand in the square and wait for us, to be honest, but let's play along," I said skeptically. "How do you sense this? Do you have a virtual map in your head and follow us around?"

"That would help enormously, but no. It's more akin to a submarine sonar, in that I sense range and direction. It's a sensation unlike any other. Imagine describing the colour pink to a person who has never had sight. It's not like a sound, but if it were, it would be like a mosquito when you are farther away, and a motorbike when you are closer. I can gauge the direction closely. Walls and barriers don't seem to effect it, which plays into the entanglement theory in that it happens through a dimension that is not impacted by walls. Range or distance are more difficult for me at first contact with a new person, and I can be fooled. If all sources were equally loud, I could gauge distance by volume. But some people radiate more strongly than others, so I have to guess a lot about the distance aspect. What really helped me pin you two down was when you flew over me in the blue helicopter. I knew how far away you were, and it somehow sharpened my ability to track you. Once I have acquired that detail about how strong you radiate, it sticks with me and I can be much more accurate each successive time."

"There are about seven billion people in the world, Moy Lei. How do you pick us out of the noise?"

"Actually, I only appear to sense certain people. Only the people with an intense and urgent interest in me, I guess. The rest I am not attuned to. I've only sensed you for about a day now. I am only aware of a dozen or so people at present. Haha, obviously. I assume some of the members of the Kanbo – her clan – who know I am missing. I can feel them, but I can't distinguish who is who, just that they are physically close to Haha and are attuned to me.

"The sensation gives me more information than just distance and direction. I called you 'white souls' earlier. That is my made-up name. I've only known about my ability for eight months. I was raised to avoid triggering my peanut allergy and have stayed away from them for a lifetime. I believe Haha, or someone guiding her, might suspect peanuts are a trigger for my abilities. I have not dared to ask. A friend served a meal cooked with a small amount of peanut oil several times over the period of a week. It was in a dish that we had on a Sunday, and then leftovers several more times reheated. I had a small allergic reaction, plus other transitions where these new abilities manifested, although it took me weeks to puzzle them out and that they were related to the meals. I had no idea of the threat they represented at the time, but it is in the nature of my upbringing to be secretive, and so I kept quiet and researched. Our Kanbo has archives that go back into the clandestine history and it was there, in our Arcania, where I learned about the myths of Boku-yōkai, and the importance of diet and interaction with chemicals.

"As I was doing my research, I realized there were two distinct groups of people I could sense. I called them 'white souls' and 'dark souls.' From my admittedly odd perspective, one group was typically made up of well-meaning, altruistic people and the others were family, if you get my drift. Then one day I sensed a third type. Haha was hosting a monthly meeting of the Jonin, the most senior rank of the Kanbo. I'm not involved with them enough to know them personally, or exactly how many they number, but I figure four to eight Jonin run the Kanbo. I was dropping off Haha's birthday gift at the hotel they were using, and she met me in the car park. It was in Las Vegas at the time of the big concert shooting last October when that asshole opened up from the Mandalay Bay. Although we were at a nearby hotel, and actually not in harm's way, rumour spread quickly that many hotels had active shooters loose inside, and this activated the Kanbo contingency plan. The Kanbo were evacuated, and during this emergency, for a brief period, I heard this third type of person. If a 'white soul' is like a quality motorcycle – distinctive but smooth and muffled – and a dark soul is similar – but more like a quality car – this new soul is like a muscle car with tailpipes designed to be as noisy as possible. I got the overwhelming sense of fierce, raw power dwarfing the normal traffic. Our limited archives referenced this third type in only one book, and I had missed it on the first scan through. It referred to them as Boku-yōkai 'Adepts,' or in another section, as 'demon-priests.'

"I only heard the 'demon-priest' in the Kanbo that one time but could track it enough to know it was one of the Jonin moving together with the group as they evacuated. I've spent months now locating bits and pieces of data about them, and as you can imagine, information is scarce. Whereas I can manifest my tracking ability, and perhaps another two to three skills, the 'demon-priests' have a much greater range and strength of magic. Remember, they probably have access to the arcane information passed from generation to generation about how to trigger the powers. I found a document that suggests that using these skills is very draining, and they can only operate for an hour or two, then need to rest. This is why we are waiting here. Waiting for the Boku-yōkai, who is lurking just outside of the walls of this cathedral to be drained of energy.

"The texts suggest that historically, some demon-priests apparently act alone, others in a sect. Numbers appear to be incredibly small. Perhaps 20 to 30 demon-priests in the whole world. I don't really know. I'm guessing, really."

"What made you leave home suddenly, and fake an abduction?"

"I sensed something change, and I panicked. Some prey can sense a predator even though they can't detect them with their regular five senses. It's a primal feeling. I woke up to it one day and knew in my gut the devil-priests had become conscious of my interest in them. I had no awareness of their presence directly, no range or direction. Just that they were stalking me. Perhaps I searched in the wrong database and alerted it somehow, I don't know. But it is aware."

"Why not confide in Chiyome? Couldn't she protect you?"

"She would feel compelled to try, as I've said, but you should see what these Adepts are capable of. The evil accounts I have read and their amazing skills. The Jonin have not had a new member for almost a decade, and most have been in place for several decades. If this thing is a Jonin, it knows us backwards and forwards and has hidden in plain sight for a long time. I have gotten close to the group and tried to sense it, with no hint of success. I think it could kill any or all of us whenever it chooses. So, I fled here. I know it is difficult for the Kanbo to follow, due to the inter-clan prohibitions. If one of the Kanbo follows me here, it might be the devil-priest and that will give me valuable information. And I wanted to contact Ellison."

"You've mentioned Ellison several times in past tense. Has he left the country?"

"Roughly 14 hours ago now, I suddenly sensed another Adept. It felt different to the Kanbo Adept. Slightly less powerful, I think; definitely a dark soul and very close by. I walked around and triangulated where it was located, which proved to be Dr Ellison's house, down behind the south square. I sensed the devil-priest move off, and I risked going to investigate. I found Ellison tied to his bed, dead, and cut up like a human sacrifice. I think parts of him were...taken."

"Ugh, that's gross. You poor thing!" Marcy had seen many grizzly scenes in her career and knew more than most the traumatic impact seeing such things can have on the mind.

"It was awful, especially as Ellison believed that Boku-yōkai have a history boosting their powers further through cannibalism. In the same way cord blood and stem cells assist, he had data that the consumption of certain portions in the older parts of our brain, the amygdala for instance, played some part he didn't yet fully understand."

As if suddenly slapped, Moy Lei snapped to attention, her eyes bugging wildly. Her head pivoted this way and that, and quickly settled on a spot well to the right of the nave of the cathedral. Her eyes began to track farther to the right, away from the main entrance, around the corner, and down the side of the church towards the entrance by the transept, the aisle that cuts across the floor from side to side.

"It's here, suddenly close, and coming quickly," she whispered, frozen to the spot. I looked at Marcy whose eyes were closed, and she was rocking slowly back and forth. I shook Marcy's arm, but she was non-responsive, almost trance like. I hated myself but this was no time to pussyfoot about, so I slapped her firmly on the cheek. No reaction. Then the world began to slow down for me, as if I was being dipped into treacle or toffee. It was an effort to move, and my lungs felt full. I fought the effect.

"How do we fight it?" I pushed Moy Lei and tried to get her to snap out of her apparent panic attack. Her breathing rate had skyrocketed and she was sweating profusely. At least she could still talk, although her voice was strained.

"I thought we would be safe here. I thought they could only be active for an hour or two at a time and could not come into the cathedral. It's built on top of two converging ley lines. The energy is supposed to be too strong for Adepts to be near, hence a place of sanctuary. I can feel the lines and they burn me. I am less capable, and so I supposed I was less sensitive. Perhaps the opposite is true. I'm so sorry. My ignorance has killed us."

"There must be something we can do!" As the words left my mouth, an immense wave of fear and helplessness flowed over me; a dam bursting. Like Moy Lei, I found myself sweating and panting for air. Most people talk about a fight or flight response to a threat, but there is a third 'f': Freeze. Rabbits and smaller animals often play dead while predators go by, and I felt like a mouse facing an imminent attack from a tiger. I was suddenly insanely terrified. My lizard, primal brain had taken over. I wanted to run, but I couldn't. I was rooted to the spot. I slipped my shaking hand into my jeans pocket and pulled out the camping knife. It was stiff from lack of use, but I managed to extend its seven-inch blade and angled it towards the door Moy Lei was now looking directly towards.

"It's here. Right upon us," Moy Lei whispered. The Cathedral was huge, and the door some 80 feet away. Hardly close. What did she mean by "right upon us"? I looked left and right, and then glanced behind me. About 12 feet away, the air shimmered. I stared at it, and dragged myself around to face it, the effort of changing positions daunting, and the anxiety associated with moving and possibly being discovered by the menacing threat, intense. I felt certain we were about to die, and my mind went to Marcy. Whatever this bastard was, it would not have her. I took a step, and then another, and put myself between her and the shimmer. I focused all of my mind on it. It slowly materialized into a soft-grey silhouette, slipping away again if I relaxed even a jot. It had no features other than being distinctly male looking, but its posture looked relaxed and confident. Its head cocked in curiosity as it stared at my efforts, perhaps impressed I could sense it was there at all. Moy Lei was still looking in completely the other direction. Then the outline of the man seemed to tire of me and gave a shrug. It reached behind its back and pulled out a pistol. It began to raise it, slowly pointing it at me. I considered throwing the knife, but it just seemed hopeless. My spirit broke and I caved and looked at Marcy, tears rolling down my face. The blade slipped from my grip with a clatter.

"I'm so sorry, honey," I cried to Marcy. The figure brought the gun all the way up. For some reason I began to count out loud.

All of a sudden, with a massive popping sensation that had no noise associated with it, all of the pressure vanished. My vision had a clarity it's never had, and my hearing seemed to expand to the point I could have heard a flea walk across a dog's back four miles away. The grey figure coloured in instantly: Red sneakers, blue jeans, a green Barbour-style waxed jacket. Where the head should be was a pink cloud of exploding brains and other bodily mess. As the body began to crumple lifelessly, the world sped up and a soundwave from a muffled rifle-shot assaulted my new super-hearing. I grabbed my ears. Marcy was coming around, too. Moy Lei had collapsed but seemed awake and shocked more than anything. I lifted my hands from my ears and tried to listen. I heard a noise from above and looked up. Ian Po's face was peering down at me from the balcony, leaning over the barrel of an Ultimate Ruger rifle, complete with noise suppressor.

"Are you guys OK down there? I thought you were going to stand there while that arsehole shot you!"

4: DEEP DOWN

Heads turned at the suppressed shot echoing around the cavernous space, but Ian escaped notice secreted in his perch near the ceiling. No one could see Moy Lei, who was prone on the floor, or the bloody corpse of the demon-priest – crumpled a few yards distant – due to the position of the pews. I quietly signaled for Moy Lei to stay down. I whispered the name of our accommodation and told her to slip out, under the pews, and meet us later. I covertly signaled Ian to withdraw, too. We would have to call the police, but no sense in everyone getting tangled up any more than we had to. We certainly could not tell them the full story.

Back in the square, when Moy Lei had told us we were in danger, I had activated my phone's silent alarm feature. I can do it with touch while it is still in my pocket. It is designed to call for help if I feel I am in danger, for example if someone tries to kidnap me for ransom. It signaled my team that we were in danger and constantly streamed my GPS coordinates to them, and they had rushed to support us, having just arrived in town.

Marcy was coming out of her trance, and her eyes fell on the corpse. In a very unlike-Marcy moment, she screamed. That noise brought people running. I quickly pulled out my phone and dialed the emergency services. I was reporting that a man had been shot as the bystanders began to gather. Marcy recovered quickly and went straight into cop mode. She pulled over some velvet rope barriers and closed off the scene, making sure everyone stayed back. She was dying to ask me what had happened, but we couldn't talk openly.

"I didn't really see what happened," I said pointedly to her. "I heard a pop but couldn't tell where it came from. Then you screamed and the man was down. He's clearly dead." She got the message and confirmed loudly she hadn't seen the shooter or incident either.

The police arrived quickly and secured the building, but there had been time for both Moy Lei and Ian's team to clear out. Since we were closest to the body, we were questioned the most. We were separated and each gave a statement at the scene, and then another at the police station. We were both tested for gunshot residue and searched for weapons. I admitted to the camping knives, but this was not an issue. Marcy's status as an ex-cop helped, and the gun with the victim's brains and fingerprints on did, too. They could tell he was involved in something nefarious, and not an innocent bystander. I could tell the detectives were leaning towards some gang on gang theory and didn't distract them from it. We were both asked about an Asian woman who other witnesses had reported as standing near us, and we both had the same thought, saying it was probably just another tourist we had been standing near. We hadn't seen her doing anything unusual and we just chatted briefly about the cathedral.

We were released within a couple of hours. Ian was waiting outside in his Audi and whisked us back to the hotel. Moy Lei had not appeared and we invited Ian and his team up to the suite to compare notes. I ordered us all dinner to be delivered to the room, and when it had arrived, I conferenced in Kelsie and kicked off the debrief.

"First things first, Ian. How are you doing? Shooting someone is traumatic."

"OK, I think. A stiff brandy would help. I'll have a few sleepless nights I'm sure."

"The VPD always made us talk to a counsellor after any violent action. Don't be too manly. It helped me every time," offered Marcy. Marcy hadn't known that it was Ian who had shot the assassin until we were on the way back from the police station, and she had been both appreciative and guilt-ridden since.

"Thanks. It was so weird. I arrived and saw you, and you looked like you were worried about a threat in the vicinity. You were all looking about as if trying to locate someone. I decided to go high and do overwatch and sent the others to scour the perimeter for threats. They reported nothing found, by the way. I climbed up to the gallery and unpacked the rifle. I just had it set and when I peered down, I saw the guy in the green coat. The guy I shot. I had this crazy instinct to look away, and even walk away and leave you all to it. I actually began to move back and turn, then caught myself. Why would I do that? It was crazy, I'm sorry. I feel so bad."

"Don't be silly," I said.

"Anyway, I had to fight to refocus on covering you. I found I could scan the area, with effort, but it was most difficult to look at that guy. Part of my brain registered this was really weird, but mostly I just wanted to forget everything and wander off."

"We are very glad you didn't," said Marcy warmly.

"It got real when I noticed him reach for the gun. I guess the adrenalin rush helped me fight off whatever was happening to me, and I was able to really zero in on him. He had somehow been a blur before. I would never have been able to describe him afterwards. But when I managed to concentrate properly, when he drew his weapon, I could see him clearly – and can still picture him now. When he raised the pistol, instinct took over and I..." He drifted into silence. Marcy took over the story.

"I don't have much to add. It's like I nodded off in the middle of it. One minute I was listening to Moy Lei's bizarre story, and then I rocked myself awake suddenly and saw you, Ethan, then looked around and saw the guy on the floor. I had no idea Ian had shot him until you told me in the car coming here. And I can't believe I yelped like that. God! So embarrassing." I put a hand on her arm and took over.

"Whatever it was, it affected us all differently. Moy Lei seemed to know the guy was close." I didn't want to tell the rest of the team about devil-priests yet. Marcy and I had to discuss how much of this we would accept as truth first. "Close by, but she was also somehow convinced he was way off near the door; a good 80 feet, or more, away. Perhaps there were two different people."

I paused, trying to get everything straight in my head, then continued.

"I was assaulted by something. It was like a drug effect. The world was distorted. I lost emotional control and felt paralyzed with fear, even before I saw the gun. It seemed like time wasn't working properly. I could do nothing to stop the guy. He could have easily killed us, if that was his intent – and I think it was. Ian, again, man. Thank you!"

"It's what we do, Ethan. No need for thanks. Unless it's that brandy." I took his hint and called room service and ordered a bottle of their best.

"What about a nerve agent, or a gas?" This from Ian. "If we were all at different distances from the dispersal point, perhaps we would experience different effects, right?"

"Something to look into, I agree. I don't know much about such things. I thought nerve agents typically have lasting physical effects, such as blisters or coughing, which we didn't experience. A gas with a hallucinogen could be a possibility, although it didn't seem to affect the guy who you shot. Do we know who he is?" I realized as I asked that if anyone knew the answer to that last question, it should be me, having spent most time with the police. Everyone shook their heads "no."

A tap on the door interrupted us and we took precautions. Each of us pulled a pistol from the cache Ian had obtained for us, and we fanned out around the room. We expected the brandy but were taking no chances. I peeked out of the peephole and saw Moy Lei on the other side. I cracked the door open and checked she was alone, then let her in. A brief round of introductions followed, and she stepped forward and gave Ian a thank-you hug." Her eyes were puffy; she had clearly been crying.

After we had discussed a strategy to protect us all, the team took their leave. We had rented the whole of the third floor and had rooms for everyone, even if that meant some hot bunking, sharing on a shift pattern. Ian went off and told the hotel staff that, being eccentric billionaires, we wanted no hotel staff or other visitors on the floor without calling ahead. The team rigged cameras and other sensors at strategic points in the hotel and grounds, networked together, and routed the data to Kelsie's team in Vancouver, who would hopefully be out of range of any 'magic.' We would be constantly monitored, backing up our own efforts

We had enough food left over for Moy Lei to sate her hunger, and we ordered up some lemon tea at her request. She had been back to her rental unit and grabbed a small bag with fresh clothes and would stay with us overnight in an adjacent room. Before she ate, she used our shower, as she hadn't dared have one when collecting her bag. She emerged as her tea arrived and sat down and pecked daintily at the food. She was very thin and wore shorts and a tank, ready to retire when we had finished the debrief.

At five feet six — appearing taller due to her light frame — she looked fit and agile, but not hard like someone who runs or cycles excessively. Some Asians have porcelain-white skin, but Moy Lei's was dark – almost olive in colour. She had an intricate body-length tattoo of a thin tree, which started on her left instep and twisted in thin, spiky lines of varying widths to her neck, and then up and over her right ear to her temple. It swirled lightly around her torso and down her arms. The lines were so subtle that the effect was not overpowering. The tree had occasional white, narrow flowers, and some small red, blue, and pink buds. It was both beautiful and mystic.

Her thick, black hair was drying straight and dropped below her shoulders; it was cut in a sharp, level line across her mid-back. Her face was long, her nose thin, her cheekbones soft; she wore no makeup. Her left ear was studded with a six-pointed, silver star through the lobe, and five small spikes ran in a line around the top edge of her ear.

We were all exhausted. We talked over the day's events, and aside from confirming the experience was consistent with reports that Moy Lei had read of devil-priest activity, we had no real new information. She could not account for why she had thought at the cathedral that he was farther off than her radar suggested. I brought up the subject of Chiyome.

"Your mother will be expecting to hear from us. We need to make a plan."

"I'm OK with you telling her you located me. Tell her I have run away from her and I'm well, and that I plan to contact her soon myself. Then you can return to Canada – and safety."

"Ethan and I haven't had a chance to discuss this yet," said Marcy cautiously, looking at me for support to continue, "but I don't think we can walk away. Whoever is behind this probably knows about our involvement. I doubt we will be safe back home, and probably will put others in danger if we return to Vancouver. I believe we have to resolve this by locating the threat and mitigating it." That's my girl. Direct and in your face. "I also think we need to tell your mother what is going on..."

"No, that can't happen. Even if you can convince her not to attempt to identify the devil-priest in her group, I don't think you can communicate with her without being discovered. If the Adept knows we are onto it, it might choose to kill everyone there. That's totally off the table." Moy Lei was adamant, but I thought I might be able to convince her.

"If it's possible to talk with her in secret, I think I know how. Earlier, you asked us to 'suspend disbelief' and hear you out. I'm asking you to do the same now." She did, and we kicked around a plan. She was smart and well informed, and her input elevated our sketchy initial plan to the level of a half-assed plan. It would need more work, but it was a good start. After an hour, we had something no one was comfortable would work, but we were agreed it was our best path forward. I retrieved my laptop from the luggage Ian and the team had brought with them from Gatwick Airport, and contacted the dark web site Chiyome had given us to communicate with her. It was essentially a drop box. We would leave a message, and she would post one back at some future point if she wished. We would have to check back. Our message was:

> "CONTACT MADE. BEARPAW. SIGNIFICANT COMPLICATIONS ENCOUNTERED. NEED TO BRIEF YOU IN PERSON. ALL COMMUNICATIONS DEEMED INSECURE. INCLUDING THIS ONE. YOU HAVE EXTENDED YOUR TRUST, AND WE HAVE DELIVERED. YOU NEED TO TRUST US ANOTHER TIME. WHEN CAN YOU BE IN TIMMINS, ONTARIO? ALONE!"

'Bearpaw' was a codeword known only to Moy Lei and Chiyome, prearranged in case of trouble. I hit 'send,' and Moy Lei retired to her room. We called Ian back and got Kelsie onto a conference call. We spent 30 minutes making arrangements for our return to Canada the next morning, and then let the team get some rest.

*

Marcy and I were exhausted but still buzzed. We decided to slip down to the bar for a drink. It was a risk, given we had enemies at large, but sometimes you just must go with – or in this case, against – the flow. The small bar was quaint; styled like a library, books lined almost every inch of available wall, and it smelled of Charles Dickens and old paper. The period furniture and staff uniforms matched perfectly. It was also full to bursting point, a wedding group occupying most of it. We were not really hungry, but they found us room in the restaurant, so we took a seat and waited to order. Our table was on a slightly raised platform, and we could see across the room; yet at the same time, it felt intimate, being nestled behind an ornate pillar and burgundy velvet drapes. While we sat, Marcy let her leg drift towards me under the table and ran her instep up the side of my shin. Then she continued up to the lower part of my thigh and smiled at me suggestively. Leaning forward with coquettish grace, she slowly peeled her blouse down, exposing part of her shoulder, then ran her finger discreetly over her new tattoo. *Oh, oh.*

The tattoo was of a phoenix rising. It was a recent addition to commemorate the beginning of her battle to leave behind the scars from her abused childhood, which were compounded by what she witnessed during her career as a police officer. It was both a symbol of moving on and up, as well as a connection to us and adventure into BDSM experimentation. Mostly for fun, and partly because it felt naughty and right, she chose 'Phoenix' as her role name when playing dominant to my submissive. I didn't have a name yet, and maybe never would. Gwen had suggested that some people create characters that they step into and out of as a way of framing or 'ringfencing' kinky play. Marcy had considered this, but decided it wasn't for her. She wanted to be herself, not an avatar, but at the same time enjoyed the idea of having a play-name. We had agreed that whenever she presented a phoenix in some manner, whether as a picture or when used as a codeword, it indicated she wanted to play and was taking charge. I guess she had some steam to let off tonight.

Gwen had also clarified for us, that BDSM is different from abuse or a pathology by being *fully* consensual. Even if one party chooses to give up control to another, there are prearranged limits and boundaries, and the encounter is deemed 'consensually non-consensual.' I could opt out, but with little Ethan leaping around in my lap already, I chose not to. I smiled and sat back, signifying that from this point onward, she was the boss.

"I'm ordering from the hostess for you tonight. Whatever I say, you have to go along with and seem happy about it." Not waiting for a response, she took my menu and the wine list away and placed both on her side of the table, alongside her own. She continued to stroke the inside of my thigh with her instep, occasionally extending her leg and reaching almost to the top of my inner thigh. The tablecloth kept things well hidden, despite us sitting on a dais in front of 30 people. The hostess came by shortly afterwards and we chatted for a little while about the castle history, options on the menu, and our plans while in town; we were more than a little vague about the latter.

"What canna start you two off with? You look proper thirsty." Her voice rose and fell in a stop-start Geordie accent.

"I'll have a large glass of Chardonnay," Marcy replied. The server scribbled this down on her pad and looked expectantly at me. Marcy didn't give me time to speak and cut me off with a firm tone.

"I think tonight he'll have a Bacardi and coke. Diet coke if you have it. Keeps him in shape. Tall glass if you have one. Double shot of Bacardi." The server looked from me to Marcy quickly a couple of times, then smiled and scribbled that order down, too.

"Do you want anything to nibble on?" she asked, a subtle, playful change in her tone. This time she addressed Marcy only.

"I'd love some bread, with butter and a nice balsamic perhaps."

"Of course. And him?" She didn't even turn my way.

"He's fine for now, thanks."

"Right-o, then." She smiled and bustled off.

We both laughed out loud once our quick-on-the-uptake hostess had left to fill our order. Of course, Marcy hadn't finished with me yet.

"Go to the restroom and remove your underwear, Ethan. Bring it back here discretely and place it in my purse. Come on, hurry up. You need to be back here before the drinks, otherwise I might make you lose the pants, too." I was out of my seat briskly and returned within 90 seconds. I reached down and picked up her purse, just as the server returned. I tried to ad lib doing something meaningful with Marcy's purse, but nothing came to me. Then I tried handing the purse to Marcy, as if she had asked for it, but she just sat and smiled politely, hands firmly on her knees. I put the purse in my lap and made a meal of opening it, while the server positioned the drinks in the right places in front of us. When she had gone, I hurriedly placed my Saxx into the purse and zipped it shut, then returned it to Marcy's side of the table.

The bread arrived and we were asked if we wanted anything for dinner. It was getting near the end of the evening, so Marcy just ordered a dessert for us both. We made small talk for a few minutes, then Marcy told me to lower the zip on my pants and "let some air in." I felt quite exposed, even though everything was covered by a table cloth. Marcy withdrew her foot, slipped it into her sling-back and reached down to pull the rear strap up over her heel.

"Stand up, and step around here next to me," she ordered sweetly. I complied, checking carefully that nothing was visible through the open fly that shouldn't be. I stood awkwardly by her chair for a long ten seconds.

"My shoe's strap needs to be tightened up a hole. Kneel down and attend to it!" She was really enjoying causing me great discomfort. In truth, it just looked to the world like a man helping his woman with a fiddly shoe strap, but to us the buzz-feeling of psychodrama was building. This behaviour was unsettling as I had no idea where she was going next – but I was determined to keep my nerve, whatever happened. She was clearly in the mood to create chaos for me. As much as I was feeling embarrassed, I was also getting pretty horny. None of this felt undignified or unwelcome; it felt exciting. An anticipatory rollercoaster flipping between panicky dread and sexual thrill, as she set me risky challenges and then I accomplished them.

"Sit now, the dessert is here." I sat back down and quickly flipped the napkin over my crotch, as little Ethan was pressing to find his way out to be friendly and horrifyingly engaging. The hostess asked if we wanted anything else, so Marcy ordered us another round of drinks as well as the cheque.

When the hostess had left, Marcy asked, "Is he hard?" I looked around to see if anyone could have heard the question. I didn't think so.

"Very."

"Then I'll give you a choice: You can either pull your penis out of your zipper under the table or, alternatively, you can call me Mistress Phoenix for the next ten minutes, whenever I ask you a question. What's it to be?" I really didn't think I was ready to go as far as appearing overtly as a sex slave in public, so I opted for the former, reached down, and eased him out. I carefully adjusted the napkin so it didn't look too tent-like. Just as I got organized, the hostess returned with the bill and offered it to Marcy, who accepted and inspected it.

"Honey, pass me your visa."

I had to tilt my hips to reach into my back pocket for my wallet, steadying the napkin with the other hand. I took out my credit card and handed it over. Marcy gave it to the server.

"I'm sorry, we've just arrived from Canada. I appreciate this is indelicate, but what is normal for a tip here?" She addressed the hostess as if I didn't exist. The hostess was clearly having fun at my expense, too. The women were sharing a moment.

"Well, Miss, if you are fully satisfied with our service, ten percent would be bonny. But there's no obligation. I am enjoying looking after you two tonight. You are...refreshing." I wasn't sure what that meant, but it was said with a fun and friendly tone.

Marcy scribbled a tip and passed the bill to me. She had added 50 percent.

"Total and sign that, Ethan. Thank you." I did, and the hostess tapped the numbers into the card machine and let me enter my PIN.

"Thank you both. Have a fun night. Let me know if you need anything else."

The server left and we giggled like idiots. Marcy's face is confident and pretty when at rest; but when she laughs, it is like all of our cares have evaporated and she draws me into her world and lifts me with her girlish charm. At these times, I forget she is a hard-as-nails ex-cop.

"I hope this giggling isn't making you soft. I want you to think of me: I'm wet and interested. In fact, I see you have some ice cream left in your dish and a little juice from your strawberries. Take your finger and swirl it in the bowl, then rub the mix all over your shaft for me. I want to taste it on you when we get back to the room. Oh, and make sure you get a little on your pants, next to your zipper. I'll let you zip yourself up before we leave, but I want people to see that mark on your pants." I glanced around and when no one was looking, I did as instructed. I was starkly aware of my musk and the sweet smell of berries and vanilla blending. We sat and looked at each other. We were the only people in the room as far as we were concerned. She leaned forward.

"So, you seemed very interested in my horse-riding outfit earlier. You like?"

"I like. Very much. You have a riding crop." A statement. Not a question or a suggestion. I held her eyes to mine with all my willpower. She explained what she had learned about Catherine 'Skittles' Walters.

"I'm a little scared of it, if I'm honest. I don't want to hurt you," she said, her mind back in her past somewhere.

"Do you know how to eat a whole elephant?" I laughed as I asked this silly question.

"Er...with salt? No. I don't."

"One bite at a time. Let's just go slowly." I reached over and took her hand and gave it an encouraging squeeze. She giggled again.

"OK. Let's get out of here. Zip yourself up." I did so, stood up, walked behind her, and eased her chair back as she left the table. She led the way to the door with a slight sway, leaving a little 'sass-trail' in her wake for me to wade through. We got to the corridor and she stopped. There was a little side room, where perhaps a dozen other guests were finishing their food. In the centre was a white stone statue of a woman with a pleasant face, in a Greek-era outfit.

"Dare for you, Ethan." She handed me the sunglasses from her purse. "March in there and put the glasses on the statue. Take a photo and bring it to me upstairs. Take your time. Walk up, in fact – I'll take the elevator."

She left me contemplating the least embarrassing way to complete her challenge. I decided there was no subtle way to do this, so I took a breath and strode in. I placed the glasses on the face of the statue. They drooped. Apparently ancient Greeks had smaller faces than modern men and women. I took a picture, then rearranged the glasses and lined up to take some more shots. A woman seated close by smiled and raised an eyebrow.

"Sorry. Scavenger hunt. I'm a Canadian." I said the latter as if it would explain everything. She laughed and leaned over to tell the other five people at her table. The pointing started. I retrieved Marcy's Oakley sunglasses from the statue and swiftly withdrew. I tried to leave some sass in my wake, but I probably just looked awkward.

The restaurant is in the basement, and we occupied the third floor. I climbed the stairs, and each level had two long flights, so I was breathing a little harder when I reached the second. One of my team was seated casually on a bench with a magazine; on guard, but not obviously so. We chatted for a moment and I continued on my way. I checked the camera and sensors on the way up and gave Kelsie a self-conscious 4500-mile wave. I was acutely aware of the red stain on my fly. I let my hand dangle casually in the way, hopefully masking the red mark from her 4k vision.

Due to the irregular nature of a castle, nothing is square. Our room is off the wide, main corridor, just past the third suit of armour. There was a small swing door, another corridor perhaps ten feet long, and then the door to our actual room. The short corridor only leads to our room and nowhere else, expect in one wall there is a closet, for linens and other supplies, I imagined. The Brits do this stuff really well. On the floor in front of our door was a leather case, complete with a padlock and on our door was a pink post-it note.

"All your clothes, phone, key card...everything..., in the case. Lock it up, then knock loudly. I may consider opening the door — PHx." *Gulp.*

I slowly complied with the note and was quickly feeling very vulnerable. As I dropped the last piece of clothing in and 'snicked' the padlock closed — standing completely naked in the corridor — I tried to remember the laws about public nudity in England. It says something about our new game that I had thought to look them up on the plane. There was some legalese, but it boiled down to that you can be nude, as long as there was no attempt to shock others. If the police, or anyone really, suggests you cover up, then you really should. Well, either Marcy would have to give me the key, or someone would need to lend me some clothes to comply with such a request.

I knocked loudly. No reply. I waited. Knocking a second time might get me into more trouble. She must have heard, unless she was in the bathroom. After a long twenty or so seconds, the door cracked open and Marcy's face appeared in the gap.

"Give me the case." She opened the door just wide enough for the case to fit through and I handed it to her. The door closed again. I waited. Nervously. Looking at the door that led out to the hallway, which no one was likely to open, but... Marcy opened the suite's door and handed me a folded-up headscarf.

"Blindfold yourself!" The door closed again. I positioned the soft cloth over my eyes and tied a double knot behind my head. I adjusted the scarf until I could see nothing. And waited. I heard the door open again. Hands on my shoulder turned me about, then grabbed my arms and pulled my wrists together roughly behind my back. I felt a leather belt cinch tightly around my wrists, and then a moment later, a second around my elbows, drawing them together and forcing my shoulders backwards and upwards. A pause, and then the door closed once more.

I was blindfolded, tied up, naked, in a corridor, awaiting discovery. I was sweating. On edge. My world was both zoomed in to the tight space behind the scarf, but also expanded trying to hear any sound. I realized I was standing with most of my muscles tensed. I was at more than half-mast and could feel cool air around my testicles.

I thought I heard someone walking down the corridor, but they didn't stop or open the swing door. I was listening hard for Marcy coming back to open our bedroom door, when I felt her hand cup me very softly. She had closed the door but stayed outside with me. OK, now at full attention. She ran her tongue slowly around my nipple. Keeping me cupped with one hand, she lightly grasped my shaft and played with it. She pushed me slowly back against the wall, which was cold, then I felt her lick the length of me. Then her mouth was over the head my penis and she was sucking slowly. I felt my balls tighten in her grip and goosebumps erupt on my shoulders. I was panting a little. She stopped suddenly, then I heard the beep noise as she opened the door with her card.

"OK, you taste of strawberry and vanilla. And salt. You can come in now. You got me horny," she whispered, close to my right ear. She led me slowly into the room and turned me around. The door clunked closed behind us. I felt the four-poster bedframe behind my knees as she pushed me, slowly, first to a sitting position, then continuing more firmly until I was lying on my back. My arms were pinned beneath me. She grabbed a handful of my hair, pulled my head forward, and propped a pillow under it. I felt the bed move, then weight shifting, and suddenly she was astride me, pinning me down more firmly, her hips over my tummy. Her womanhood was bare and grazed the hairs leading down to my manhood. The inside of her muscled thighs gripped my waist loosely. I felt her hands on the scarf as she slowly removed it. She sat back. Wow, what a sight: black riding boots; open, black horseshow jacket, which I could see in the tall, tilting mirror behind her had a vent through which her bare, curvy bum shone; a black riding hat; and nothing else but a big smile. She reached over to the pillow and grasped the handle of the Skittles crop. She put the leather tag on the end of the crop under my chin and pushed my head back, so I was looking straight at the ceiling.

"Hmm. Tough decision. Which of your heads should I ride?" I wanted to ask *why not both*, but I sensed she was talking to herself more than me so I stayed quiet. She resolved to mount the lower head and eased backwards until the tip of me touched her. Reaching back, she held my balls so that she could guide me in, then kept sliding backwards slowly, until I was fully engulfed. She started slowly moving her hips in all sorts of fun directions. Every few seconds, she gave me a gentle swat on a nipple, or my arms or shoulders. She threw the crop off to the side, and we really started to gallop.

*

When we woke, I checked the site and found a message from Chiyome. "OK-TOMORROW – 5 PM LOCAL – WHERE?" I left an address and signed off. We ate breakfast in our room.

We left Moy Lei, who would collect her things from her rental place and then travel south with Ian and the support team as her personal guards. We would rendezvous with them in London once we had met with her mother in Canada. We checked out at the front desk and walked to the helicopter, with the bellman four paces behind us carrying our one bag. He was dressed in period livery, creating a strange scene indeed.

I did a thorough pre-flight check, then spun up the engine and we lifted cleanly to Newcastle airport, a short ten minutes to the north. We had a long-range Commander aircraft waiting on the tarmac, and I settled the Eurocopter nearby. The private terminal operator agreed to ensure the helicopter was returned to the rental company. We walked across the tarmac, boarded the jet and, once we were satisfied no assassins lurked in the cockpit, it took off for Timmins, Ontario.

With the time zone winding back five hours, it was only 11:15 am when we landed after our seven-hour flight. We were early for the meeting but still had much preparation to complete. We suspected Chiyome would be taking precautions and, despite our suggestion that she was to come alone, we worked on the assumption that she would have her people watching us.

We wandered into a café by the airport and had a light lunch, in full view of anyone who wanted to watch us. At 2 pm, we returned to the hangar and stepped into a Robinson R66 — a five-seat, light helicopter — and flew off over the horizon at top speed and low altitude. Once away from the populated area, I dropped to treetop height and weaved around in the rolling hills. We were pretty confident the anyone watching would lose our trail with this manoeuver but, just to be sure, I landed in a clearing and pulled out a case from the stowage locker. Kelsie had flown into Timmins overnight, and placed the case in the chopper, which had been under guard until we arrived. We changed into fresh clothes from the case and dumped everything we had brought with us. It was a very long shot we were bugged but we took no chances. Leaving our old clothes behind, we took off again and made one more stop to check arrangements for our meeting, then settled down on a small peak to the north to wait for the agreed time.

Kelsie had a team in a small motel, three miles from the rendezvous site. They had dispatched three quadcopter drones in the early hours, and each had landed in a position from which their cameras could watch the meeting location and the roads around it. At 4.30 pm, two ultra-quiet, electric, motor-glider drones were launched, too, and were drifting in lazy circles over the same area at 2000 feet; they were practically invisible to the naked eye. At 4:40 pm, I spun up the helicopter's engine, lifted off, put down again at the motel, where Marcy hopped into a rented F150 truck and drove to meet Chiyome. By 4:50 pm, we were all set, and I could see Marcy and all of the area around the site on the array of screens in Kelsie's temporary operations centre.

I walked out and restarted the R66 and was able to keep in touch with everyone by a private, encrypted, radio link. At three minutes to 5 pm, a white Chevy Saloon came out of the garage of a farm house a mile from our meeting site and made its way to park next to Marcy's truck. As it pulled up, Marcy reported that Chiyome appeared to be the only occupant. Kelsie relayed that she could see Chiyome leave her vehicle and talk with Marcy. Marcy handed a pre-written note to Chiyome that explained we had good reason to think her Kanbo might be compromised and perhaps she was bugged, hence our precautions. The note also contained our plan for the next hour. Chiyome must have accepted our plan because Marcy proceeded to casually lean on her car – our signal to proceed as planned – as the two women made small talk.

I immediately lifted off and covered the ground to the site in a couple of minutes. I settled the R66 on the roadside, 40 feet from where the two stood. They both climbed into the back seat and buckled up. We lifted two feet, spun 180 degrees and then sped up, keeping as low as possible. We skimmed the ground for 600 yards, then I climbed up, over the tree line, and away. We repeated some evasive manoeuvers, including stopping for Chiyome to change clothes and leave them behind. Not knowing her shoe size, we provided her with three sets of white sneakers. She chose the largest, but they were a little big for her. Short of aerial surveillance, we should be untrackable.

We flew south for ten minutes and descended to settle on the pad at the Kidd Mine. I own a significant portion of the mine, and its zinc and copper operations had proven quite lucrative over the years. We were met by the site manager, with whom I had arranged for a personal tour for the three of us. He handed us helmets, reflective jackets, and – in case of any emergency – a personal respirator each. He then gave us a quick safety talk. We then proceeded to the shaft, where he led us to the bottom. Kidd is one of the deepest mines in the world, and we were now 10,300 feet below the surface, surrounded by metal ores. We had no real idea of the capabilities of the Boku-yōkai Adepts, but if this didn't throw them off, we were fucked. We asked our guide to give us some space and he walked away out of earshot, no doubt questioning the sanity of eccentric billionaires.

Chiyome looked at us and raised an expectant eyebrow.

"I am pretty confident my operations are secure, but I admire your diligence at ensuring we are not overheard for this meeting." A little sarcastic, but there was a hint of respect. "I think it is time you told me about my daughter."

Over the next fifteen minutes, Marcy and I took turns to explain the events that unfolded from the time we had arrived in London. We didn't name Nigel or mention our electronic surveillance capabilities, but otherwise shared everything. Moy Lei had prepared a note, which was now in a sealed envelope, and we passed that over to Chiyome. She opened it and read it. I was impressed how unphased she remained throughout, but I could tell the news of the devil-priest had shaken her, as had her daughter's near miss.

"Thank you for saving her life, Mr Booker. Ms Stone. Mr Po obviously can't know of my existence, but please take care of him for me. I am indebted to you all."

"She seems like a nice kid, for an assassin's daughter," said Marcy, a little pointedly. "What do you think of all of this Boku-yōkai stuff? Of course, we are skeptical. But we also can't explain what we experienced."

"I've read some of our arcane literature. I've had a little exposure to some very unusual happenings. To be honest, I, too, find it a stretch; but as you say, if not magic, then what? I can't fault my daughter's logic. If there is an Adept in my Jonin, and if they have the abilities that are claimed, then I have a wolf in my house, most likely hiding in plain sight. They would be lethal and have had years to plan contingencies and create a near infallible information network. I take back what I said about your preparation for this meeting. Perhaps this is barely adequate, but I'm not sure what else you could do. It would be hard for me to move against such a cunning enemy and survive if I don't have a clear idea who it is and – ideally – what they are actually capable of achieving with these alleged, unusual powers."

Chiyome paused, and we were all quiet for a while. We were committed to the next step but hesitated, as it would essentially recommit us. It also bought Chiyome a moment to process the tale we had dumped on her. Eventually, I took a breath and forged ahead.

"We have a few questions and a proposal for you, Chiyome. If we follow the logic that your Jonin Adept became aware of Moy Lei some time ago, then why trigger their counterpart in England when they did? What set off that sequence of events at that time? It appears to have happened within a very short of space of time since our last meeting with you in Vancouver. It implies that that he or she are aware of us. How certain are you of the woman who was with you? Cho was her name?"

"One hundred percent, otherwise she would not have been there. She is one of a very small number of people who I consider show me unwaveringly loyalty. But that's the point, I guess: Someone has fooled me quite cleverly if we believe what we are saying here. But on the other hand, Cho is not Jonin, and was not at the Vegas meeting in October. At that time, she was assigned to the Toussaint family in Mississippi."

"I suppose you won't provide us with a list of the Jonin?" I said it wryly, but she ignored me.

Marcy picked up the conversation. "I don't see much use in going directly at your Jonin. The Adept will see us coming from a mile away and it won't be a happy ending, at least not for us. I think Ethan and I are in grave danger. I think they know who we are and what we are capable of, but would come at us anyway."

"I concur," said Chiyome, nodding.

Marcy continued to lay out what we had agreed ahead of this meeting. "Moy Lei plans to chase down other Boku-yōkai, for her own safety and for yours. We also won't be safe while this Adept has us in their sights. We are going to pool our resources with your daughter and go after your problem. Our intent would be to identify them, from a distance. We would then relay the identity to you. Could you then neutralize the threat?"

"I don't want my daughter in any more danger. Can you protect her?"

"We don't know. Can you? If she does nothing, is she any safer?" asked Marcy.

"I will be ready to take on the Adept if you can identify them," responded Chiyome, with conviction in her eyes.

It would be interesting to see how that would happen, but we were glad we would not have to go after them ourselves. Marcy and I are not killers, although this would be self-defence. This next 'ask' would be a tough one for Chiyome to deliver, but I put it out there anyway.

"We have no real idea what we are up against. It would be helpful to get access to your information on the Boku-yōkai." The queen of assassins was silent for several long moments. But then assented.

"What you ask will take some time to separate and acquire if I am going to do it deftly. Look at the website in 72 hours."

We discussed several more points and then retraced our steps to Chiyome's car. Forty minutes later we were wheels up for London on the chartered jet.

5: DEAD MEN WRITE THE RULES

[GWEN] — I had known Ethan for a few years before we became friends. He very kindly donates some of his wealth each year to the University where I once sat on the Donation Distribution Committee. When I retired from teaching sexual sciences to third- and fourth-year students, I yearned to cross *cool coffee shop owner* off my bucket list. I'm not a lover of coffee, but having spent so much time studying in coffee shops over the years, I felt that I knew how to make the best atmosphere in the world. Ethan not only helped me find space for The Crazy Bean, he also offered me the chance to rent my suite in the Booker Building, right above the shop (albeit 26 floors above).

Ethan also lets me use an office on the 20th floor for my other small business. I maintain a very small and exclusive client list for people wanting sex and relationship counselling. I maintain my qualifications so that I can practise. I am also part of a group informally called Kink Aware Counsellors. I have spent the past five years becoming very well informed on non-traditional sexual and relationship subjects, and their truths and myths. The Kink Aware group spends most of its time educating other psychologists and counsellors on the new information available from studies and surveys on sexual activity and psychology. The data is undermining long-held beliefs about human sexuality and might trigger the biggest sexual revolution since the 1960s. And I think that is awesome!

There is a fundamental change in thinking called for, now that the two leading governance bodies in the world of psychology are doing a complete about-face, upsetting a range of long-held beliefs. In Europe, the World Health Organization (WHO), and in North America, the American Psychological Association (APA), maintain their respective 'bibles' that document human behaviour. These are segregated into what is deemed 'normal' and what is not, and what should be done clinically about either. These publications – the International Classification of Diseases, (ICD), and the Diagnostic and Statistical Manual (DSM) – have existed for decades and, through many revisions, have maintained the firm position that most forms of sexual behaviour unrelated to the pursuit of procreation were deviant forms of sicknesses that could require treatment. Homosexuality was chief among these illnesses and, starting in the 1960s, took 50 years to reach today's status in the UK and North America, which is that psychologists deem it normal behaviour. Legally, too, in most of the western world it is considered normal. In about a third of the western world, same-sex marriage is allowed. The media has largely embraced it, and at last we see eminent role models who happen to be gay or lesbian promoted in all walks of life. Yet there remain significant areas that are much more conservative. There are still 14 states in the USA (Alabama, Florida, Idaho, Kansas, Louisiana, Michigan, Mississippi, Missouri, North Carolina, Oklahoma, South Carolina, Texas, Utah, and Virginia) that maintain anti-sodomy laws, despite the federal Supreme Court ruling in 2003 invalidating them all. In the more progressive of societies, although we enthusiastically support the concept of homosexuality, we are still learning how to feel entirely comfortable with it.

The world of "*kink*" is on a similar liberalization trajectory but lagging by 20 to 30 years. The WHO and APA categorizations have reinforced the stigma in the general populous about kinky sex. For two decades in my case, and 120 years for my colleagues and their predecessors, it was our job to diagnose and treat people who had fetishes and unusual, often frivolous sexual interests. We were doing that work diligently, in private and often in courtrooms, too.

It is very hard for a group of experts to admit that what they have believed, taught, and prescribed for most of their careers is at best uncertain, and in many cases might have been doing more harm than good. In the early part of this decade, the APA recategorized most activity that would fall into the definition of BDSM from a pathology to a paraphilia. The former a disease, the latter a sexual preference shared by only a very small portion of the population but is otherwise deemed normal. Like anything else, as long as your paraphilia doesn't cause you or others distress — other than dealing with the impact on you of society's stigmatic view of your preference — and that any activity is genuinely consensual, it is no longer considered a disorder. This year, the WHO indicated they were essentially following suit.

It is interesting that this kind of pivot takes years. The decision made by the WHO this year will be formally endorsed in 2019 but won't really come fully into effect until 2023. The long cycle is not (only) red tape; it is because it is smart to go slowly to make such fundamental change, for the following reasons. Remember, courts have ruled on cases involving child custody and work termination based on these laws, which are now changing. A whole profession with big egos — mine included — must rethink treatments, approaches, language, case histories, and a myriad of aspects of what we do. But more than that, we have to make a belief transition, and get our heads *and hearts* around it. It has been far easier for me because I have enjoyed BDSM since my teens and the world is aligning itself to my belief, not moving away from my long-held views.

I was out with a small party of progressive colleagues celebrating the announcement that the WHO had taken this aforementioned bold step, when I got the call from Ethan asking for my help. He didn't tell me the details but essentially wanted my assistance contacting an ex-colleague in connection with a case he was working on in London.

Dr Naomi Harroway is considered a leader in stem cell research. She lived in London in 2008 and was studying the science of regenerative therapies during the explosion of the subject onto the world stage, and was part of the transition from questionable experimentation to a viable, if controversial, science. She met Jane Eldridge, who worked with me here at our university, when we were away at a conference in Massachusetts, and they fell in love. As a researcher in neuroscience, Jane could keep up with Naomi in deep conversations about cells and brains, which left the rest of us way behind. Hearing them passionately chatter and babble away in what sounded like their personal foreign language was refreshing. After a year of dating, they wanted to marry, and Naomi relocated to Canada where same-sex marriage had been legal for five years already; it would not become legal in the UK until five years later. I knew Jane well, both socially and professionally, and attended their beautiful and touching wedding.

In 2015, Jane was killed in a road accident. She had been full of life and the pair were laughing their way through the shops on Robson street when Jane stepped into the road and was crushed by a city bus. Naomi witnessed the horrible sight. Jane died, and Naomi's heart broke at the scene. Over the next three months, Naomi had a total breakdown and, although I didn't have a formal patient-therapist relationship with her, as a close friend I offered as much support as possible. But slowly and certainly Naomi pushed us all away and became reclusive. Eventually she relocated to south London, and we've all lost touch. It's so sad. Once a year I visit Jane's memorial on campus and talk to her about Naomi for a brief, personal moment. Tissues are involved.

Ethan's ever-diligent team, while doing research for his case, came across my relationship to Naomi and he asked me to contact her to provide an introduction. I briefly explained the circumstances. He asked if I would be willing to fly to London and try to reach out in person. Apparently, the case was important. I packed enough clothes to spend two weeks away. Gia enthusiastically agreed to dog-sit Elvis, who had started pining as soon as I reached for my suitcase. I was pessimistic that time would have healed enough to let me rekindle any sort of relationship with Naomi — if anything, seeing me again would pick off any scabs that may have formed — but for Ethan, I would willingly try.

When you first meet Ethan, you immediately intuit he is confident from accomplishment, not wealth. You sense he is compassionate and empathetic, yet incredibly independent in an infectious way that lifts you up to stand on firmer feet yourself. He is powerfully built and gorgeous, but genuinely unaware of how striking he is and the effect his natural charisma has on his admirers. This innocence of course amplifies their desire and interest no end. He is the whole package, and you would *never* think of him as incomplete or out of balance. Until you see him with Marcy, and you realize he had been missing an essential part of himself. Some musicians are great soloists but come alive playing in a band. Marcy is his difference between going happily through life, and actually living life.

Marcy is black and white. Very little grey. Her typical approach is as straight forward as possible, at full speed. Not that she can't be subtle and tactful, because she can. But she will tell you exactly what she is thinking, doing so with a mature finesse.

Our first real meeting was full of fireworks following an embarrassing misunderstanding, but we quickly became fast friends. I think I was able to help her repackage her feelings towards sex, and how abuse and BDSM are different. I shared a wealth of information with her, and to borrow from the famous Mark Twain quote, good information "is the enemy of bigotry." Perhaps the words that allowed her to fly free were from a conversation about how most of our beliefs and stigmas came from great yet 'faulty' science, from the likes of Ebbing and Freud in the late 1800s. Those adventurers into a complex, unexplored, and undefined realm created a great framework, but had biased data — or no data at all — to validate their beliefs; a creed that itself was a product of living in a truly repressed society. In such a society, and without the likes of the internet and its anonymously gathered data, most people would not discuss their sexuality. It just was not done, and if anyone would, admitting to being sex positive was almost a social crime, despite what people practised behind closed doors. So, the new science was tested and validated by studying people in jails and asylums, or reading stories written by the likes of the Marquis de Sade, a man who was incarcerated for much of his adult life. Or Sacher-Masoch, who was benign but loved to be dominated by women, and if possible, women wearing fur. Venus in Fur, which became a Roman Polanski movie and a Broadway show, is an example of his work. De Sade and Masoch were where the terms sadist and masochist were derived from. With such pitiful data, and nothing to challenge it, the relatively immature science defined kink, homosexuality, and almost any sex not directly pursuant to reproduction, as bad.

Marcy summarized my sermon back to me at the time.

"I get it. The rules made by a bunch of dead guys still dictate to us today. The new data just now becoming available is a potential game-changer, and we are abdicating our responsibility if we do not take an openminded look at it." As I said, she is black and white, but not narrow minded or inflexible. I have since proudly incorporated her words into my counselling of others.

*

Kelsie booked me a fabulous first-class flight and I was chauffeured to the airport and fast-tracked through all the checkpoints on both sides of the Atlantic. As I led my suitcase out of customs, a cute woman in a suit was holding a card with our agreed word on it, "Robinson." Ethan insisted on using a codeword rather than my real name, as he worries about kidnapping. It's less likely to happen in London than other geographies, but it has become part of his normal way to do things wherever he travels, as his wealth makes him a potential target. I thought he was being paranoid, but he explained it is more common than you think for bad people to turn up at the airport, copy a name off a legitimate driver's card, stand closer to the arrivals door than the legitimate driver, and intercept their customers. Their victim happily lets the kidnapper carry their case to the awaiting car – into which they climb through the door being politely held open for them – and then bad things happen. In many cases, they are just robbed and dropped off again. They can be taken to cash machines and forced to drain their bank accounts, and to places where they are forced to use their credit cards. In extreme cases, they are held for ransom.

In Ethan's world, you have the driver's name and he has to confirm he knows your real name before you go with him. Quite smart, and there is no hardship to it. The Robinson codeword is Ethan's little joke, referring to the book and movie called The Graduate. In the movie, Ann Bancroft plays the woman of the world to the innocent but horny young Dustin Hoffman's 21-year-old character, which is the point of Ethan's wit. Ann goes on to seduce Dustin but, as Ethan knows, he is not my type. The cute, female, Town Car driver holding the sign might be. Coincidence, or did Kelsie ask for a female driver? That would be her style. Efficient and funny.

In no time at all, I was dropped off outside a charming pub just across from the Colliers Wood tube station, in southwest London. The car drove on to drop my luggage off at wherever Kelsie had booked for us, and I wandered in to the bustling bar through the wood and glass door. Like most pubs in the London suburbs, it was eclectic and busy, but it took me no time to find Marcy perched at a garden bench drinking a glass of white something. She hopped up and we hugged like old friends, and she went off to buy the first round. Chardonnay for me. The order reminded me how confused the Brits and Canadians still are about the metric system. We Canadians drive in kilometres and order wine by the ounce, whereas the Brits drive in miles and order wine in millilitres. We were soon seated under a warm sun, drinking 250ml drinks, enjoying a cool breeze and girl-talk.

"Ethan is about 15 minutes away. He had some business to attend to, unrelated to our case, seeing as he was in town. This case is a bit confidential, and a little odd, so I hope you won't be offended if I don't share too many of the details?" Marcy was uncomfortable from having to hold back information from me, an inveterate nosy parker.

"And you know how much I love to poke at secrets," I teased. "Seriously, it's OK. What can you tell me?"

"We have a client who has an issue that relates to stem cell research. It's fairly esoteric stuff on the edge of the field so we wanted to find an advisor and, according to the research we've done so far, there are not too many with Naomi's level of insight. We certainly have other options, but when we saw the connection to you, we thought we would start with her. You said she wasn't well?"

"She wasn't well when I saw her last, but we've lost touch. I'm not sure how she is these days. Her partner died in an accident and it really knocked Naomi sideways."

I'd noticed a group of men across the garden looking our way a couple of times. Marcy confirmed that they had been getting louder over the past hour as they worked their way through several pitchers of beer. My spidey-sense made me glance at them now, and sure enough, they were elbowing each other, pointing our way, and getting a little too macho. It was a mistake to glance, as it only encouraged them. Two of them stood and wandered our way. I gave Marcy a look that alerted her to trouble coming, and she sat back in her chair and somehow radiated unfriendly vibes, which unfortunately flowed over the heads of the prowling drunks.

"Buy you ladies a drink?" This from the taller one. He was Caucasian, late 20s, thin, barely filling out his 1970s Stranglers punk shirt. His jeans had holes in them, but not the sort you pay extra for. His sidekick was stocky, pale, and perhaps a younger, smaller brother. He was much better dressed than his buddy. Obviously thought himself a bit of a clotheshorse. Shame about the fluffy beard.

"No thanks. Nice of you both. We haven't seen each other for a while and need the time to catch up," explained Marcy pleasantly, giving them an easy exit.

"That's OK love. We've never met either of you, so it will take a long time for the four of us to all catch up. We'll buy the first round. What'll you have?"

"No offence, we'll let you get back to your group over there. We are not feeling very social. Again, thanks, but no thanks." *Still polite, but a bit firmer. Not quite 'piss off.'*

Then the stocky one really put the cat among the pigeons. "You two just planning a little girl-o-girl thing then?"

I really hate Neanderthals like these. I felt my head swivel slowly their way. I heard Marcy whisper under her breath, "Oh crap." She sensed my rage welling up and pointedly glared a warning at me as it took shape and leapt up, and out of my mouth.

"Well I for one would. She is a cutie, isn't she? But she's got more testosterone than your whole schoolboy gang over there put together and she has a real man who takes her to bed. I'll have to settle for you two flakes, I suppose. I hate to lower myself to twerps who don't understand a polite turndown when they see it. But I am hungry, and you two would make nice snacks." Their eyes bulged with anger, which only encouraged me, I'm afraid. "But if we do this, it's my rules. And I'm bringing my strap-on; I have a much bigger dick than you two, I bet. Go sit down and let me finish catching up, and I'll come collect you on the way out and we can go and play!" I stopped. The garden had gone very quiet.

"Or we can put that smart mouth to better use," the tall one said, after a short pause. His face had gone as red as beetroot and I saw my 'intimidate-the-bully' gambit hadn't worked as I'd hoped. Marcy stood up and stepped between us.

"OK, that was fun, but it's over. Fuck off and sit down."

"But we came all this way!"

"It'll be embarrassing going back with egg on your face, but better than me putting you down on the ground. I'm a cop and you won't be either my first or my biggest dance. I want to get on with my conversation, so either take a swing at me and take the consequences, or go back to your seats." She took a couple of steps towards them to back up her words with action. I had no doubt she could contain these two, but if the rest of the gang decided to join in, some of them would get hurt. The gang stood up and started to walk over. *Dang*! Marcy changed positions and shifted her weight onto her back leg. A fighter's stance. I pushed my chair back and stood up, pulling the almost-empty Chardonnay bottle from the cooler bucket and flipping it around to use as a club. The remaining wine spilled onto the grass at my feet. What a waste.

"I've got 5000 pounds to bet that the girls win! Any takers?" boomed a loud voice. Heads turned. Ethan was leaning against a post, watching. He'd taken his jacket off and his physique looked pumped. His voice was playful but his eyes were murderous. He looked hard, fit, and threatening. "What do you think, Derek?"

Derek, who was Marcy's bodyguard today, was sitting at a table nearer the fence and had been waiting for Marcy's signal to dive in. He dropped his newspaper, stood, and slowly removed his jacket, too. Derek used to be a bouncer apparently, and he knew how to intimidate punks.

"I want to bet with you, not against you, man. I've seen her spar with Gia, and Gia was an MMA fighter. But I disagree with the blonde lady over there. I think these punks are smarter than she said. I think they know when to walk away, and I think they will even clear that lady's bill on the way out. They did offer to buy a drink after all."

The momentum had changed so much in our favour now that two men and a woman we didn't know stood and faced off with the gang. The gang were looking more and more isolated and unhappy by the second.

To his credit, the taller one saved some face. He made a 'tsk'-ing noise and pointed at Marcy and smiled. Then said, "Respect!" in a gangster voice, which didn't really suit a white guy. He pivoted, dipping slightly to kick off his gangster walk and lead his boys out of the pub. A server started to object, as they hadn't paid, but Ethan leaned over and I heard him whisper to her, "I'll cover them. Let them go." He walked over, kissed Marcy's cheek, and sat down next to us; Derek returned to his newspaper. The garden settled back down to their conversations, laced with the dissolving drama, and the server brought us all another round. On the house this time.

"Think I need your help to kick their ass?" Marcy grunted, semi-jokingly.

"Not when you have Gwen as back-up, no!" he said, deadpan. "In fact, I was betting in your favour, in case you didn't notice." Marcy leaned over and kissed his cheek back in mock forgiveness.

We talked about different ways for me to approach Naomi. Ethan's team had been surveilling her, which felt intrusive and quite wrong to me and I said so. But I conceded that there wasn't much choice and, aside from tracking her movements, the observations were not invasive. We'd learned her cellphone number and I could call her; but if I did, she might not pick up or, worse, answer and refuse to see me. I could walk up and knock on her door when we knew she was home. The third option was at a coffee shop, which for the past two mornings at least, Naomi had visited at 8:30 am. She took a laptop and spent 30 minutes sipping an espresso while perusing news and research. After much debate about pros and cons, we opted for the last option. We would come back in the morning; I would be waiting for her and would try to open a dialogue.

Before leaving for our hotel, I suggested we do a walk by Naomi's home. Having a better sense of how she lives now might help me reconnect with her the next morning. We drained our glasses and set out along Merton High Street. We would turn right on Leyton Road, then right again onto James Street, where Naomi rented an upstairs flat in number 44. Ethan dispatched his Audi Q5 and driver to the far end of the street so we would walk past Naomi's apartment and then depart in the car and return the next day.

I didn't realize how wound up I was until we were halfway up Leyton Road. A door ahead flew open and a woman with red hair – dressed for the gym – zipped out holding a black cat under one arm. I jumped out of my skin and put one hand on my chest. She locked her door, crossed the road and, using a different key, she opened the door of her neighbour's house, deposited the cat on the mat, and locked up again. She climbed into a tiny Yaris and drove off in the direction we were walking. I realized I had been holding my breath.

"Easy now, Gwen," laughed Ethan.

"It's alright for you toy-detectives. You do this for fun. I'm feeling guilty spying on my friend and terrified I will mess this up for you two."

"Sorry, I was just trying to calm you down."

"No, my fault. I'm being silly." We carried on.

All of the houses on James Street were connected in one long, two-story terrace of matching light-brown brick dating from the late Victorian era. Each had a grey slate roof and a tiny gated yard that spanned the width of the house, but was only four feet deep and separated the house from the sidewalk. Most occupants stored their garbage and recycling bins in this small yard-space, and each bin was a matching grey or blue per council code. You are struck by the sense of uniformity; but then you realize that each house has unique doors and windows, and some have small add-ons like loft extensions and, suddenly, the uniformity morphs into chaos.

Number 44 had a sturdy white front door with a black knocker but did not have the double porch like most of its neighbours. The windows had all been replaced with white, double-glazed units sporting faux lead-line lattices that attempted to project a quaintness of times gone by, but resulted in a cluttered, overly busy look. The upstairs front window was apparently Naomi's and had green curtains. That shade of green had been Jane's favourite.

Ethan's surveillance was electronic, with tiny cameras concealed in a parked car monitoring the front of the house. Through this camera we had seen Naomi arrive earlier, and as there was no rear exit, we knew she was home. We were hurrying past when her face appeared at the window and our eyes met. I panicked and stopped. I was sure she recognized me. I thought that if I spooked her, she might not go for her regular coffee in the morning and might even leave town. I went with my gut and waved to her, then walked slowly over to the front door. Ethan and Marcy carried on – heads down, looking guilty – and left me to it. I didn't knock. She had seen me approach; the pressure of knowing I was on the step was already enough. I gave her time to process this surprise and stood tensely waiting to see if she would open the door. I anchored my feet, suddenly conscious that I was rocking back and forth.

"Who are those people, Gwen?" Naomi's voice through the door.

"Hello, Naomi. How are you, hon? They are good friends of mine. Can I talk to you? If you don't want me to come inside, I see a pub down the street where we could talk. I'll buy you a drink if you like."

"Have you known them long? Those friends?" *Unusual question.* She sounded a little paranoid, which renewed my concern for her welfare. If she was still sick, I would advise Ethan to back off.

"Ethan, for years. He's my neighbour. He's always talked about Marcy, but I have only got to know her well in the last two months. They live together now, so I guess they are both my neighbours. Really nice folks." There was a long pause, then the locks clunked and clicked. She opened the door and quickly pulled me inside. She relocked the door, turned, and melted into my shoulder in tears. I wrapped her up in a hug, then realized that I was crying, too. Tears freely flowing down both our faces.

"God, look at us. Come up, I'll put the kettle on." She led me up a flight of stairs, past a sitting room, and out to the back of the house. The tiny kitchen was clean and tidy. She hugged me again, then showed me to a chair tucked under the small rectangular table that hugged the back wall. She busied herself with kettles, cups, and cupboard doors, and I sat quietly. My instinct told me to let her drive the pace.

The last few years had not been kind to Naomi's face, which seemed to have aged ten years, not three. She retained her boyish figure and, if anything, had lost a couple of pounds, which made her look a little wiry. Her day-to-day attire was still a tank top and jeans and, as I noted from the surveillance photos of outdoors, a snug leather jacket. Her tight dreadlocks rolled off her head and almost to her waist, ending in about a dozen tails. They started from five crisp braids, which ran back from her forehead like rows of crops that had been planted and tended to all this time by diligent farmers who used to be soldiers sworn to military precision. Stylish, not grungy. Her mulatto skin was still smooth and glowing, but her face was thin and had a tendency towards looking mean; a look that she had honed to keep away unwanted attention. Her left eye hinted at being lazy and was offset by her right eyebrow being a little high, but both were anchored neatly around a razor-straight nose. Her lips were thin and gave her an intelligent air and, although puffy now from crying, her eyes were quick and beautiful. The whole ensemble was both lithe and elegant, and totally captivating.

"Sugar and milk?" I answered yes to both. She brought over two cups and a small plate of cookies. Her hand trembled slightly as she set them down. Her nails were bitten down to the quick.

"I think about you and our group from Vancouver often. I miss you all terribly," she said, looking off to some distant place.

"Are you still finding it hard to talk about things? I miss her. I go to her memorial site and, although I know she's not there, it comforts me," I said, softly.

"I really miss her. But I've made my peace with her not being here anymore." Neither of us had used Jane's name.

"Are you back at work?" I changed the subject. I knew she wasn't.

"No. Well, I do some research from home occasionally to keep the wolves from the door, but I don't work for a company or go to an office or anything. I rarely leave the house."

"You know that's not healthy. Are you seeing anyone?" She would know I meant a therapist, not a girlfriend.

"No. But I'm feeling well. You know, healthy. I know this is going to make me sound bonkers – and definitely like I need a shrink – but I'm convinced that there is something sinister going on. I'm not hiding at home because I'm depressed; I'm here because I'm terrified."

"What do you mean?" I suddenly felt very uncomfortable, my neck hairs standing up.

"It started with Jane's accident. Honestly, I relive that moment so often I wonder if my memory is faulty. We were chatting happily, holding hands, looking at shoes in a window. We had an anniversary coming up and she wanted to buy me something. She stopped and looked puzzled, then turned and looked across the street. Her face changed. She smiled almost like she recognized someone she knew, but there was no one there. I saw clearly. It's usually a very a busy street, but right then there was an absence of people. She squeezed my hand then took off into the road smiling. I didn't recall any of this at the time, we were so intent on saving her. But lately, I went over it and I'm sure she felt she saw someone she wanted to talk to."

"She might have, and that's tragic, of course. But it's all in the past now, surely. Nothing to be done about it. She wouldn't want you holed up and missing out on life." I squeezed her hand.

"Yes, but that's not all. Other people are dying."

"Other people?"

"Eight people who I've worked with over the years have also died in accidents. I heard about Bob Mayes; I wrote a paper with him in 2008. He died unexpectedly in an accident, so I contacted Joyce, his widow. We met for dinner and she told me the story. He stepped off a flat roof. He was up fixing a leak and she was watching from a window. He just suddenly looked up, smiled, and walked. It was as if he thought there was a bridge. Didn't hesitate. The penny didn't drop for me. Then I heard about Carol Bravoski. We were lab rats together in our clinical research internships. Walked onto a train line. Her husband thought she had seen someone she knew. Probably a big coincidence, I know, but I'm wired to be drawn to such anomalies, so I had to research it. Eight people in the field of regenerative research have died in similar circumstances. That is statistically relevant."

"Have you talked to the police?"

"And say what? Besides, no one has died in England. The eight deaths are in six different countries. And... sometimes I feel like I am being followed. I never see anyone, but I'm sure that some days I am being watched. Some days I have terrible fits of fear."

"Is that why you were asking me about Ethan and Marcy? How long I've known them?"

"Yes. I'm suspicious of everyone, Gwen. I hate myself, but I'm terrified. I think it must be something to do with big pharmaceutical companies. They spend billions, and you hear stories about their cutthroat tactics. I am so happy to see you, Gwen, but you shouldn't hang around. I could be putting you in danger."

"Come here, honey!" I leaned over and we hugged. She was reluctant to let go, and so was I. "Listen, I didn't expect you to agree to see me if I'm honest, but I am so pleased you let me come in. I had tried for a long time to reconnect with you, but you wouldn't let us come close. Of course, it's not a total coincidence that I was walking past your door now." She tensed a little. "Ethan and Marcy are detectives. Well, private detectives. Marcy was a real police detective until recently, but they both do private work now. They just helped take down a ring of human traffickers in Mississippi. They are good people, doing things for people who don't have many options. Sort of like Robin Hood and Maid Marion. They haven't told me about their case. Confidential and all that. But they had hoped to talk to you about some aspect of it. I don't know what, but they had hoped you would be some sort of technical advisor."

"I'm not sure I would want to get involved in something that might bring me even more trouble. I'm struggling to cope with what I already have."

"Look, you have to make your own determination, but I would trust them with my life. In fact, I have. Perhaps whatever has you scared actually relates to what they are working on. Perhaps you could help each other."

She sat quietly for a while before speaking.

"I guess I can't live like this forever. I have to take a chance at some point. If you think I can trust them."

"I do. I think you should hear them out and if you are not interested, they'll back off. I'm sure of it. And if you decide to share it, I think you could ask them not to act on your story unless you agree to it. They are two of the most ethical people I know. And they laugh in the face of danger!" I said, in a dramatic British accent. We both started laughing. A silly, tension-relieving chuckle, which built into a wave of giggles. We both stood and hugged again.

"I've really missed you Gwen, you crazy bitch."

6: THE WRONG PROBLEM

[ETHAN] — We had both grabbed a few hours' sleep over the Atlantic, and a few more after reaching our Wimbledon hotel at 4 am, but I wasn't ready to face the day when my 9 am alarm sounded, seemingly seconds after my head hit the pillow. We had a brunch meeting planned with Naomi and Gwen for 11:30 am, so with my emphasis favouring the third of the following options, I rolled over and suggested to Marcy how we could start our day.

"We could grab another hour's sleep, or... find some running gear and race around the common, or... see how many orgasms I can give you in an hour; set a new record." She rolled over and snuggled in, and I thought she was going to say "yes" to option three, but it turned out she had other, quite evil, plans.

"Actually, no. I have a better idea. Don't think it escaped my attention that you solved the case of 'the missing Naomi' yesterday, Slave-Boy."

"Oh. Crap," I gulped, suddenly feeling very nervous. And excited. Little Ethan had been at half-mast but was suddenly poking Marcy in the belly and twitching for attention. She wrapped her fingers playfully around him and nuzzled her lips into my ear and whispered.

"I'm showering first. Then you, but don't come out of the bathroom without permission. I have a surprise for you!"

Fifteen minutes later I was toweling off when Marcy, speaking in a mock British accent ordered me out of the bathroom.

"Hurry up, Ethan. I've laid your clothes out on the bed. You have three minutes before we are out the door – however you are dressed – so I suggest you don't dilly dally."

Marcy was ready to go, dressed in jeans, ankle-length leather boots, a white T-shirt, and the raincoat that we had acquired in Durham. I approached the bed apprehensively, and saw she had laid out my coat, a red golf shirt, jeans, and socks and shoes. *Seems OK*, I thought, until I lifted the shirt to put it on and detected someone – who was now grinning like a Cheshire cat and waving scissors she had somehow obtained – had cut away the crotch of the jeans. And then I spotted there was no underwear in sight. I put everything on quickly, conscious of my time running out, and glanced in the mirror. With the thigh-length coat done up, nothing looked amiss. But underneath, from the top of my thighs upwards, the jeans consisted of the belt, then a strip of material on each side to hold up the pant legs, and nothing else. Buttless – and frontless – chaps, but in dark denim.

"Come on, then. There's a shop I want to go to, which will be open at 10 am. That's in five minutes." As she said this, she reached over and tugged me by the collar so that the coat rose up an inch or two, and I quickly, and obediently, scooted behind her out into the corridor. We waved off the protection team that had started to follow us, and we went outside. I carefully stepped down the three stone steps to the uneven sidewalk, and we turned right and headed down towards the high street. I had my hands firmly placed in my coat pockets to hold everything down, but Marcy wasn't about to make it that easy for me.

"Hold my hand, Ethan," she laughed, "and take your other hand out, too. If you try to stop gravity from taking its course, I'll have you march with your hands on your head."

"Yes, Phoenix." It struck me that was the first time I had used a title in our play, so I asked, "Or should I say Miss, or Mistress?"

"While no one is in earshot, let's try Mistress or Phoenix. I'm not sure I will like it, but only one way to find out. I like calling you Slave-Boy, so get used to that. Slave-Boy."

"Err... Yes, Mistress. May I ask where we are headed? And how long we will be outside? It's rather chilly, you know."

"Suck it up, Slave-Boy. You like it when I go commando in a skirt." She gripped my hand. Then, in a slightly more serious tone, changed the subject.

"What did you mean when we were in bed, just after landing in Durham, when you said that you don't see yourself as a shy exhibitionist? We never circled back to that topic. You got all alpha-brat on me as I recall, and we became distracted."

"Only that I think an exhibitionist likes the part where people are staring at them, even if they have to be teased out of their shell. Shyness aside, I think they get a kick from being observed by people, and perhaps showing off, whereas I genuinely fear being caught and being unable to do anything about it. The threat of forced exposure turns me on. Either forced physically, like being tied up and unable to cover myself; or like now, psychologically, where technically I'm only forced by my commitment to obey your directions. The odd times I've actually been caught naked, such as by Gwen on the roof that time or when you marched me naked down the nude beach in France carrying my clothes in a locked bag, I found deeply embarrassing. But if I'm honest, I do enjoy enduring those moments, too. It is thrilling, but it's definitely enduring, not basking in it, like I think exhibitionists do. That's akin to when you spanked me. Did I love the pain? Definitely, yes. But the real high came from the buildup of dread — that's important — then being pushed to my limit or a little beyond even; and enduring it. I get off on being able to prove to you, and myself, that I can withstand what you throw at me. That sounds vain, but it doesn't feel that way to me."

We rounded a corner, and Marcy suddenly stopped and pointed down at a tin can that littered the sidewalk.

"Why do people litter, Ethan? Be a good Slave-Boy and pick that up, will you?" she ordered. The twinkle in her eye and evil grin made it clear she had been searching for some reason to make me bend over in the short coat. I looked around and the coast was clear, so I quickly scooped it up and tossed it into the trash can that was just a few feet away.

"Another question for you, Slave-Boy," she said, once her laughter at my awkward manoeuver had abated. "Right now, I think we are doing really well at dangling your dignity out there in the wind – pun intended – but there might come a point when I want to step things up even further. But you can only be so naked, or almost caught. You can't get more nude than fully naked, or closer than 'almost' caught. How do I add more danger for you? Any suggestions? Or would you prefer me to work it out and surprise you? I worry about surprising you, because we are supposed to be discussing or negotiating limits in advance. It's hard to surprise you if we just agreed to do something."

"Yes, it's tricky. I see that," I exclaimed, with exaggerated anxiety in my voice. I was caught and confused between not wanting to shoot myself in the foot, and wanting her to have room to push my limits. "I like the surprises, and you are so good at them. How about we say I fully consent to you surprising me? How's that? If you leave me a short window to use my safe word, it would be ideal, but I know that is not always possible in that instant of surprise. I have to accept that if it goes a little too far, I am responsible for that, too, and will have to get over it, as I am asking you to push me *and* surprise me."

"Any guidelines?" she asked. I'd spent some time thinking about what drives me, and shared part of it with her now.

"I would hate my predicaments to upset unwilling participants. The idea of unwittingly shocking kids, for example. And yes, I know playing these games we can't always think of everything, but assuming we can somehow mitigate those risks, my thrill centres around the dread and psychodrama building up to the maximum. At a location where nakedness is accepted – a nude beach, for example – the risk of shocking others goes away, but my embarrassment doesn't at all. You can totally mess with my head, but it's different again in a space like here, on the street. I feel pretty confident that here, you wouldn't ask me to strip right off and walk naked, but I can really fret about an awkward flash." I paused, both worried and excited about what I was about to say.

"I recall being disciplined by Pa once, where he took his hand to me. I can't recall what I had been up to, but I remember thinking I had been in the wrong. It wasn't a hard smack; it was more of a shock, as I never thought he would *ever* smack me. Afterwards, knowing that he would follow through if I went too far, I always knew he would go further than I would." I froze, suddenly thinking of Marcy's abusive parents. *Idiot. Where was my head*? I rush to fix it. "Marcy, so sorry. I know today we would consider that abuse."

"Maybe," Marcy chimed in, squeezing my hand to let me know I hadn't accidently brought out her own demons from her past. "I think you ended up respecting him, rather than fearing him. Neither of us condones non-consensual corporal punishment today, but I can tell you first-hand that true abuse never ends in respect."

"Good to know. My point is, in scenarios like here, today, I know you can push my limits quite a lot, but you won't go too far on a public street, so my dread is contained within known limits. But if on a rare occasion you went significantly past my comfort zone, proving you will occasionally terrify me, then every scenario has unconstrained dread, which I think deep down I would love, in my fun but slightly weird way. I would never want it to breach your comfort zone, though. Anyway, I can't see how we would do that, do you?"

"Hey, I'm not afraid to tell you to strip naked right here and now." I stared at her in disbelief, but she continued. "OK, I am too scared, I'm kidding. But maybe I can order you to strip, and then it becomes your problem. Are you going to chicken out or not? I could always tell you to stand down at the last second if you looked like you would really do it. Or maybe I wouldn't. You would never know, would you?"

"No, Mistress," I replied, ruefully, "and I think you are going to be very good at tormenting me."

Marcy laughed loudly. "Anyway, you've given me some ideas. And I hear you are saying that you are consenting to me trying what I think is just on the line – and you are accepting the risk of me getting it wrong – to maximize the surprise element, the psychodrama, and the dread elements. Enough of that! This is perfect timing. I think we might find some things in this store that could help me." With that, she stopped and pushed me into a sex-toy store. We had apparently arrived at our destination.

Marcy shamelessly marched up to the only assistant, who looked like she had just finished straightening up after opening the shop for the day, and addressed her in a voice filled with confidence, which I suspect she didn't truly feel.

"Morning. Can I ask, did you happen to see that Julia Roberts movie where she walked into a fancy store, and because she wasn't dressed appropriately, she was shooed out, then later popped back to show how much money she had spent elsewhere?"

"Yes, I think the famous line was "Big Mistake," wasn't it, love?" replied the assistant gamely. She had a strong London-cockney accent.

"That's right. Well, it's your lucky day, I think. We need to stock up on BDSM equipment, and we are OK for money. There will be a couple of items we want to take with us now, but could we leave you a pile of things to ship to Canada for us?"

"'Course love, no worries," answered the assistant enthusiastically. "My name is Geri, with an 'i'; and yes, before you ask, mum idolized the Spice Girls. If there is anything I can do for you, please don't hesitate. Did you want me to close the shop so you can shop privately?"

"Oh no, I rather think not," Marcy laughed, somewhat evilly, glancing pointedly my way. I smiled uncomfortably back. She continued, "Is it OK if we try out things we like? We will buy any items that might be a hygiene issue." Geri nodded, obviously not believing her luck.

Marcy pushed me to the back of the store.

"No kids or parents here, Slave-Boy. Handcuffs first, I think." With that pronouncement, Marcy pulled a pair of metal cuffs from a box, tested that the key worked – smart Mistress – and with all of the skill from her years in the Vancouver Police Force, had my arms pinned behind me in an instant.

"Now Slave-Boy," she laughed, "I don't think we have time to shop for outfits today, but I would like you to order something very sexy for your Phoenix to wear. Do you know my bra size?"

I guessed. "36c?"

"No!" she exclaimed, oddly delighted. Then she reached in and opened the top button of my coat. "Oh, didn't I mention that for each question you get wrong, we undo a button?" *Oh... Crap!*

A very long 30 minutes later, we stepped back onto the street. Marcy had me hold a small bag she and Geri had laughed over, but had not shared what the contents of the bag were. An embarrassingly large selection of restraints, equipment to inflict many different types of sensations, blindfolds, and gags were set aside, and would be on their way to Vancouver today, in a discreet but bulky package. Marcy had me email Darcy to expect it and say that it should avoid the usual inspection my incoming mail typically receives.

At various moments in the shop, Marcy had my coat wide open, with little Ethan completely exposed. But like some sort of magical puppeteer-cum-burlesque-master, she positioned me so that at no point did Geri, the store cameras, or the two other customers who wandered in actually catch a glimpse of him. But there were some very close calls. Marcy marched me back to the hotel wearing the one purchase we had with us that she had allowed me to see; a pair of wicked nipple clamps, which I was painfully aware of with each step. Geri had informed us that they were painful to put on, painful to wear, and to expect them to be even more painful when taken off and the blood rushes back to revitalize the nerves that semi-shut down after five minutes of being clamped. With safety ever in mind, she warned us not to leave them on for much more than ten minutes if we didn't want to risk lasting damage. “For best results, five minutes on. Five minutes off. Repeat,” she had laughed. Good to know.

Marcy had actually planned everything so well that we arrived back at the hotel with just enough time to complete my ordeal before we had to shower and dress to meet Naomi and Gwen. This entailed her re-cuffing my hands behind me with cuffs she pulled from the bag with a flourish, mounting me and riding me to orgasm. And, just as I climaxed, she pulled off the clamps. Oh boy! Geri was not wrong.

*

Gwen had stayed with Naomi, so our security team camped outside of number 44 overnight and delivered them safely to our hotel just after 11:30 am this morning. Right after Marcy and I finished out ‘shopping.’ Talk about plans going wrong last night, wow. Not that Gwen did the wrong thing in going directly into Naomi’s flat; quite the opposite. Having been caught walking past, her reaction was the only right one. It was getting caught in the first place that was ‘amateur hour.’

I was surprised Naomi was willing to hear us out, but she apparently had quite a story of her own to share. Gwen had been cryptic, saying only that Naomi was terrified of something or someone. Naomi felt her life was at risk, and that sharing what she knew might exacerbate her situation. Through Gwen, I assured her that we would not use what she told us – at least not without her consent. As the four of us sat down to a light breakfast in a rented meeting room in our Wimbledon hotel, we were spellbound by her amazing tale. She was equally enthralled with the story we shared. In our telling, we did not name Moy Lei or Chiyome, or even hint at their backgrounds.

“You know,” said Naomi thoughtfully, as she digested the information, “it’s not impossible that there is something to these phenomena. Many of the jigsaw pieces are accepted science today. The inhibitor to believing it all combined isn’t that it is totally fantastical, rather, it’s that no one has put the pieces together before now. You know, the notion that if it were possible, it would have been done already, therefore it is not possible. Good possibility theory, terrible logic. The trouble with jigsaw puzzles is once solved or if done too frequently, they feel stale and we move on to another puzzle. To solve this Boku-yōkai problem, it seems you need to combine unrelated data; puzzle pieces from different puzzle-boxes. Diet, entanglement and molecular biology, DNA, and so on. Not impossible, but infinitely more abstract. Working on any one box of jigsaw pieces would get stale quickly in today’s world. There are infinite puzzles with more intuitive paths to solution to pursue, so this aspect could easily get ignored.”

"How is it our ancestors could have solved the puzzle?" I asked.

"Two easy potential answers to that, and there could be others of course. Maybe they weren't trying, for example. Monkeys with typewriters eventually writing Shakespeare, as the saying goes, wouldn't have to solve written language. To harness their triumph, they still don't need to comprehend the words; they just need to recognize that something of value happened, and attempt to recreate it. That is easier in some cases if you are not burdened with science and knowledge.

"Or, perhaps it's because their societal rules were different. We have been taught to think in a certain way. Methodologies and practices, cross-reference verification, linear and critical thinking, and so on. This is why the puzzle pieces in different boxes elude us. They might have simply emptied the contents from all of the boxes onto the floor. Some of the newer research techniques used in big data analytics today are successful because they take humans out of the equation. We can't be random enough, or objective enough. We always introduce subconscious bias because of our experiences and beliefs. Sometimes, nowadays, we give machines very loose guidelines about data sets and ask them what they make of the data. Artificial Intelligence is better at this than we are, as they process so quickly. There is a lot of rubbish generated, but we discover many nuggets we humans would have filtered out, if we had been left to do it ourselves."

"How can our diet create special powers? That seems impossible," probed Marcy. I admit, I was struggling with this, too.

"Well, consider this simple example: I know a private pilot who flew his plane for an hour in the hot sun. He lands and updates his logbook and the rental documentation for the plane. He tells me he struggles with four fairly simple calculations. He might have taken off with 1341.2 hours recorded on the engine. On landing, the meter says 1342.6 and he must record the difference, which is 1.4 hours. Another example is they record pilot hours as 0.1 for 6 minutes, 0.2 for 12 minutes so that 1.0 = 60 minutes. If you fly for 25 minutes you round to the nearest multiple of 6 in this case to 24 minutes, in other words 0.4 of an hour. If you started with 100 hours, you would update it to 100.4 hours. Sitting here, that is not super hard math — especially with practise — but after a hot, high-stress hour in a cockpit, the math becomes difficult and most pilots use a calculator to do – or at least check – their work."

"I am a pilot, and totally agree," I confirmed. "I get embarrassed using my phone to calculate such simple things, but I often make mistakes if I don't."

"Exactly. But what my friend noticed is that if he ensures he is well hydrated, he doesn't make the errors. He can land and struggle with the math, glug down some water, and then that same math is suddenly much easier. In a very short space of time, like five minutes. Simply drinking water increases his brain function. He quickly changed his habits and now drinks during the flight to keep his brain sharp throughout."

"But that's water restoring his degraded brain-function. Someone who can't do calculus can't suddenly do it by drinking water." *Good logic, Marcy. That's my girl.*

"True, and a good point. But the concept is extensible. It's really about getting the body to change how it works by altering chemistry. Our whole body is an ongoing electrical and chemical reaction and we can change the components to a degree by changing how we fuel it. We have become adept at introducing agents outside of the norm to alter our normal operation. Athletes sometimes take a range of drugs that enhance their physical performance. Why not mental performance, too? Doctors give us drugs that we don't naturally find in the food chain when we are sick. We change brain chemicals routinely to influence depression, and a range of other imbalances, with synthetic chemicals. We've never found drugs that make us smarter or turn us into superman, but all of the ingredients are there to imply such a thing is possible."

"What about the concept that we have dormant parts of our brain that might have a purpose we don't currently use?" I asked.

"Opinion is split on that. One major camp believes that such parts of our brain are no longer required, but evolution has yet to catch up and dispense with them. Hangovers from prehistoric man. The other camp suggests that we use them every day and are just not aware of it. They are responsible for intuition and extra-sensory perception, that sensation that when we are being talked about. That camp would be closer to your client's claims. These are not mutually-exclusive ideas: We may have both brain parts waiting to fade away, as well as brain parts in use without us knowing about them. The idea that someone could activate a brain function that could render them effectively invisible is clearly several steps up this thought ladder, but it does feel like it would be part of the same stream of logic. If such a thing existed."

"How would that work though? How could we not see something we are looking at?" I asked.

"I don't know, but the brain is always filtering out data. There is too much to absorb, so we take shortcuts to prevent ourselves being overwhelmed. If you can influence or hack that process, you might create the illusion of invisibility."

"Give us an example." Gwen was getting in on the act now.

"I'm tempted to ask if you've ever watched a teenage boy clean his room and see how much mess they don't see. But a great example that I know is the basketball test. Can we bring up a browser on this big TV in the corner?" We fiddled with the TV until we had my laptop plugged in and projecting my screen onto the TV.

"OK, let me type. No one look." We closed our eyes until she said we could look.

"Right. Girls against boys. I'll start the video and you will see two teams playing basketball. One team in red and another in white. Girls, you count how many passes the red team makes. Ethan, you count the passes the white team makes. Both teams have to discount any pass that bounces off the floor. I will grade you on who gets closest to the real pass rate. Ready?" She quickly started the video, which lasted twenty-five seconds. It took me a while to work out what was happening, as it wasn't straightforward team-play. There were just three players per team, and both teams had their own ball, which they passed backwards and forwards within their group; no one made any attempt to find a net or steal the other's ball. Both groups stepped closely around each other in a random, complex pattern, so I had to focus hard to separate the fast-moving chaos. When it stopped, I was confident there were thirty passes for my team, excluding the three that bounced.

"OK. Girls?"

"Twenty-eight."

"Ethan?"

"Thirty."

"OK, great. I didn't actually count, but let's say you are both right. Next question: Did the gorilla dance across the screen from right to left, or left to right?" All three of us looked at her, confused. What gorilla? She replayed the video. Ten seconds in, a large man in a gorilla suit danced into the shot from the left side, and then body-popped and robot-danced his way in front of all the players, before shimmying out of the shot to the right.

"Is that the same video? I would swear it wasn't there."

"Yep, same video. I hacked you. I talked you into being very focused on one task, and by making it competitive really pressured you into wanting to be successful. Your brain filtered out anything irrelevant to the task. It's a key skill to our survival as a species and part of our base wiring, but it can easily be hacked. In fact, most of our brain works on similar shortcuts, and the more primal and necessary they are to us, the less we realize we are using them at all. And so, when they are hacked, we may not even realize. This also relates to some mental illnesses, where people hallucinate and don't realize it, for example.

"What we are exploring today is *How can one brain hack another remotely*? I essentially just did that using my voice and a video. This 'magic' we are wondering about is really doing the same thing through an irregular communication channel. Audio and vision may still play a part, but there is something *undiscovered*. Well, at least by us. Entanglement theory has some of that possibility embedded in it, as it appears to access other dimensions, but there are other potential channels."

"Such as?"

"Amplifying brain waves? Radio and microwave communications are really just electromagnetic waves created in one place, and then travel to another where they are decoded. The brain operates on electricity and radiates a tiny amount: How much of that could be amplified or in some way transmitted to influence the electricity of another brain?

"Or let's consider pheromones. These are akin to smell, but work on a smaller and more subtle level. They are chemicals that are secreted through the skin, particularly in mammals and insects, which change social behaviour in receiving individuals of the same species. There are different types that serve different functions: alarm, food-trail, or sex pheromones, for example. These are well documented in insects and rats, but not so much in humans, partly because we have a more developed ability to override such primal inputs than, say, a mosquito does. But there are some good candidates for our puzzle."

The 'primer' pheromone differs from all others in that it signals something is changing around us, so pay attention. It puts us on alert, but there is no specific message. The 'signal' pheromone – GnRH – functions as a neuro-transmitter in rats and elephants to make them lower their forelegs so they are well positioned for sex. Neuro-transmitters in general are how most of our brain triggers activity. A great place to hack. Some species of animal release a volatile substance when attacked by a predator that can trigger flight in aphids, or aggression in ants, bees, termites, or in members of the same species. For example, consider wasps. The Southern Yellow Jacket use alarm pheromones to alert others to a threat; in the common paper wasp alarm pheromones are also used as an alert to incoming predators. Pheromones also exist in plants: Certain plants emit alarm pheromones when grazed upon, resulting in tannin production in neighbouring plants. These tannins make the plants less appetizing for the herbivore.

"Ethan, what you described is not too far from such behaviour. And thinking about it, using diet to control which pheromones we release is directly connected to the science your client talked about. The challenge is the degree of control and subtlety employed here. Obviously, pheromones could not explain your client's claims to sense you from a hundred miles away, or in a rainstorm."

"More importantly, how do we combat it, or at least negate it? Wrap aluminum foil around our heads and wear a gas mask?" This from Marcy.

"That's as good as anything I could suggest," sighed Naomi. "We need to know how this works – at least on some level – before we can defeat it."

"Would you be willing to study it personally? There would be some risk, of course. When we contacted our client, someone with whatever this magic is came after us. And our client could locate us with some sort of supernatural radar, so we have to assume the Adepts can do that, too."

"Yes. If what you say can be observed, I would give my right arm to unpack the science behind it. I'll help." Unequivocal. "I'm all but a prisoner in my own house anyway. It's not clear if your clients are related directly to my fears, but I have to do something. Can you protect me?"

"I would love to confidently say yes, but we don't really know what we are up against. I can guarantee you any reasonable defence we can think of — money won't be an issue — but there is no guarantee of success. But let's see if we can get you a test subject to study first. Before we all commit."

I stepped out of the meeting and went to Moy Lei's room. I shared what we had learned. In conclusion I said, "Here is what I am thinking: You once said every story needs a crazy professor, and I can provide a possibly crazy scientist and a laboratory on a deserted island. We can set up in a location that can only be reached by helicopter and surround it with guards. It would be safer than London, at least, and we share everything we learn from studying your brain with you, so if nothing else you would be better informed. Nothing about your background and the Kanbo needs to surface. I think your biggest concern outside of being studied is what else happens to the knowledge we might obtain. Outside of our own safety, Marcy and I have no interest. We can be trusted to keep quiet. Our scientist will have knowledge, but no proof. We would retain and, if appropriate, destroy data and samples. I don't think she would tell anyone what she discovers, and if she did, who would believe her? That said, she would be putting herself at grave risk by joining us and like we do for you, I take looking after her wellbeing seriously. She would be an equal part of our team."

"Ethan, you had me at 'crazy scientist.' It's not like I have another plan. Where in the world can we set up? I would still like to be outside of the easy reach of Haha's Kanbo."

"I have to do some research, but I agree. So, let's stay in Europe." We walked back to the meeting room together, and I did the introductions. Next, we decided to widen the circle of knowledge a little and approached Kelsie and Ian's support team about our fantastical situation. We were very clear about the risks and stressed this project was entirely voluntary, but no one hesitated. Two other people also joined us. Kelsie had requested we included Julie Gonzalez, a researcher on her team in Vancouver. Although both Ian and Kelsie were more than proficient, Julie was apparently a savant when it came to unearthing nuggets of interest from complex data. The other inclusion was Gwen; she was insistent about staying close to Naomi. We were not sure about adding Gwen until Moy Lei pointed out that she might already be on the Boku-yōkai radar. We knew we could protect her better if she was part of the team. She was in.

*

After an afternoon of planning, Marcy had one last surprise in the bag from the shopping trip. We had decided that Ian, Moy Lei, Naomi, and Gwen would dine together in the hotel, while Marcy and I would eat out at the Italian, just across the road. We were spruced up and about to walk over when she drew me aside and sat me down on the bed.

"Ethan, I'll admit to being in two minds about this. When Geri suggested it earlier, I was caught up in the excitement, and must admit it seemed like a hoot; but now it seems a little weird. Don't laugh at me, but I nearly threw this particular toy away and said nothing; but here we are. Anyway, as always, feel free to shut me down. I brought home one more toy I didn't tell you about. I hadn't even known such a thing existed, if I'm honest."

"Now I'm curious," I interjected during her nervous pause, trying to head off the obvious panic that was welling in her voice as she worried unnecessarily about taking a risk. "Out with it. I promise not to judge. Or laugh. Or run."

"Hmm. Wait until you see it, first."

She pulled out a device that resembled a cross between a tiny bird cage and a metal sculpture of a penis. It was gunmetal grey, and had wires that connected it to a small, black, plastic box with a little light on. I looked at her, puzzled.

"It's a male chastity cage. If little Ethan misbehaves, he gets locked into it. It has a small padlock, and I'm the key holder. He stays in the cage for as long as I say. Maybe five minutes, but maybe five hours. Or days. Would you dare give that power to me?" She fingered a small metal key, which was on a jewellery chain around her neck, like a key pendant I've seen many women wear.

"And the wires and the black box?" I asked, haltingly.

"That's a surprise for later. What do you think?"

"I don't want to boast, but I think it looks pretty small," I offered.

"That's by design, silly. When you are in there, you are not supposed to be able to get hard when wearing it. Geri said if you like wearing it, it's best to invest in one that is custom made. It should fit snugly but shouldn't pinch. Unless you like the pinch, of course, and then you can get one with spikes that prick you if you get hard. It's supposed to be fun talking dirty to you, with your trying to avoid the discomfort of an erection."

"Hey, let's give it a whirl. You checked the key worked, right? I don't want to have to call the fire brigade."

It took 15 minutes of pushing and shoving, and the strategic use of some thread from the hotel sewing kit, before we had it on. Marcy gave me one more chance to back out before snapping the tiny padlock on with a 'snicking' noise, which sent a shiver through me. Now it was on until Marcy decided otherwise, unless I chose to embarrass myself with a visit to the Emergency Room at the hospital, or purchased and very carefully used a pair of bolt cutters.

The device had a thick, hinged, metal ring resembling a handcuff, which we opened and looped behind my testicles, then closed over the top of my balls and the base of my penis combined. It was tight-fitting, but easy to put on when unlocked. Once locked, the small circumference would never let it slip past my crown jewels. The harder part was getting my penis flaccid and small enough to slide into the cage-like tube, which was marginally big enough for little Ethan to go into. Every time Marcy got impatient and tried to help, he expanded again. But with some fumbling, eventually he was inside it, peeking out through its bars. The two pieces then push together, and the padlock stops them coming apart again. You can't remove the ring because you can't open the cuff-hinge when the lock is on; and you can't remove the cage as it, in turn, is locked to the cuff. There was no way to pull myself back out of the cage or touch myself. Maybe even peeing would be impossible without a mess.

We noticed the black, plastic box had a belt clip, so I pulled on my trousers – à la commando – and clipped the box on the inside of my trouser waist, out of sight. The wires ran from the cage to the box, and the box had a little red light flashing patiently away. I walked around the room to test things out. I was very conscious of both its weight and grip; but more so that any chance of a future orgasm was totally up to Marcy at this point. I resolved to be very well behaved.

We could smell the Italian food almost as soon as we stepped out of the hotel, but when we pushed our way through the restaurant's front door, we were assailed by the most wonderful, garlic, butter, and onion aromas. There were two female greeters at the door, so I stepped forward to claim our reservation. The women smiled expectantly, and I opened my mouth to speak but the strangest shriek came out as a small electric current shot through my penis and I almost levitated in surprise. I glanced back at Marcy, who was looking innocently at the ceiling. Now I knew what the wires did.

I tentatively began to ask for our table and thankfully, this time, nothing happened. Until we were half way to the table when a second jolt struck. I'd been half expecting it, but still. The greeter sat us down, set us up with menus, and let us know that Stella would be looking after us tonight. As soon as she was out of earshot, Marcy collapsed into laughter and, after a few seconds of trying to look serious, I followed.

"How are you doing that?" I demanded of her.

"How am I doing that, Phoenix, I think you mean." I nodded, obediently, and she continued. She was coyly fingering the key on her pendent. "This chain looks like jewelry, but it actually connects to a small transmitter in my bra. There is a wire running down my back, under my hair. On the key there is a micro-button, which when I press..." I jumped again.

Stella chose that moment to introduce herself, and I suffered several shocks in the two minutes it took me to order us our cocktails. As she left us to fetch the drinks, Marcy continued her explanation.

"Your cage has ten levels, and that jolt is level one." She lifted her left arm and reached under and fiddled with the transmitter through her sweater. "'I think it's at level three now. Do you want to feel it?"

"Err... do I have a choice?"

"Well, you could always use your safe word, I guess." She pouted, with mock disappointment. Teasing me. Daring me. She looked deep into my eyes and started to count backwards from five, slowly. I braced myself, tempted to yell uncle. When she got to two, a much stronger jolt struck. Crafty.

"How was that, big Ethan?" she asked sweetly.

"Certainly got our full attention."

She fiddled with the transmitter again. "That's probably level five now, but it's so hard to tell through my clothing. OK, here's the game: Every time the staff are at our table, if you use any of the following words, we get to find out what level five feels like."

"*We* get to feel? Is it shocking you, too?" I quipped back.

"Good point. It's just you. For that I'm adding extra words to your list. Silly boy. The words are please, thank you, cheque, bill, ta and any type of grape varietal. Or wine."

I began to sweat, which I suddenly realized would probably make a better connection and increase the shock.

We left the table 90 minutes later. I had done very well at finding alternate terms for the shock-words, even when Marcy had me ask for the sommelier and had me engage in a long debate about the merits of different wine regions. But I slipped enough to learn that level six was my limit. Thankfully, Marcy backed it off at that point.

The final surprise was back in the room, where Marcy threw a pillow on the floor and stood in front of it before explaining that the cage was staying on until she had a satisfactory orgasm. I sank to my knees with a pretend sigh. A slave-boy's work is never done.

*

Over the next 48 hours, we located a deserted island off the Scottish coast that was inaccessible by sea. It had been a Special Boat Service training base up until 2012. The SBS is the maritime sister to the British Special Air Service, or SAS. We leased the Isle of Standoch's facility for three months and began flying in supplies of three types: Type one was everything practical, such as food, generators and furniture; type two was defensive equipment, both electronic, and things that go bang; and the third type came from a list of research equipment generated by Naomi, which included portable brain scanners and equipment to extract blood and DNA samples, plus the tools to analyse results. Gwen slipped out and came back with her contribution: A well-stocked bar and several good books. I was relieved she didn't give us a suitcase full of sex toys.

While our logistics efforts flourished, Julie set about gathering data. She was careful not to search for anything we believed might trigger interest, such as terms like Boku-yōkai. I checked Chiyome's dark-web portal daily and left updates, but nothing arrived. I didn't press her. She knew what was at stake. On the third day, Julie called a meeting to share some information. We were just setting up the conference bridge when Moy Lei burst into the room.

"Trouble is coming. I just sensed three new people looking for me. They are not Adepts, but they are very dark souls."

"Do you think our target has hired a hit squad?" Marcy was on her feet.

"Whoever it is, they are not close. If I had to guess, I would say they are on the far side of London." I glanced at Ian, who was already texting from his encrypted phone with his team, ensuring they were alert.

"Let's outpace them. Leave here quickly and fly up to the island," I said.

"Or we can set a trap and catch them. They might be able to tell us something about our adversary," suggested Ian. Marcy shook her head. She could see the same issue as I could, but she demonstrated why, in her police job, she had been the task-force commander; her grasp of strategy and tact at handling her troops was excellent.

"I like the way you are thinking, Ian, and thanks for being ready to get into it with these guys. But let's say we capture one or all of them without injury to ourselves: What do we do then? I don't think any of us are ruthless enough to interrogate them. It was hard enough for me when I was a cop, but back then I could threaten jail time. I'm not going to start breaking fingers. I also worry that these three are a decoy. Lure us out of our den here, away from innocent bystanders, then send one of the magic guys on us. Moy Lei doesn't detect one, but that might be because it hasn't yet been given us as a specific target. It might still have been instructed to move to a position nearby. We would have very little time to react if it was close when it was set on us. I say we move, but not to the island. Let's keep that to ourselves until it is completely ready to be defended."

I took over. "Ian, once we have heard what Julie has to say, can you organize transport? Get us helicopters with decent range and create a route to accommodations, somewhere in Europe that is difficult to reach by plane or foot. Cabins in the alps, that sort of thing. Every day or two, depending on Moy Lei's radar, we will hop around and stay ahead of them and any other threat that arises."

Julie and Kelsie appeared on the video conference screen, and we caught them up then listened to what Julie had to tell us.

"I've sent you a package with a lot of new information. I set up 27 cross-binary..." she started enthusiastically, but Kelsie cut her off.

"They don't need the details of the technology, Julie, however exciting it is. Just give them the key conclusions." You could tell Kelsie was very proud of her prodigy but smart enough to avoid killing us with information we could never comprehend. And had little desire to, frankly. Julie was a little disappointed but carried on, her bubbly enthusiasm intact.

"Two significant finds so far. Firstly, I don't think your analysis of the eight deaths is accurate. Well, it is accurate, but not complete or thought through. Err... sorry." She was suddenly worried Naomi would be offended having her research challenged by a youngster, but ever the woman of science, the professor was patiently waiting for Julie's hypothesis.

"The key to it is to remember there were nine deaths, not eight. Jane Eldridge also died. You didn't include her as you see it as a separate event, but I don't think it is. The eight you considered all have a strong tie to stem cell and other regenerative sciences, but Eldridge doesn't, other than through marriage. But, all nine of them belong to a related but critically different set. This is where I think you had been solving the wrong problem. If I apply this new set as a filter to untimely deaths in the brain-research family of candidates, the number is actually 36, not eight. All 36 were neuroscientists involved, to some degree, in studying the areas of the brain that don't appear to have a clear purpose at this point in time. Two thirds of the deaths were people involved in research into the new theory about how consciousness functions. The Three Super-Neurons Theory."

There was silence. I sensed Kelsie had coached Julie before the call, to pause at this point before rushing on to her second finding.

"Oh, God. Does that mean Jane could have been murdered?" This from Gwen, who unconsciously reached for Naomi's hand.

"I don't think that's certain yet, Gwen, but I think we have to consider it a likely possibility. There could be many explanations, but a cult-like group protecting their secrets would fit this picture. What's your second piece of information, Julie?" I wanted to keep things moving. I was very conscious of danger approaching.

"The second interesting data point: On the assumption that stem cells are involved, we created a data set of their commercial and medical shipments and sales. This includes publicly available data, plus data Kelsie somehow obtained for me from private databases, including many from the dark-web sources." I assume our friendly hacker SkyLox was involved. *Smart thinking, Kelsie.* "There is a finite number of stem cell and cord-blood sources. The most and best stem cells come from a blastocyst. I've prepared a quick recap." The screen filled with diagrams.

"Egg and sperm unite in the fallopian tube and begin to divide and multiply, becoming a small number of cells that know how to grow into many different cells to create all the components to make a body. These we call stem cells. Later in the process, cells are locked into their intended use. A nose cell can't decide to be a toe cell, and so on. But at the early stage, they can be anything the body needs. A blastocyst is the glob of cells about four to five days post-fertilization and might contain 50-150 stem cells. Current thinking is that this is the optimum point in the process to harvest the cells for Invitro Fertilization, or IVF treatments. Ignoring the controversy of terminating life before it really gets a foothold, harvesting can be from a uterus under traditional fertilization, but today is most commonly the result of IVF pairing in a laboratory.

''Identifying sales and shipments from the uterus is almost impossible, but 8% of the overall inventory we've isolated came from natural birth termination, and that data was exclusively obtained from the dark-web source incidentally. The other 92% come from IVF labs across the globe, with various levels of official standing from top research hospitals, to private clinics, right down to criminal operations.

"That's the supply side. What about demand? Obviously, the majority of product goes to legitimate research labs. Many western countries strictly control – or in many cases prohibit – such research, and strong inventory control is in place. It was easy to scope this group, but it only represents about a quarter of the demand. Many countries don't have a policy in place nor the ability to police one, and so we turned quickly to distribution analysis, which gave us better data.

"You can't just FEDEX this stuff around, as it needs certain environmental conditions maintained, such as temperature. We focused on such transportation methods, primarily. We've mapped everything out and have a fair picture of the landscape, but isolating our 'people of interest' from the clutter is difficult. Our target might receive the actual delivery for their use, but it's more likely they are piggybacking on deliveries made for other purposes. We were unable to find data that pointed to suspicious activity in the USA. That avenue appears to be a dead end. But we might have had a break in Europe. We focused on the smallest deliveries. Most go to independent private research facilities. A few don't, but most of those have a rational explanation. We found one that we can't explain and suggests a physical follow-up is required." Odd phrase. I guessed that is how someone who spends most of their time living in a database might talk to us 'physicals.'

"A shipment, a few cells per month, goes to the equivalent of a refrigerated post office box in Porto, Portugal. There is no record of it ever being collected – again, Kelsie will have to fill in the gaps on how we obtain that data – but the inventory count for packages is always zero. In all other sites, inventory count increases with delivery, then decreases with consumption or resale of the cells to other parties. At our anomalous site, cells arrive according to the shipper but don't according to the receiver, and have done so smoothly for five and half years. It might be nothing more than poor record-keeping, but it is one of the more interesting anomalies.

"That is all we could come up with. I'm sorry, but it has been a bit hectic." She seemed very sincere that her incredible feat was insufficient. I think she hoped to crack the case in 24 hours all by herself.

"That's incredible, don't apologize. You've done wonders in such a short time," said Marcy. "Is there anything else of note delivered to that address?" *Good cop question.*

"Jeez, I'm so ditzy. I need sleep. No, nothing there. But I should have mentioned that the same credit card that maintains that account is also used in Lisbon. Shopping, mostly for agricultural supplies. Some exotic herbs and cheeses. And a few ounces of cesium and selenium. An odd mix."

"You said the Porto site gets regular deliveries. When is the next one due?" Ian asked.

"The day after tomorrow, if the frequency is maintained."

No one had any more questions.

"Go and get some sleep, Julie. Excellent work. Thanks, that was incredible." I could feel Kelsie brimming with pride. On the screen, it looked like Julie had already moved on to the next data sequence and forgotten us; she would not sleep for some time, I guessed.

We wrapped up the call quickly, grabbed everything we brought to the hotel, and checked where Moy Lei's radar said the current threat was located. We had a thought that we might be being herded into a trap. We literally flipped a coin to select a random direction, which resulted in us leaving the hotel slightly towards the threat, before looping around and heading in the opposite direction. Two choppers were ready for us at Redhill Airport. Four hours later, we were touching down at a private chalet near St Moritz, Switzerland.

7: TWO ISLANDS

[GWEN} — St Moritz is beautiful all year around – an alpine town nestled in a valley flanking a windless, mirror-like lake – and the sight of it took our breath away. We were perched on top of a sharp peak in a wonderful building which was too small to call a castle, but too castle-like to be anything but. Unless you flew in and landed on the small helipad, as we had, the only way up was by cable car, which was now locked off. Even so, I had heard the boys discussing a parachute attack and a climbing assault, which they eventually discarded. Apparently, we had rented the place for a week, but were planning to be out of here within 24 hours, on to our next hop. Moy Lei's remarkable radar led us to believe the three 'dark souls,' as she called them, were still in England somewhere, but creeping slowly closer. I loved the term 'dark soul,' and discussed it with her at length.

It felt so good to be back in touch with Naomi. I secretly admit to myself that I've always had more than a soft spot for her. I fully respected Jane and Naomi's relationship while they were together, but I was always drawn to Naomi – and a little inappropriately attracted to her. In these odd circumstances, I wouldn't pursue my long-standing feeling for her, but I wanted to be close to support her, and hoped something might naturally develop through our renewed proximity.

In the meantime, Naomi had retired for the night, Ethan and the gang were off doing something logistic, and Marcy and I were having a glass of wine in a fabulous medieval equivalent of a bay window, overhanging a thousand-foot drop down into a lush valley across the lake from the town of St Moritz. If beauty were a prerequisite for hosting the Olympic games, you could see why it's been here twice, in 1928 and 1948. It should come again.

St Moritz as a name for the town's location is first mentioned around 1137 AD. The village was named after Saint Maurice, an early Christian saint from southern Egypt said to have been martyred in 3rd century Roman Switzerland, while serving as leader of the Theban Legion. An astonishing 6666 Roman soldiers converted to Christianity en masse and were martyred together in the year 286 AD. Pilgrims traveled to St Moritz often, to the Church of the Springs, where they drank from the blessed, bubbling waters of the Mauritius springs in the hopes of being healed. In 1519, Medici Pope Leo X promised full absolution to anyone making a pilgrimage to the Church of the Springs. Now here, in 2018, Marcy was again apologizing to me — over bubbling Prosecco — for not including me in the 'cone of silence' from the beginning. I absolved her, too, and put her at her ease.

The topics came and went, and we babbled like old friends, but conversation eventually made its way around to Marcy and Ethan's art class antics. I had arranged the introduction to the university professor, and she told me how she enjoyed teasing Ethan in front of the group. She also hinted he might never go back to a certain castle up in the north of England. I suspected it would always hold fun memories for them both. I also learned something else from her, as I had never heard of the Skittle's Crop.

She leant forward and whispered conspiratorially, already blushing.

"You've been a sport with data and advice on certain topics, Gwen, and I want to pick your brains a little more. I need to stop talking to you about Ethan's and my sex life, but I'm kicking around a couple of scenarios where I tease him with my... er...vibrator. My vibe. God, sorry, I still feel so awkward talking about this stuff. I don't need ideas as I already have a game in mind, but I worry that bringing another 'penis' into the room might upset him. I suspect many women have a vibrator, but using it with your man...? You hear stories about male egos...you know... Anyway, what can Dr Gwen the Magnifico tell me? Do you have any real data on the subject?"

"Sure, no problem. OK, basic ground rules: Anything concerning BDSM requires consent, but there is a spectrum to consider. If you just tickle his balls with a vibe, although a purest would suggest you discuss it, most people don't. It's basically harmless, and it's impractical to discuss every detail. If you plan to surprise him with a strap-on, or insert anything where the sun doesn't shine, you definitely should discuss it in advance and again, closer to the session."

"Why twice?"

"Because he might be OK with it in principle and say yes, when discussed in advance. But then you get to it, and perhaps he is not feeling clean, or in the mood. Or conversely, if you haven't discussed it in advance and spring it on him at the last second, it can be overwhelming. He could say yes when he really means no. Or say no when he is actually curious. There is a lot in between those bookends, of course. The bigger stuff, you talk about; you can make a judgement call on the little stuff."

"Got it."

"Then there is a different dynamic, which is where you are coming from, I know. Some men can get intimidated just having a vibrator around, whatever you do with it. Just knowing you have it, without even seeing it, can be an issue for some. They compare themselves to it, often subconsciously, and worry you prefer it to them. This is a tricky subject, because many times women actually do prefer their vibe, often subconsciously. At least at some level. You never have to dress up for your vibrator, or humour/disappoint it if you are not in the mood. Especially for women who have more success with clitoral stimulation, a vibe can work for you more often than a man can. Men, or any partner, can be great at providing clitoral stimulation, and you can have a great time. But if you like sex to culminate in intercourse, it's hard for both parties to climax at the same time if you rely on men to multi-task. The old adage is mostly true: Men can't multitask. But in the heat of our own orgasm, women are not so great either, to be honest.

"The issue is more about physiology. Men's bits are easy to get at, easy to understand, and easy to please. Everything is on the outside, and it's typically keen to perform. Women's bits are hidden, mysterious and finicky by comparison. I'm going to digress into the history of masturbation. It's not directly relevant, but it is interesting and good background." We refilled out glasses and settled in.

"A month ago, we talked about how uptight the Victorians were, and how anti-sex they became towards the end of the 1800s. I think I told you that masturbation was seen as something akin to the gateway drug. The basic premise was that for men, only the weak minded would desire sex. You have to submit to intercourse for procreation purposes, but otherwise, it is a distraction at best, heinous and deplorable at worst. Women were never considered weak minded, as they were not really considered to have minds of value in the first place. If they had urges, or 'attacks of hysteria' — a word derived from the Greek word for uterus, by the way — it was not a mental weakness; it was perceived as a physical ailment. Always polite and condescending, were the English.

"So, oddly, if men had the urge they were encouraged to see a prostitute rather than take matters into their own hands, so to speak. There is some belief that women, by contrast, were sent to a physician. Sound silly? I told you John Harvey Kellogg invented cornflakes to settle stomachs in the belief it quenched these immoral desires, whereas spicy food was considered to sometimes stimulate arousal. One well-cited account of history is that if women needed treatment, they could go to a physician who would exercise the hysteria through manual stimulation of the labia and clitoris. It sounds like a choice job for the men, but remember that, to men of learning, sex was considered a weakness, so they saw this work as demeaning and labour intensive. As I said earlier, hard work because women's parts are hard enough to make work in an intimate setting, let alone a doctor's office. So, men did what they do well, and invented a labour-saving device. To save themselves labour of course, not for our benefit. I should say, more recent analysis of these claims isn't necessarily disputing this all happened, but it is failing to find the same evidence the original authors based their account of history on.

"The first vibrators were hand cranked and go back as far as 1734. Think egg-beater-like devices. Later, someone invented the steam vibrator. I think it was Dr George Taylor in 1869. I would have to double check. But thankfully the fashion caught on. General Electric, GE, started producing home appliances in the last decade of the 1800s. Their general purpose, electric vibrator was their fifth domestic electrical product, launched in 1900, preceded by sewing machines, fans, kettles, and toasters. We had electric vibrators before electric irons, washing machines, and tumble dryers. They were sold to cure a range of non-sexual ailments of course, not specifically as a sex toy. They were advertised until the 1920s, when they started turning up in pornography.

"In the 50s and 60s, Kinsey, Masters, and Johnson did some breakthrough research into the male and female orgasm. They pretty much proved not only how our lady-parts all work, but that we have longer and more orgasms than men. That is, if we know how to go get them. On average, men orgasm for seven and a half seconds, compared to over 15 seconds for women. This is partially why some men can feel threatened ,of course. We women can outpace them in all respects, especially with a vibrator to help. We have longer orgasms, and recover faster, and some of us can actually have multiple orgasms. Men typically can't keep up in the same way but, of course, they have their own benefits from their simpler engineering.

"But the scientific publications from these noble sex researchers were not accessible or understandable to your average layperson, and less so if you were female back then. The whole sexual revolution of the 60s didn't occur because we found our clitoris, and it didn't really help us locate it, either. It occurred because condoms and antibiotics became widely available.

"But in 1972, Alfred Comfort published *The Joy of Sex*. Basically a layperson's guide to the female anatomy and how to treat either nicely. You could get the book from the local store, and it showed us where our bits were and encouraged us to play with them. It boldly went as far as to suggest we take some quiet time away from our male partners, take a hot bath, put some candles on, and discover how to orgasm. Many women had never orgasmed; and for those that had, it was not something they could easily reproduce. It takes focus, practice, privacy, and the right mood. But *The Joy of Sex* pointed out that once we know how it all works, we can show men what we like. Most men were not ready for us to show them how to 'do their job.' Another potential threat to manhood.

"The momentum began to build, and in 1966, Jon Tavel patented the marvellous invention of the basic cordless vibrator, from which the spectacular variety of products we can enjoy today emerged. However, it was shops and home sex-toy parties such as Ann Summers in the UK and the various Love Shops we remember opening in Vancouver who brought them to the mass market. And eventually, on-line shopping combined with television shows such as Sex in the City made them more accessible and permissible to use. For many today, if they found out their partner had eight different vibes –

one for each day of the week plus another for birthdays – they'd probably think they were extravagant, but not kinky per se."

"I don't want to imagine how many you have, Gwen. Don't tell me. But you've always got some good statistics. Does every woman have a vibrator now?"

"This is an area where there are many data sources and they all have similar results. Somewhere between 40-50% of women report using a vibrator today, up from 1% in the 1970s; around 20% of men admit to using or owning one. The figure for men used to be much lower and has shot up in recent times, too; in fact, that number is a global average, and the UK and North America would be nearer 30%.

"Then there is the law. It's rare to see anyone prosecute offenders under some of the arcane – or odd – laws, but in Arizona you can only own one dildo or vibrator. In Texas you are allowed up to six or seven. In Georgia, all sex toys are banned. Anyway, my digression has digressed."

"So, people – in some geographic areas more than others – are getting more and more comfortable with the use of realistic-looking sex toys, often even considering using them themselves. Going back a few decades and thinking of men with a sex toy conjured up creepy sex dolls, often the inflatable type. I think men were set back by such things. More recently, non-humanized vibrators for men – handheld units much like those we women use – have taken off. I attribute the upswing in admission of use to the reduction in stigma for this very positive change. In fact, it is increasingly common for a man's first vibe to be bought for him by his female partner. But the 'orgasm gap' – the different frequency for men and women's orgasms in heterosexual encounters – is very real."

"Orgasm gap?"

"I read three recent studies reported in *Psychology Today*; between them, they worked with nearly 20.000 people, making their findings quite significant. According to the reports, for people in longer-term, committed, hetro relationships, men orgasm about 85% of the time, and women only around 70% of the time. A modest 15% gap, but we women would welcome any improvement, of course. Yet in quick hook-ups or one-night stands, the gap is a whopping 52%, with men reporting 91% and women a mere 39% of sex resulting in an orgasm. Imagine taking your vibe out on a one-night stand to even the odds. Fair, but many men, and women, would still see that as rude, even if on a more regular basis they were open to vibrators. In lesbian relationships, the success rate is way above women soloing, or with a guy. Sorry hon, we sapphics have more fun." We both laughed hard and I saw that both of our glasses were empty again. I refilled them both.

"Statistically you might be right, but Ethan and I are batting 100% orgasm rates for both of us for both regular sex and our more creative moments. He is wonderful. God, I'm blushing again!"

"Fantastic. But the male ego is as unpredictable as our lady-parts. Ethan seems relaxed about sex, but I wouldn't assume. You could just ask him of course. He is probably very approachable if you are tactful. I think you would be fine to ask him outright. But if you want to sneak it up on him, you could do it in stages."

"What do you mean?"

"Maybe start with him seeing you use one, but not all the way to orgasm. Just a teasing warm-up. Maybe tie him up, tickle him with it a bit, then let him see you enjoying it. Then when you are both riled up, toss it aside and finish without it, just the two of you. Then you could talk to him about how he felt about it later. Another approach is to use it on both of you, but make him come with it, rather than making yourself come with it. After a few times, then maybe it is your turn. That sort of thing. Go slow and talk about it."

"So, I shouldn't just ask him if he would be intimidated if I had a bigger dick than he does?" joked Marcy, echoing back my stupid comment to the thugs in the pub garden. Then she caught herself and realized she didn't feel comfortable with her own joke. Then she looked at her glass, then back at me, and snorted with laughter. What a great gal.

*

I was grateful to be included in the detailed briefings, what with my being something of a tag-a-long. It was 1 pm and we had reconvened as a group for the second time since landing at St Moritz. Kelsie was giving us an update, and it seemed the Scottish Standoch facility had been made defendable faster than expected. This was partly because Marcy's little brother, Max, had joined our little band and had taken personal charge of that operation.

Until recently, Max was undercover Canadian Forces in Europe helping with the war against ISIL, but he resigned his commission after falling head-over-heels with Gia. Gia had been Ethan's personal trainer, is an ex-Olympic Taekwondo competitor, a mixed martial-arts fighter, and one-time involuntary prostitute. A story for another time. Max and Gia had been busy establishing a new charity supporting sex-trade victims, but when Max heard that his sister was once again under threat, he insisted on becoming involved. Ethan had agreed, and Standoch seemed the best use of his numerous skills.

"That's fantastic. Thanks, Kelsie and Max," interrupted Ethan. "I think we should divide and conquer at this point. Moy Lei, Gwen, and Naomi will head out in an hour to Standoch. We've rented a place near Criccieth in South

Wales. Spend a few hours there, to get the dark souls turned around, then fly up to Standoch and dig in. Max, any resources you need, Kelsie will help obtain, or at least provide funding if you have your own sources. Ian will come with Marcy and me to Porto, but his security team will travel with Gwen's team, as their protection.

"Marcy, Ian and I are going to observe the Porto collection site. If our anomalous delivery sticks to its schedule of 3 pm tomorrow, the delivery should 'disappear.' Our job is to find out how. As this could potentially be a Boku-yōkai Adept at work, we need to keep our numbers on the ground very small and take every precaution we can."

"How can you protect yourself against such a thing?" Moy Lei was quite agitated.

"To be honest we are fumbling in the dark – and we know it – but we plan to take advantage of what at least appeared to work in Durham Cathedral. The Adept may tune in to us once we take a personal interest in them. At this point, we don't know who they are, so we hope they will not know about us either. We are trying to consciously focus more on the delivery trail than on what might be at the end of it. If anything."

"That is correct. I think there is a low risk that they can sense you this way. At least, as far as I know," confirmed Moy Lei.

"We plan to get to the site tonight, set up as much video surveillance as possible, and then back away to a safer distance. Marcy and I will stay at least a quarter of a mile from the collection point and not monitor it directly. Kelsie has agreed to monitor the site remotely and give us constant verbal updates. This way, we will have no direct knowledge of the Adept, and hopefully Kelsie will be too distant to be a concern. Ian will stay at least two hundred yards away from us at all times and cover us with a sniper rifle. As in Durham, hopefully being so peripheral will prevent him from being affected if we come under attack, and he can save our butts again, if required. We've already fitted his sniper scope with a camera, which Kelsie will also monitor; this way, if Ian can't see an attack, perhaps Kelsie can warn us via audio. That's the best we could think of at this point. Anyone offer improvements? No. OK. Wheels up for us in 45 minutes. Before we depart though, Naomi: In London, Julie mentioned a theory. Something about three Super Neurons. Can you bring us up to speed on what that research field is interested in?"

"Yes, of course. There are still many mysteries to solve, but with advances in DNA research, various forms of electrical and magnetic imaging, and so on, we are getting a good handle on how our brains work. We've mapped out much of where things happen, and a little less of how they happen. For example, we know which parts of the brain deal with speech, emotion, vision, etcetera. We know that the nervous system is involved, in that neurotransmitters – chemical substances produced by neurons – that transmit nerve impulses to the various synapse points. The synapse points are interfaces to the body's systems such as glands, which might release adrenaline or dopamine, or control emotions, heartrate, or the muscle-control systems. Most of these complex mechanics are understood to a great degree but, despite all of this, there has been little success as to which part of the brain contains our consciousness. Our life force. That is, until a few years ago.

"Three neurons that, up to this point, had not been deeply investigated, became an area of focus. They are unique in that they don't appear to relate to anything specific — which is partly why they have been ignored to this point — and they are connected between themselves and to all major systems throughout the body. They are also larger than other neurons, both in terms of their core as well as the length of the tendrils and pathways, hence the term 'super-neurons.' In the absence of any other purpose, the emerging theory is that if not within these three super neurons, where else could consciousness reside? Not exactly clinically compelling, but it is clearly salient. Research has been slow, but perhaps that's because so many researchers in this field have come to untimely deaths. I still can't believe no one put that connection together before." Naomi paused and took a sip of water, seemingly lost in thought about lost friends and colleagues.

"Is there any way these three super neurons can be responsible for the powers we are talking about?" I asked, fully engaged in the medical aspects of this problem.

"Who knows. If they relate to consciousness and overall command and control of the mind, then we could hypothesize they would be a factor, but we are really just guessing. Jane certainly never discussed super-natural potential with me at any time."

Ethen cleared his throat, then took back control of the meeting. "OK, that is some really compelling information. Thanks for the context. We have to get moving soon, so is there any other new information or questions?"

"Once last point," interrupted Kelsie. "As instructed, we have set a filter on the credit card used in Porto and Lisbon so we can see transactions, but not details about the owner." This was an added precaution to stop an Adept sensing we were interested in them personally. Just their account. "Aside from the single monthly payments in Lisbon and Porto, we've detected a range of six to nine additional transactions monthly. They look like daily living expenses: groceries, gas station, utility payments."

"Do you have a location? Porto or Lisbon?"

"Actually, neither. They are all in the Azores, specifically the island of São Miguel. While most of you are headed to Standoch, I think the rest of you might end up going to a second island."

8: STANDOCH

[MAX] — There was a heatwave in Portugal, and Ethan and my sister were sweltering at 110° F. In South Wales, it was a rare 101 degrees, warming Gwen and the gang a little more than expected, though it was nicely tolerable.

Yet here on this rock — which I was already beginning to hate — it was 39 ° F at 1 pm and will drop rapidly to one or two degrees above freezing when the sun dips into the black, churning sea. Standoch might not be a sun destination, but it is certainly a great place to defend. From up in the air, it looks like a giant molar, thrusting up from an angry boiling ocean that hasn't settled, even to a simmer, once in the 50 hours since we touched down. On average, the cliffs rise up nearly 200 feet from the ocean swell, and the lowest cliff top is 116 feet above the whitecapped water below. There is not even a suggestion of a bay or landing area anywhere on Standoch's gnarly circumference. At 3500 yards at its longest and 2400 yards at its widest, Standoch is a natural fortress.

On arrival, we deployed the best sensors Ethan's money could afford, and there were more coming. Every inch of sea around us, as far out as a mile, is covered by at least two cameras watching on all visual frequencies, plus spectra our eyes cannot see, such as infrared. The skies out to twenty miles are covered by radar and laser, and both sea and air are also covered by complex audio-scanning. On the island's tabletop surface, we positioned omni sensors every 1000 yards, which scan for all of the above plus rapid heat changes, vibrations, and changes to the makeup of the air. A strange scent or smell such as a rubber sole, aftershave, toothpaste, or gun oil will be picked up at 1 part per 3 million.

We constructed 15 towers and installed robot controlled, fully automatic, 50-calibre machine guns, and laid 600 armour-piercing antipersonnel mines. Essentially, if anything happens on the ground outside of our 100x100 yard base, it gets torn up by unforgiving firepower, without anyone on site lifting a finger. This was all by design in case a Boku-yōkai Adept distracted the human guards with their strange power. Anyone approaching by air within 600 yards of the island will come under fire by infrared-guided machine guns, which would easily shred a helicopter at half a mile, even if it were skimming the waves. We couldn't let this happen without human intervention, given it was possible helicopters servicing nearby oil platforms could stray into these areas, but our air defence could be released either by us here on Standoch, or remotely by Kelsie in Vancouver. To turn off our ground defences, which are fully automatic, it would take both Kelsie and me to key in a code. One of us alone cannot shut it down.

After we had secured the island, a fleet of six heavy-lift helicopters began arriving from various areas on the Scottish mainland, carrying cargo that consisted of generators, food, and all of the comforts of home we would allow ourselves during our mission on the island. Each loading area on the mainland was monitored from both here and Vancouver, so we knew precisely who was on each chopper, both through visual means and by aircraft weight. If an Adept had snuck on board, they would have been noticed and we would not allow that flight within range of landing on Standoch. Again, it took a green light from both sites to allow the flight to touch down.

Four full-size trailers had already been flown in and settled on blocks and hooked up to newly-installed, redundant generator power. These trailers housed everything we might need for the analysis of Moy Lei's physiology; from EEG and MRI, to bodily fluids, and any range of tests we could think of – and a few we don't know exactly what they are but sounded good. The site was secure, and already 50% operational as a research base. People were housed in the two, small, concrete buildings left behind by the SBS, which we had refitted quickly with camp beds, microwave ovens, and heaters. In one of three new half-sized trailer was our operations centre. Both Kelsie in Vancouver and our team here on the island have 24/7 real-time video of all access locations on Standoch, from which we can control our defences.

I had brought along some recently retired ex-colleagues, each with a background in military operations including six who have special forces experience in Iran, Afghanistan, or the former Yugoslavia. A strict rotation of staff on shifts was in place and things were mostly running smoothly. To avoid sharing any sensitive — and let's face it, unbelievable — information with the broader team, I warned any attack might use a new psychological warfare technique, and possibly chemical and other agents. Gwen, Moy Lei, and that group had just been cleared to lift off from Wales, to arrive directly here in just under four hours' time. I was as happy as I could be with our defences, under these unusual circumstances.

Before leaving Vancouver, I had inspected the Booker Building defence arrangements and made some adjustments, including the addition of four of my ex-special forces friends to the team protecting the building. Ethan maintains four very capable teams on a regular basis, one of which was Ian's team who were busy escorting Gwen and company. The other three were on a two team on, one team off pattern, defending the Booker Building, which was essentially on lock down. Again, to open any door into the private areas, someone both in the control centre there and here had to enter a code. My ex-special forces team members were floating freely, covering anything they thought a risk.

I couldn't think of anything else to put to work to defend the people I love, and yet I was still fearful. Give me an enemy I understand, and I will kill it. What Ethan had briefed us on was something beyond my ken, and I refused to become overconfident. I had wanted to bring Gia with me, so I could protect her here. Don't get me wrong, despite years of military, special forces, hand-to-hand training, which I have put to use in the field on too many occasions, Gia would (and did once) kick my ass in a close-quarters encounter. She is a hard ass of the first degree. But given our foe's unknown capability, I would have preferred her here behind our longer-range defences. But Gia – being Gia – was set on both protecting the Vancouver team, as I wouldn't be there to do so, and also to expanding our outreach to human-trafficking victims around the world. Our charity effort was just getting off the ground and she would not lose momentum. I nearly didn't get on the plane, but I knew that if I didn't, she would lose respect for me for failing to respect her ability. This sucks!

*

Gwen, Moy Lei, and the others had landed, and after a brief meal and wash-up, had ventured into the trailers to begin working on understanding how our strange new friend, Moy Lei, ticked. Blood and other samples had already been taken and were being analysed here at Standoch. A mirror set of samples were sent to laboratories in Geneva and Norway. I was off shift and should have been resting, but along with everyone in our inner circle not occupied with critical activity, I watched as events in Porto unfolded via video.

Porto is by any standards a beautiful city, at least where the Douro River separates the Gaia zone — which houses approximately fifty port-wine manufacturing and tasting companies — from the steeply-tiered old town full of history. The old town's castles and churches, and its tall, narrow, yellow, pink and red terraced apartments date back to the 1400-1500s and are captivatingly beautiful. Buildings on both sides of the river escape the sun's force under a carpet of orange roof tiles that shimmer in the afternoon heat. Both banks were connected by the intriguing, two-level, Dom Luis I Bridge to the east, and the long- spanning Arrábida Bridge to the west. The whole panorama is overlooked by the spindly Igreja dos Clérigos – or "Church of the Clergy Man" – bell tower, a baroque- era boutique church that stands on the skyline to the north.

Ethan, Marcy, and Ian had already scouted the offices of the shipping company. and we expected the stem cells to show up in the next hour or two. Nothing seemed untoward. It was a small office nestled in a narrow square, with a large refrigerated area accessible from a small loading bay. Ian — who was least likely to be known to any party — had posed as a prospective customer and taken a short tour. He had mapped out the premises with a hidden camera in his jacket pocket and strategically placed several 'disguised' cameras around the premises. These would stream video to us for the next 36 hours before their batteries ran out.

Before entering the site, the team had released three small surveillance drones, which Ian had piloted to overwatch positions where we could observe the comings and goings of the loading dock, as well as each side of the building. By swiveling the cameras, we had good lines of sight up and down the surrounding streets and all approaches to the vicinity of the company. The team on the ground had then withdrawn. Ethan and Marcy proceeded to a rooftop bar on the second story of a port-tasting company, out of sight of the delivery dock. While they sat surrounded by electropop music, 670 yards across the Douro River, Ian was on the 4th floor balcony of a 400-year-old Airbnb rental with a rifle zeroed in on the exposed patio where Ethan and Marcy sat. Next to Ian were controls for the three drones, and he was capable of repositioning them to follow or observe anyone of interest, but he was currently locked out of the system. Darcy Fullerton, Kelsie's sister and designer of these specialized units, was remote controlling all three from Vancouver. Each had been modified following last month's incident where the drone pilots had seen an attack on Ethan, but at that time had no capability to take offensive or defensive action to protect him. Each of the three drones now carried a small flash-bang grenade, which wouldn't harm a target but would incapacitate them for 12-20 seconds with unbearably bright lights and loud noise.

Ethan, Marcy, and Ian were out of the real-time visual surveillance loop, in an attempt not to alert the Boku-yōkai to their proximity. We hoped this strategy would keep them off the Adept's radar. We didn't know how effective that would be. Kelsie, Darcy, and I were the only people with eyes on the target, albeit remotely, keeping the rest of the inner-circle team – including the onsite team – updated with real- time audio updates via discrete earphones. As a further edge, Kelsie had persuaded our friendly white-hat hacker to access the GPS of the truck that was delivering the stem cells. We had been tracking the refrigerated van for 90 minutes and it was now entering the city; we waited for it to approach the dock.

At 5.04 pm Porto time, the van backed into the loading bay amid the reverse-drive warning system's harsh shrieks, which echoed around the ancient stonework. The driver climbed out of his cab and stretched, then wandered to the rear of the vehicle, already wilting in the stifling heat. A staff member from reception came out, chatted for a couple of minutes and, judging from the expressions and gestures, they were possibly discussing Portugal's surprise, premature exit from the World Cup in Russia earlier in the month. They eventually walked over to the back of the bay and pulled forward several trolleys, which they set up behind the truck. The driver then broke the seal on the refrigeration unit and opened the van's rear doors. The two men extracted approximately 20 packages of varying sizes and laid them out on the assembled trolleys. The driver closed the refrigerated doors and they began poring over the dispatch paperwork attached to their respective clipboards.

They were animated at first, but after about 30 seconds, they suddenly paused and just stood quietly. An elderly man in smart grey pants, a white shirt, fashionable yellow scarf, and a jaunty, pork-pie hat detached himself from a small alleyway to the east. He strolled casually over to the trolleys and inspected the delivery. The two men stood still and stared off into the distance while the interloper located a package, which was perhaps has big as a soccer ball, and placed it into an insulated bag that hung limply from his shoulder. He then quite casually drifted back into the same alley he had arrived through just moments before. As he strolled away, the driver and reception worker reanimated – as if nothing had happened – and continued with their work and conversation. That was very scary. The first direct evidence I had personally ever witnessed that something supernatural lives among us. I realized my skin was clammy and the hairs on my neck stood on full alert.

The scene on my monitors shifted suddenly, as Darcy lifted the drone we were watching 400 feet into the air and began to track the individual. On two other screens, we saw the images from the other two drones also move, leap-frogging forward to cover potential egress paths for our target. In 30 seconds, he simply exited the far end of the alley and walked to a taxi that was waiting at the side of the road. The car pulled away and we tracked it through the streets towards the airport. Our drones did not have the range to cover the 30-minute drive to the airport, but we had planned ahead. With the credit card intelligence in mind showing the link to The Azores – São Miguel in particular, the team had set up remote surveillance at the airport earlier in the day, in case that route was used by our target. They had placed 15 small cameras discretely across the terminal, piggy-backing over the airport's Wifi system to send the video feed back to our monitors. We were all relieved to see the taxi pull up, its door open, and our target step out as casual as could be. As he stepped through the departure doors and up to the check-in counter, we got our first good look a Boku-yōkai Adept. He was nearly six feet tall and skinny. Almost gaunt. He was African-American, with very light skin and with sunspots on his cheeks. His short, curly hair was white, and he had the bespectacled, kind face of a man in his late 60s. He had added a light sports jacket to his outfit; it must have been in the taxi. He ambled slowly but confidently through security with a small leather backpack, which presumably held the refrigerated bag. He approached the counter for São Miguel departures, checked in, then sauntered into the security check point and out of the range of our cameras.

We lost him at that point and wondered how he intended to get the package through the security area where a small bottle of shampoo would be prohibited, but perhaps this is another area where someone with his apparent talents has advantages. The team on the ground had travelled in two separate taxis to the airport's private terminal. Ian arrived 30 minutes later than the others, as he stopped to recover all three drones and the base station. At 6.34pm, our private jet departed for São Miguel, but would arrive too late to see where our target went on arrival.

*

Thirty-six hours later, we were sitting down to our morning teleconference and a modest breakfast. We at Standoch were taking turns preparing food for the group, and results were mixed. Today's wasn't bad: Gwen and Bobbi — an ex-Foreign Legionnaire — had plates stacked with crepes, honey, and raspberry jam. And enough hot coffee to float the island. Bobbi left us to it as Kelsie, Julie, Ethan, Marcy, and Ian came on line, and Naomi, Moy Lei, Gwen, and I turned our chairs to face the big screen at the end of the table. As usual, 'queen of operations' Kelsie ran the meeting like a military encounter.

"First up will be a security update for all sites, then a target location update on São Miguel, followed by a report from Naomi on medical findings. Anything else for the agenda?" There was not.

"Vancouver, São Miguel, and Standoch all report as secure. Any changes to report?" There were not.

"Update on the London triple-threat location?"

"As far as I can tell, they are still grouped together and closing in. I would estimate they are on or near the Scottish coast adjacent to our position. Presumably trying to decide how to get to us here," reported Moy Lei.

"We are ready for them," I chipped in, "but we should not assume they are alone anymore. If they are, it should be easy, but we should be prepared for something unknown, bigger, and more complex."

"I'm confident you are as prepared as you can be, but get anything else you need to keep safe," reassured Ethan.

"OK, moving on." prompted Kelsie. "Target tracking. Ian?"

"Good news here. We think we have him. We focused on the north-east corner of São Miguel based on the few credit card hits. I talked to the owner of a grocery store and showed her a picture of the target. She definitely recognized and spoke passionately about him. Apparently, he hosted his usual monthly cookout for the community yesterday. At Furnas, the underground volcanic hot springs bubble close to the surface where there is a picnic area by the lake. You can bury pots of food to cook in the underground hot water stream. Sounds like he routinely buries enough food to feed anyone on the island who needs a good meal and it has become something of an island ritual. I think I translated this right, but the locals refer to him as "Saint Somersby." Aside from this monthly appearance, he keeps to himself at a small farm just outside the village; but locals with problems visit him, and he is thought of as an altruistic community-figure and man of wisdom.

"We located the farm and surveilled it with drones from a distance, and Kelsie advised we have a couple of shots of him on site, working in his greenhouses. Arial views show a small cabin, completely surrounded by a few hectares of greenhouses. We haven't moved close in with the drones for fear of alerting him, but now have drones covering anything that looks at all like an exit from the property. To back up our helicopter-type drones we are shipping over two airplane-type, long-endurance drones that should be operational tomorrow and will cover the site from three thousand feet and be able to keep up with cars should he take to the road."

"Are you thinking of making an approach?" I asked this of Ethan.

"We are not in a hurry. I'd like to learn more about what we are dealing with. Perhaps this would be a good time for an update from Naomi and Moy Lei, if there is nothing else on the target." Ethan didn't add that we were concerned we still had no word at all from Chiyome. Naomi took over – excited and animated – keen to share her discoveries. I noticed Gwen looking on with pride.

"I've worked at the leading edge of science for decades, yet in the last 48 hours, we've discovered things I had never even heard about. We have a long way to go before I can talk confidently about this, let alone explain how it is working, so forgive me if I am vague. Here is what we have observed so far.

"To pick up on our discussion on super neurons, you will recall that all observations since discovery have talked about three larger-than-normal neurons that perhaps account for our consciousness. We know they are connected to each other, and to all major control systems. Using MRIs and other scanners, we can monitor when they are active and what appears to stimulate them, but little else. Amazingly, Moy Lei has an extra super-neuron. There has never been a report of four, as far as I can discover. This is ground-breaking science. The fourth neuron is slightly smaller than the other three but equally well connected, and although smaller, it is still far larger than regular neurons.

"The three super-neurons are interconnected to everything as I said, but each seems to have a bias – or affinity – to a group of key systems. An example might be that the neuron we commonly call the Alpha has more affinity to motor control; that is, how we control our muscle movement. Moy

Lei's forth super-neuron seems to have affinity for the right, superior, temporal cortex, which enables humans to translate spatial awareness. For me, this is how I know how close I am and how I am oriented to objects near me, and which way I would walk to get to, say, the medical trailer. In Moy Lei, her enhancement could relate to her unusual 'radar' like capability. It also appears to have an affinity for the amygdala, a structure in the brain that is responsible for processing emotions such as fear, anger, and pleasure, which underpin our survival mechanisms. Maybe it has affinity to other areas as well, which we have yet to map.

"Kelsie somehow managed to obtain a copy of the coroner's provisional report on the man who attacked you in Durham. He is still unidentified. Due to Ian's excellent marksmanship, there wasn't much brain left to examine, so there would be no way to confirm if this individual had a similar, additional super-neuron, but we did confirm an additional unique feature akin to Moy Lei's. Both he and Moy Lei share unique DNA. You probably know that DNA carries the genetic code for each human. The complex double-helix of chromosomes is the information, the codes, our cells follow to build us, including our strengths and weaknesses. For example, weaknesses might be hereditary genetic diseases, and strengths might be superior athletic or cognitive ability. Leading edge science today is allowing us to repair defects by altering a patient's DNA, which causes the body to better defend itself. An example might be to boost the body's defence against cancer, or repair deficiencies in the immune system.

"In the best layman's terms I can think of, normal DNA has two types of grooves or channels — the major and minor — through which proteins make contact with the base pairs of coding. Through these conduits, we stimulate the release of amino acids and other chemicals to control growth of our bodies building blocks. Both Moy Lei and the Durham assassin have the same design as us, but their grooves are approximately 13% larger. It might not sound like much, but it is astounding and significant. Speculating, this could allow them to create different proteins and amino acids than you and I do. That means they could build physiology we don't possess, potentially using stem cells introduced through their diet. Why, I don't know, but it's not unreasonable to link that to other data we have and form a picture supporting some of the unusual phenomena we have observed. Again, I want to stress, this is barely a hypothesis. I would laugh at anyone bringing this to me as a theory.

"Next, we measured Moy Lei's brain activity when she uses her 'radar.' We saw significant brain activity in what we are calling her Delta, or fourth super-neuron, and the spatial awareness area of her cortex. But Moy Lei has also confided she has additional capabilities. They are quite undeveloped, but she demonstrated them for us. She is able to influence emotions in others. We created two pods that were isolated from each other for the five senses – sight, sound, smell, touch, and taste – plus all electrical radiations we could filter. I had one of Max's team members sealed in one pod, and Moy Lei in the other. She can concentrate, and thereby induce happiness and nervousness in another subject. It also affected me. She is broadcasting, not targeting. I can see brain activity streaming from her amygdala to the Delta neuron, and that pattern replicated in the other subject's amygdala."

"Can you speculate how that happens?" Gwen was prompting her to guess, which was obviously an alien urge to the scientist part of Naomi.

"There is nothing I can think of that enables the link, but there definitely is a link. Entanglement Theory is as good as anything. My guess, and don't hold me to this, is the Delta neuron is a transmitter, which can connect to other people's brains and stimulate certain activity." The conference call was quiet for some time as we all processed this, but them Naomi indicated she had yet more to share.

"The other interesting indicator Moy Lei shared, is that somehow peanuts play a role in her eco-system. Peanuts are rich in minerals, and one of them is selenium, which also plays a role in several of the neurological and cellular systems we have already discussed. It is a very effective electrical conductor, and in all of us we see trace elements of it in our brain. But if I eat peanuts, there is no change of selenium or electrical efficiency in my brain. We gave Moy Lei a controlled dose of peanut oil and see two marked effects: Firstly, her physiology sped up in all respects. Peanut allergies, especially if they trigger anaphylaxis, cause the body's defence systems to go into overdrive. So that is not unusual in one sense, but in Moy Lei it has an additional dynamic. Our brains make up about 4% of our body mass yet consume 20% of our blood oxygen and our body's electrical energy. In a normal anaphylactic event, this stays about the same in a subject, or even possibly declines as a ratio as resources move to the areas that react to the peanut, such as swellings or creating additional mucus etc. In Moy Lei, we see her lungs beginning to over-react with the small dose we gave her, but we saw her brain dramatically increase the proportion of energy and blood flow. I would estimate perhaps up to 33%. Again, this is unprecedented and very significant as an increase. The second aspect is a doubling in the communication between all four super-neurons. I can't really explain the purpose of this, but I can observe it.

"My last guess is sort of a summary. The Adepts seem to be more developed than Moy Lei. It might simply be training and practice, but I suspect that additional diet, including stem cells, could be allowing them to further develop and evolve their physiology beyond Moy Lei's nascent ability and biology. From the postmortem details of the Durham assassin, and from the description you've shared of Saint Somersby, both appear overly thin or malnourished. That could be a result of driving their physiology past the point that they can sustain weight. Also, whereas Moy Lei begins to trigger an anaphylactic reaction when exposed to peanut oil, the two observations of Adepts suggest they operate at a higher supernatural ability without such a debilitating reaction. I suspect the four super-neurons are working together to mitigate the allergic reaction yet harness its energy. Like a supercharge. Alternatively, they could have used stem cells to modify their body in some other way to counteract the extreme allergic effect. But in summary, Moy Lei can link her brain to others' brains, or if not link, broadcast to them, to transfer emotions and perhaps other control patterns, and to a point, she can increase that ability through her diet, in particular with peanuts. But after a point, her body will go into shock due to the allergy and she will shut down and be debilitated."

"Any idea how to block the transmission, or otherwise defeat their power?" I asked.

"None, sorry. I can't detect the interbrain link, so I don't know what to suggest. We plan to begin experimenting with that today. That's all I have to report."

"Right, that was our agenda. Other business. Next steps?" Ethan typically steps in at this point of our meeting, as he did again today.

"Max, prepare to defend or, if required, evacuate Standoch. Moy Lei and Naomi continue their research, of course. Lastly, I think I'll go to talk to Saint Somersby."

"What?" said Ian, Kelsie, and I jointly, all in unison with Marcy saying, "Not without me you won't!"

9: THANK YOU VERY MUCH

[ETHAN] – I had to impose my authority during our meeting this morning, but I have to admit the rebellion was understandable. Max, Ian, and Kelsie were concerned for our safety and, of course, they were right to be. I was pushing things faster than was prudent. I didn't want to say it out loud, but my overriding concern was the silence from Chiyome. We should have heard from her by now, and no news was probably bad news. My gut was telling me that – somewhere – a clock was ticking faster than we knew, and events proved me to be right. It turned out to be the saddest of days.

My plan to mitigate any supernatural powers that Somersby might weaponize was ingenious – or so I thought. I'd been racking my brain regarding countermeasures and came up with the idea to carry a backpack containing a rapid deployment, anesthetic gas. I'd had some flown in and had Ian rig a mechanism that enabled the gas to be released remotely. I would wear 360-degree video and audio sensors, livestreaming back to operations. If I were attacked Kelsie or Ian would release the gas, which would knock me out, but hopefully also Somersby. Ian could then come in and secure Somersby and keep him unconscious until we could study him, and of course retrieve me. Far from foolproof, but a decent plan at least. Marcy added the idea of us wearing a gas mask, which I wished I had thought of, and insisted on coming with me. She argued two of us would be more effective. I didn't agree, but it was clear she was coming regardless of my viewpoint. I made a mental note to discuss hierarchy of operational authority with her, preferably not while she had me tied up over a barrel.

Ian and the twin operations centre's monitored us via our wearable cameras and several drones, including the just arrived, high altitude units. Marcy and I drove our rented compact car slowly up the 200-yard driveway to the Somersby property. Like most of the roads on São Miguel, it was spectacularly beautiful, as the entire island is festooned with hydrangeas. They grow freely along most of the country lanes and garnish every hedgerow in blues, pinks, purples, and many shades in between. The driveway was spectacular and could have been a national monument entrance way. We crept slowly along. Considering this was the most dangerous part of our trip, as a gas release inside the car was worse than pointless, we wondered if going so slowly was smart. If we lost our minds now, we were sitting ducks, although Ian had us covered from his sniper's nest on the hill off to the southeast. In the end, we approach slowly because we were scared.

We parked and stepped out onto the road, 100 yards away from the entrance to the first of the greenhouses. We had studied aerial footage and there really was no way into the cabin without passing through a greenhouse. Somersby clearly had green thumbs and a thirst for gardening.

It was hot: a breezy 108 degrees, which felt hotter in the direct sunlight or when the wind dropped speed. But the sweat pouring down the inside of my shirt and the rivulets of moisture inside my gas mask were from fear. We pressed ahead. I wanted to hold Marcy's hand, but how confident would that have looked? I was afraid. My mind flashed back to Durham Cathedral and the oppressive, debilitating fear the Adept had evoked in me. I briefly pondered if this feeling was a gentler, passive defence version of an Adept's weaponized fear that Somersby relied upon to keep away the unwanted, but then recalled Ian's report that locals often visited Somersby with their problems. I decided my trepidation was based on the real fact that all of this scared the shit out of me. I glanced at Marcy and saw she was wearing her cop face. She is a hard ass. But she was sweating, too, with unfeminine wet patches in various places.

We reached the door to the greenhouse and found a bell. Marcy lifted the corner of her mask to talk.

"Let's try the door. If we ring the bell and stare at him through the glass, your fancy gas grenade won't help us at all." She twisted the handle and the door opened. We both shrugged, and I pressed the bell. We could hear a distant chime. I followed Marcy into the greenhouse's sweltering, moist heat and reluctantly closed the door behind us.

About 30 seconds after we closed the door, both of our phones chirped a series of emergency beeps. We both read the messages at the same time: Trouble at Standoch. Another set of beeps: Trouble in Vancouver. How could they both have a problem?

"Let's back out of here!" I commanded from the corner of the mask and turned to the door. A gaunt, thin man stood 30 feet distant outside on the path between us and our car. He had haunting eyes. He was short – perhaps five feet in high heels – and he was in his mid-twenties and dressed like a hipster. Skinny red pants, slim-fit blue shirt, and a vest or waistcoat. Shiny black boots. His eyes were huge, almost bug like, and he radiated energy. His chin was wrapped in a thin, dapper beard. If this were a politician or movie star, you might call his aura charisma or stage presence. Sudden waves of terror ran over me and I quickly stepped over to Marcy. She already had her gun drawn but seemed at a loss for a target. She didn't seem to see the man in the middle of the drive, which was crazy. I pointed him out, and she looked but saw nothing, her head swiveling, seeking a target. She was panicking, which was truly scary. I've never seen her show fear. I spoke into my microphone.

"Ian. Kelsie. We are under attack, but the attacker is not close enough for gas — stand by. Stand by. Over." No answer from Ian. With a hiss of the satellite link activating, Kelsie cut in. Her voice also panicked.

"Copied, Ethan. Be aware: Vancouver is also under attack! We are breached and might not be able to assist."

[KELSIE] – As Marcy and Ethan approached the Somersby residence, our food arrived. We had ordered pizza for the team and it should have arrived 30 minutes before we kicked off the operation, but it was late. We had a call explaining the delay and we considered cancelling so that we wouldn't be distracted, but as far as we knew, Vancouver was not a target. That was my awful, fateful mistake, and it will haunt me to my deathbed.

The delivery girl arrived with a trainee who, she said via the intercom, was learning the ropes. My assistant, Elizabeth Marley, told her by video to hold and I sent down two of Max's special forces friends to collect the pizza. I triggered the door-opening switch when they were ready and asked Max to confirm it from Standoch, which he did. It felt so odd that I needed help to open my own front door. I returned my attention to São Miguel. Thirty seconds later all hell broke loose.

"Holy shit!" squealed Elizabeth. She pointed to her screen covering the delivery bay, while her fingers flew over the buttons. She expertly backed up the video footage then let it play. Two young women in jeans, sneakers, and tee shirts stood holding boxes of pizza as the door opened. They both tried to offer their boxes to the guards. One man refused and stepped to the side, keeping both hands free but near his concealed belt holster, keeping enough distance from the women to cover any moves they might make. It seemed like total overkill, but professional as hell. The other man accepted both piles of boxes and juggled them so he could sign for the order. His reactions were incredible when his colleague's chest exploded from a long-distance rifle shot. He threw the pizza towards one of the women and crouched, reaching under his jacket. The woman who wasn't dodging the pizza stepped in and pulled a wicked blade from her sleeve and rammed it up through his chin, into his brain. She sheathed the nine-inch knife in time to catch a pizza box before it hit the ground, opened it, and extracted a pair of pistols. As the two women stepped over our threshold, it struck me that I was watching footage nearly 20 seconds old. I hit the alarm and sirens sounded all through Ethan's spaces in the Booker Building as a third woman, the rifle owner, followed her fellow assassin through the door.

[MAX] – Suddenly, someone was hammering on the operations centre door and I glanced up and saw Moy Lei outside, yelling up at the camera. I buzzed the door open. Ethan and Marcy were just approaching the greenhouse, and this was poor timing for her to barge in.

"What is it? This is terrible timing!"

She gulped down a breath, having clearly sprinted form the medical trailer to our operations module. "They are coming, and fast. They've split up and are nearly here already. The dark souls."

"They can't be. By helicopter it's a 20-minute flight."

"I know what I know! They are nearly here." Suddenly, the proximity radar alarm sounded. I looked at the radar screen and three distinct targets were inbound at nearly 550 knots. Not much under the speed of sound, with today's atmospherics. I hit the general alarm, which would get everyone up and to their battle positions. I calculated that, at that speed, they would be with us in under two minutes. I keyed in the release of our 50-calibre air defences. This was no oil rig milk-run. After 90 seconds, the trailer door opened and John – my assistant – took his post helping me repel the attack. I would direct, and he would monitor and control systems. I keyed the audio for Vancouver.

"Kelsie, we are under attack. Can you notify Ethan?"

No reply. She had just been on audio asking me to let the pizza guy up. I quickly typed in the message myself and broadcast that Standoch was at *condition red*. Instead of one message appearing on my phone, which I checked to confirm the broadcast, two came in. Vancouver was also under attack. My thoughts went directly to Gia.

[GIA – Vancouver] I heard the breach alarm and leapt up off the couch. I had been working my way through reports on trafficking-victim rehabilitation efforts on my laptop. I ran for the main control room. Then I recalled that Max's new protocols meant that an alarm would automatically shut off the elevators. I stopped and reversed course, and instead headed for the stairwell. One of Max's military friends, Ji, had the door open, and he was crouched at the top of the stairs, peering over the railing. As I approached, his gun flicked towards me; when he identified me as a 'friendly,' his gun was aimed back at the stairwell.

"Ethan's Team Beta has the other stairwell covered," he said, calmly. A real professional.

We both heard it at the same moment: Footsteps running softly, but full tilt, up towards us. An impressive pace, considering we were over 20 floors up. I braced myself and watched our lone, armed defender line his gun up at the space where the attacker would appear in mere moments. A shooter's stance; feet apart, two handed, and braced. The footsteps ceased with the heavy thump of someone stopping suddenly. A metallic ball flew up onto our landing.

"Grenade!" yelled Ji, and flung himself down flat, trying to take me with him; but I had different ideas. I was at *fast speed*, a skill I was taught at the beginning of my martial arts training. The world slowed for me, which allowed me to keep ahead of the situation by microseconds. Instead of dropping, I stepped back though the door.

Whoomf!

The door shook and lights went out. As the emergency lighting blinked on, I stepped back out to see a woman moving quickly – a parkour style – not on the floor, but around the wall at least four feet off the ground. Ji was still prone, still drawing a bead on the space that the attacker *should* have been occupying, while his target shot him in the face as she was still defying gravity. A feat hard to do on the level or running downhill, and an incredible act of athleticism running up the stairs. I admired the skill, despite my shock and horror at what she was using it to accomplish.

My body had not waited for me to tell it what to do and I found I was already running towards the same wall that the assassin was traversing and, like her, I left the floor, and ran down the wall. The trick to defying gravity is to run at the wall, almost trying to run through it, rather than trying to run parallel to it. With enough speed, you can stay up for about a second and a half before mother nature tires of your antics and flings you down on your ass. The attacker was already being dragged down and recognizing that, and at the same moment registering me as a threat, she pivoted and changed directions. She branched off across the floor towards the opposite wall, still at a remarkable full sprint. With her mounting one wall, and me beginning to fall from the other, our passing point was such that our heads would pass close to each other. It would have made a bizarre sight, worthy of a martial arts movie. It still felt like slow motion to me and I could sense it did for my assailant, too. I've fought people who think at *fast speed* like me in MMA tournaments, and it is like nothing else. Moments slowed further, and I increased my pace and chose my attack. I reached out and grabbed her by the neck and let physics solve my problem for me. She was desperately trying to retrain her gun on me, but she wouldn't have time. She should have dropped the gun and gone hand to hand to block me. All I had to do now is hang on. With a jerk, time sped up and our respective trajectories created a whiplash. Her neck against my 135 pounds. *Crack*. We landed in a mess, and I smacked my hip as we crunched against the staircase.

A fraction of a second too late, I realized my error. Another woman was following her more slowly up the stairs and had me in her sights. I began a roll to my left but doubted I could break her aim. I braced for pain and thought of Max, sending my love a *goodbye*. The expression on my assailant's face changed and she began to whip her head around, sensing an attack from behind. Without a sound — but with savage teeth bared – Elvis landed square in the middle of her back and she sprawled forward, her gun slipping from her grip. As she rolled and protected her face from the massive German Shephard's teeth, I could tell she was about to reach for his eyes. No way. In one fluid motion, I concluded the roll I had started and leapt, landing square on her stomach with all of my weight and momentum, crushing vital organs. I reached down and snatched up her gun, and calling Elvis to the side, shot the assassin in the neck as she flailed.

I checked she was gone. No doubts. I double checked Ji, too; he was already unconscious and bleeding out with no hope. I took his radio mic with deference, not to disturb his last moments, and checked in with Team Beta on the other stairwell. They were two men down, but the remaining two had their lone attacker at bay. She was half a floor down from their position, trying to get an angle to get at them. I didn't fuck around. I dropped down a floor, crossed over, and blew the head off the other woman from behind with the gun I had taken from her teammate. Elvis was at my side, tail wagging. I knelt and let him lick my face, then slouched back against the wall, holding my hip.

"Double treats for you tonight, boy. Double treats." Then in my very best Presley voice, which I admit was terrible, I whispered, "Thank you very much!"

[MAX] – When the fast-moving targets were a quarter mile and 20 seconds out, their profiles changed. They swept from horizontal flight to vertically upwards, rising rapidly, easily outclimbing our ground defence. We watched them on a long-range camera as they swooped up to five, then eight, then 12 thousand feet, before reversing course back towards the mainland. Three separate, small, business jets. *Shit. An expensive decoy*, my brain registered – a little too late.

"John, check all around us!" As he was checking, I was also looking at the radar and saw two slower speed-blips upon us from the other direction. I cursed my stupidity. Bloody amateur hour. I deserved to get my ass handed to me. As I registered my mistake, we heard the air-splitting sound of three 50-calibre machine guns opening up. Within five seconds, they were out of ammo and overheated, but those seconds were lethal. Two of the guns had automatically focused on one incoming chopper and, for half of that time, so had the third one. Then the system had detected the second aircraft and switched the third gun to that target. Target one was done. Falling like a stone towards the churning, black sea, 600 yards offshore. If they survived the crash, the exposure to near-freezing water should get them before they could possibly reach the island. If they somehow made it, they could never scale the cliffs. Target two twisted and jived, and as we looked out of the window, we saw it lurch down and belly-flop onto the clifftop to the north and burst into flames. At 600 yards away, we could see a dozen men scramble out and take defensive positions. A minute later, they were oriented and someone must have given the signal to advance. They separated from cover and ran forward, guns up. To a man, they were ripped apart by the automatic ground defences.

I took in a big gulp of air and began issuing radio requests for status updates. My mind was in Vancouver with Gia, but I had a job to do here so had to stay focused. One by one, the radio reports came back that we had no casualties, suffered no damage, and were secure. The team had already begun reloading our depleted air defence. It was then that I glanced over at John to my left; he was gazing off into space and his hands were tapping oddly slowly on the keyboard. I looked at his screen and saw that he was attempting to disarm our defences. The requirement for Vancouver to endorse his instruction was the only thing that prevented us from being exposed and overrun.

"John!" I barked. "What are you playing at?"

"Ethan's over there. I need to shut this down before he gets killed," replied John, his voice distant and faint as he kept punching in the stand-down code, over and over. I drew my pistol... keeping it close to my side. I texted Naomi and advised her that John had somehow been 'hacked.' I suspected we had a Boku-yōkai Adept loose on the Island. Crap!

[ETHAN] – The gaunt man outside laughed at us and started forward. I tried to pull my gun but felt weighed down by a new, second force. I could barely resist the first wave of intense fear, but this second wave was completely overwhelming. I managed to step between Marcy and the stranger but then I collapsed to my knees. I raised my gun towards him but could not keep it aloft. It was too damn heavy. I could see Marcy inch up alongside me, equally struggling to get her weapon up. I saw her glance over my shoulder and I followed her gaze. Approaching from inside the greenhouse from behind an aisle of long-leafed shrubs came a thin old man who limped at a speed that belied his obvious age. He was staring at us, and I could somehow sense he was the source of this second, overpowering wave of emotion. I knelt with my hands at my side, powerless to act. He approached rapidly, and we had no recourse. My mind went back to the description Moy Lei gave us of finding professor Ellison's eviscerated corpse and I knew that if Kelsie, Ian, or Max didn't trigger our gas, then we would likely face the same fate. Perhaps we would be fertilizer for this greenhouse. I cursed myself for letting Marcy join me.

The old man strode purposefully past us, clicked his tongue in frustration, and then stomped to the door and peered out. He flung open the door to the outside and planted his feet on the threshold. His stance projected his whole will towards the thin figure on the driveway, who had now stopped in his tracks, and was glaring back fiercely and the older man. It reminded me of

Gandalf facing down the Balrog in Lord of the Rings. The two men faced off for what seemed like an age, before the more distant, younger man shook his head, turned, and casually withdrew. As he vanished around the corner past our car, the older man man who had appeared from inside the green house turned our way and walked over. As he did, the pressure holding us down dimmed, then evaporated over the space of a few seconds. Marcy and I struggled to our feet and we both raised our guns defensively. The old man stopped in his tracks and stared at us like we were mad. Perhaps we were. After a few seconds of standoff, he slowly held out his hand in welcome and spoke.

"I've no idea who you fine folk are, but it would please me greatly if you could lower your weapons. I'm Jim Somersby." He waited. I don't think he really expected us to drop our guns and just shake his hand 'hello', but it was a clear de-escalation signal. I looked at Marcy and she eventually nodded my way. We compromised and lowered our guns to 45 degrees and a little to the side. This seemed to make Somersby relax – just a little. I removed my mask, and Marcy followed suit. Somersby shrugged and lowered his arm.

"I would offer you tea," he said kindly, a tone used by doctors and policemen around the world delivering sad news, "but we need to go and recover your friend from up there on the hill. There is nothing we can do for him, but we should bring him in out of the heat. Guance, that man on the driveway killed him before he attacked you two, I'm afraid. I felt him attack, and that's how I realized you two were even here. I'm truly sorry for your loss." He bowed his head respectfully. Marcy was already on the move, running up the hill to Ian's surveillance post.

10: MR SOMERSBY

[ETHAN] — It was a heart-wrenching sight: Ian Po was slumped over; blood that had oozed from his slit throat had dripped down over the wooden rifle-stock and drenched his leather shooting-gloves. No signs of a struggle or that he had even reacted to the knife thrust that ended his young life. We stood quietly over his body and, using my phone, replayed footage from the overhead drones. We watched, horrified, as the Adept simply walked up and slayed him as he lay incapacitated, presumably by a similar power that had held us enthralled. I was both angry and puzzled that Kelsie had not interceded with the drones, or at least followed the attacker so that she could be tracking him right now.

Flies had already begun to gather, so I hauled Ian up onto my shoulder to carry him, then Marcy, Somersby, and I walked down to the greenhouse. Throughout this activity, Somersby said nothing. When we were inside his greenhouse, he pulled out plastic sheeting and tape and helped us wrap Ian's remains, which we would ship back to Vancouver. Ian had three daughters and a loving wife; I needed to take him home and break the tragic news in person.

We soon heard from Kelsie and Max and began to understand that there had been a coordinated attack of all three of our positions simultaneously. My anger towards Kelsie persisted unreasonably, but I bit it back, knowing it would soon be replaced – as it should be – with a cold intent to find and deal with Ian's killer, Guance. In addition to Ian, three of Max's colleagues in Vancouver were gone: two men from Team Beta – who have worked for me for over four years – as well as the legitimate pizza delivery boy, a 16-year-old named Charlie. The police were treating Charlie's death as a robbery-gone-wrong, and we wouldn't dissuade them from that notion. I would ensure the families of those we lost were taken care of financially – not that it would bring them back their loved ones. Five good people lost in the space of less than 20 minutes. Not counting the assassins, of course. The dark souls. How fitting that phrase has become.

It was daunting to think that whoever we faced could deploy three ninja-like assassins in Vancouver, a small army in Scotland, and at least two Adepts. Three if you count Durham. We didn't know where Jim Somersby fit into all of this but, so far, he hadn't been hostile towards us. It was time to get some answers. We were acutely aware that Max was dealing with a ticking time bomb: He was defending Standoch against an Adept and was in dire trouble at this very moment.

We reluctantly left Ian's remains by the greenhouse door and followed Somersby through to his house. It was a modest, well appointed, stone rancher. There were no signs of a woman's touch and the space projected the image of a man who had been a perpetual bachelor. I was shocked that it felt like a gentle place; believing Somersby to be some sort of international villain, my subconscious had pictured walls full of weapons; some as historical art, others as contemporary weapons for hunting. Maybe even stuffed heads of hunting trophies on the walls – animals and perhaps humans, too! Instead there were clocks, as well as paintings by local artists of local scenery. Bookshelves instead of voodoo dolls. The books were not combative tomes. No *War and Peace* or *Art of War*. They were mostly agriculture – and gardening – themed, fitting for his apparent greenhouse fetish, and there was a stunning array of medical and psychology texts. Somersby pointed towards his kitchen table and poured some coffee from a carafe on the counter. The millwork was all white pine and the floors covered in smart, hardy looking, square, sandstone tiles. The appliances brushed steel Bosch units. Yellow, rubber, dishwashing gloves draped over the kitchen sink's tap.

"Do you two want something stronger with this coffee? Something to eat perhaps?"

"No thank you, Mr Somersby. Just some answers if you please." Marcy spoke in her no-nonsense 'cop' tone. "Let's start by you telling us who this Guance character is, and where we can find him!" Somersby considered Marcy, while he finished organizing his coffee and taking his seat.

"I might be happy to answer some of these questions, young lady," he said, in his own blunt tone that dripped with resentment, "but let's slow down a little and straighten something out first. I sense a great deal of hostility directed my way, but Guance was following you, not visiting me. You brought him here. You realize that I just saved you both, don't you? I had no part in that death and would have prevented it if I had known sooner." He paused and took a thoughtful sip; he sat back, resetting his position both physically and in attitude, perhaps.

"I am very sorry for your losses. Sincerely, I am. But they were not my doing, and I resent your entering my house and talking to me like I'm part of whatever you've gotten yourself into. We can have a coffee and some civilized conversation, and I'll decide which questions of yours I will answer or, you can leave and take your chances. If it's the former, rather than insulting demands, how about a show of good faith? Tell me who you are and what you want with me."

We knew that Kelsie was back to monitoring our conversation and could trigger the gas; but with Ian gone, it would be a race to see who woke up first. We were younger but, with Somersby's unusual physiology, I really didn't want to take a risk unless we had to. I reached over and laid my hand on top of

Marcy's, then took over the conversation in a more conciliatory tone, despite her bristling at my intervention.

"Sorry Mr Somersby. Jim, is it? We've had a trying week, to say the least, and today was the worst of it. My name is Ethan Booker, and this is Marcy Stone. Our friend is – was – Ian Po. He was a personal friend." I hadn't realized I had paused, caught in the shock that Ian was gone, until Marcy squeezed my hand. "We are trying to help an acquaintance who feels she is threatened by people like Guance. I'll be honest: we don't know where you fit in to all of this, other than we suspected you share certain – um – capabilities with these 'people.' And from what we saw earlier, that seems to be certain now. Although while we feel that you could be a threat to us – we hope you are not – we also hope that you could be a source of information. We need to find out more about you – and them – so that we can defend ourselves and our friends. Even as we sit here, said acquaintance and some good people who work for me are under attack by a person with your unusual abilities, and I need a way to help them survive."

"Is that what the gas masks are about? You planned to gas me?" It was said with an incredulous laugh, and I admit, it was sounding sillier by the minute.

We slowly removed the gas system and lay it on the floor next to our seats. "Just in self-defence. If you attacked us."

Somersby continued. "I sense that Guance is less than half a mile away, biding his time. He's probably planning to take you when you leave. He knows he can't compete with me here, even in my dotage, as this is my territory. I am stronger here. But if you gas me, you two are sitting ducks. He'll sense it and he will come. My suggestion is you keep your finger off that trigger."

"Then he'll kill all three of us," said Marcy.

"He may, but probably not. I've lived alongside his ilk for nearly 70 years and we've not come to blows yet, despite some conflict in agendas. He has no beef with me other than my slowing him down today. But I must say, it is incredibly rare for one of the Chord to come here, let alone challenge me openly. They must be truly ticked at you. Do you mind telling me what you or your acquaintance has done to get on their radar?"

"Maybe. I appreciate this must be an information exchange, and not a one-way dialogue, but we feel quite disadvantaged, Jim. We don't know who to trust and are in a bit of a minefield of sorts." Somersby sat quietly, patiently listening to me. He opened one hand in a gesture which, while not unfriendly, could only mean we should proceed. He could out-wait us. At this point, I didn't want to say too much more, and I wouldn't reveal that our acquaintance – Moy Lei – had some abilities, or that we were very well resourced. I suspected Somersby might know if we lied, so I set out to tell the truth as much as possible.

"We were told by an acquaintance that her daughter had run away, and we set out to find her. We are private detectives. As we caught up with the daughter, a man attacked us, in a manner similar to the way Guance attacked today. I think that man would have killed us, or at least the daughter, if not for Ian: Ian shot the attacker."

"Well that would certainly get the Chord's attention, to be sure. The Chord are a tight clan and attack them and they will react to be sure." Somersby blew out a long breathe and nodded thoughtfully, then continued. "That would be why Guance killed your friend instead of just knocking him out. What did the daughter say she had done to warrant being attacked?"

"She said she became aware of someone who had these unusual abilities. She could not identify the person specifically, but believed they work as part of an organization her mother operates. She felt that this knowledge put her in danger, and she fled for her own safety. The attack on her seems to substantiate the risk she is in, but we can't really corroborate her story. She's a young girl at risk, is all we really know. And we didn't take kindly to being attacked ourselves."

"You really are in the crapper, aren't you? Tell me, did the confrontation that resulted in your poor friend there shooting that fellow take place way to the north? England perhaps?"

"Yes. Durham, northern England. Why?"

"I felt it. When one of us dies, we all get a sense of it."

There was a chime. A doorbell perhaps. Somersby jumped out of his chair with surprising deftness and took off towards the greenhouses. He shot back over his shoulder, "Sorry, I forgot an appointment. Sit tight; I'll be back. Help yourself to anything if you are hungry or thirsty." We heard his footsteps clatter hastily into the distance.

"He seems like someone's favourite grandpa, not a serial killer," I whispered.

"Do you think he is messing with our thoughts somehow?" asked Marcy. My phone beeped. Kelsie, who was now monitoring us live, answered that question by confirming what our eyes had been telling us. We straightened as we heard him coming back.

"Come, I have to leave quickly to deal with an urgent matter, and you are not safe here without me!" he commanded, a little breathlessly. "We'll use my car." He turned and we watched him retreat quickly, then after looking at each other and shrugging in frustration took off after him. We caught up to him by Ian's wrapped corpse.

"Bring him! – Guance might take him if we leave him behind." He walked on urgently. I glanced at Marcy, then she helped me put Ian back over my shoulder. Following Somersby, we went through two doorways and along aisles of planters and shrubs, to arrive at a garage. There were three cars and a small utility tractor parked in the large space. Somersby opened the trunk of a black station wagon, exposing its cluttered interior. He pulled out some boxes, placing one on the back seat of the car, then pulled some carpeting out of a corner of the garage and almost reverentially lined the trunk and help me lay Ian gently down.

"Jim. I'm not sure what's going on, but our friends are in imminent danger. We don't have time for whatever this is."

"My friends are in danger too, Ethan. Why don't we help each other, eh?" He left me to close the trunk, puzzling over his words, as he jumped into the driver's seat, started the engine, and pressed the remote that started the garage door rolling up.

"In the back seat if you don't mind," he said, nodding ahead. "I have to pick up another passenger." Looking up the road, I could see a young girl – perhaps 12-years old – standing by the main gate. Marcy and I hopped into the rear seats and closed the doors as Somersby pulled hastily out of the garage and began down the road. He stopped by the girl; she looked nervously at us through the open window, and my rusty Portuguese helped me understand Somersby tell her we were friends who could help. She had tear streaks on her face, and the beginnings of what looked like a black eye forming. She pulled the door open and slipped into the seat. Somersby took off. A quarter mile down the road, we passed a small, white hatchback with two figures sitting inside. Guance and an associate. Marcy and I both reacted angrily at the sight of him smiling back at us – Marcy's hand even grabbed the door handle – but Somersby stopped us with a command that had the pressure of more than just words. I felt my mood changing from rage to semi-ambivalence, tinged with helplessness. I settled back and felt Marcy do the same.

"Going after him alone would be a mistake. Sorry, I can't let anyone else get hurt today," growled Somersby. My phone chirped.

"OBSERVATION DRONE RETARGETED TO WHITE HATCHBACK. RELYING ON YOUR BODY CAMS ONLY TO MONITOR YOU – ADVISE IF INCORRECT – KELSIE"

At the speed we were going, we had left the helicopter drones behind, but the higher-level plane drone could keep up. With only the one unit airborne, Kelsie was making the choice to use it to track Guance. I double-tapped the microphone, our covert code for 'affirmative.' Three taps would have been 'negative.' Four, 'send cavalry,' not that we had any.

"TARGET MOVING ONTO SOMERSBY PROPERTY – NOT FOLLOWING YOU"

I knew Marcy could see the same message, so we didn't speak.

Somersby introduced us to Mariana, then explained the situation.

"I was expecting Mariana's mother. I've been helping her with her sick husband, João. Carolina has been coming to me for a year, since João's accident. Someone at a soccer game threw a bottle into the crowd and it caught him in the head. The external injury healed quickly, but his brain was damaged. A loving and peaceful man, who now has fits of enormous and unpredictable rage. I provide them with some herbs and medicine that deal with the worst, but occasionally they fail.

"The family was picnicking nearby; Carolina was to come by and collect a new supply – the concoction must be fairly fresh to be effective. João was having an episode and struck Mariana, and now has Carolina cornered by the lake. We need to get there before he hurts her, himself, or anyone trying to intervene."

Marcy gasped, "shouldn't the police be involved? They can help, not lock him up."

"Maybe. Maybe. But I've known this family for years. My father was the local doctor and delivered most of these people when they were born. I went to school with them, too. So, I'm invested. And I can help."

The road opened into a country park of sorts, with a parking area on the right, which Jim ignored and drove past at high speed. We passed some small concession stands and then the steaming hot springs, from which wafted the bad-egg smell of sulphur. We drove farther still, then broke out from the trees onto a grassy plain where the paved road stopped. We bumped on towards a picnic area, directed by a now-animated Mariana. A small crowd had gathered on the lakeshore, where a small but stocky man stood over a sobbing woman who had crumpled at his feet. In one hand the man had a picnic knife, and in the other, a stick. I felt Marcy the cop come to life beside me. She radiated an intensity which I've learned is her readying for action.

"Stand down!" demanded Somersby in a soft but firm tone, and again, the wave of supernatural pressure behind the words, which I saw Marcy struggle against.

Jim had stopped the car and was looking back over the seat at Marcy, imploring her.

"Please. I've got this. Trust me" he said more gently. She gave a slight nod. I knew that, not only was the cop alive and dominant in her right now, but the ghosts of her abusive past were demanding action of her. They were loud and persistent voices, coming from a deep, dark place. I judged her to be 'on hold,' as opposed to having stood down. She would watch for a short while, but a clock was ticking, and it had a short count-down.

"Which way is the damn wind coming from?" Jim's head swiveled as he spoke. He caught sight of the steam from the hot springs. Divining the wind direction from the path of the steam, he repositioned us upwind of João and the crowd.

He said "Stay with Mariana, please! Keep the child in the car." Then he said something in Portuguese I didn't catch to Mariana, grabbed the box he had put on the back seat, jumped out, and slammed the door closed behind him. Mariana slid across into the driver's seat and pressed her face against the window.

I took the moment to ask Kelsie over the microphone for an update on Guance. She replied, confirming he was still at the house. Searching for Ian? That was weird if true.

Somersby walked quickly to a spot about 30 yards upwind of where a group had formed around Joao, who still had Mariana's mother cornered near the lake. He put the box onto the ground and reached into it, pulling out two fistfuls of leaves. He shredded them into tiny pieces and filled his hands with the mulch; checking the wind again, Somersby threw his hands upwards, letting the leaf particles float out ahead of him, towards the crowd. He held his arms wide and aloft then let his head fall back while he closed his eyes. We watched in amazement as the small group ahead of him at first relaxed their concerned or aggressive stances, then slowly began to sway. João turned towards us, and we could see his wild eyes. His stood taller, clearly threatening harm to Carolina, who was crouched at his feet. Jim slowly walked towards him, his eyes now meeting João's. After a few seconds, João stilled, relaxed. João looked startled, but after a few seconds, he became visibly stilled, relaxed. He then suddenly seemed to realize what he was actually doing. Coming back to his right mind. He became horrified by his own actions and dropped down, next to his wife. Cradling her and checking her for injuries, crying with remorse. Jim knelt beside him, reached into his pocket, and pulled out a handful of something, which João took and ate. Jim waived to Mariana, who leapt out of the car and ran to her parents. We made to follow, but felt a nudge of Jim's power, as he held his hand up to still us.

We watched as the family came together. Mariana and Jim helped the parents to their feet; Carolina was not badly hurt, but all were shaken. The remainder of the crowd just stood, sat, or swayed where they were, oblivious of the astonishing scene we were witnessing. After a short while, Carolina led her family off and Jim walked slowly back towards us. We stood in silence as the family made its way to the car park and left. It was a truly beautiful spot: the lake, the trees, the sights of locals and tourists relaxing. I could hear the familiar accents from a small group of attractive, fun, Canadian tourists, which took my thoughts back to Vancouver and the tragic events there, and the solemn duties ahead. We watched the group mingling with a large, local family, enjoying the regional specialty – *Cozido das Furnas*. This consists of a wide variety of meats and vegetables cooked for hours in huge pots buried in volcanic steam chambers at 200 degrees Fahrenheit. God's stove. We had just witnessed a miracle, and somehow it didn't seem entirely out of place here.

Jim broke my reverie when he spoke. “Mr Booker. Ms Stone. Thank you for your trust. I suggest we put some distance between Guance and ourselves. Do you have transportation? I’m afraid I’ve been a bit of a coward as far as The Chord are concerned. Perhaps it is time to change. Let’s go see if we can still help your friends.”

Jim drove us to the airport. Kelsie had called ahead, so we were permitted to drive right up to our plane, which was warmed up on the ramp in a private corner of the airfield. The crew helped us carry Ian’s body aboard, and we carefully stowed his remains in the rear cabin. We took our seats as the captain taxied us out, and as we lined up for takeoff, Kelsie informed us that Guance was en route to the airport but still several miles away. Jim felt confident that Guance would not be able to interfere with the pilot and endanger the plane from that distance. Jim seemed exhausted from his activity; he settled back into his seat and began to doze almost instantly. Kelsie advised that the drone was low on fuel and she would fly it out to sea and ditch it as we had no way to recover it. We would lose track of Guance which was sickening, but Max’s team must be our priority. I made a silent oath for the tenth time in the last few hours that I would catch up with Guance one day, and there would be a reckoning.

We sped down the runway, lifted off, and turned north. The jet would drop us at a small strip in Scotland, refuel, and continue on to take Ian home. Our first order of business was to look after the living so our plan was to rendezvous with a helicopter and get to Standoch as soon as we could.

Once we were at cruising altitude, the steward emerged and cooked us a light meal. As the food smells filled the cabin, Jim stirred and declared himself ravenous. We ate, and with Max and Kelsie listening in over the satellite link, Jim Somersby mesmerized us with an amazing story.

History is full of incredible tales of magical monsters. Of witches, of voodoo priests, of vampires and the like. Nearly all are myths and storytelling, intermingling concepts that are partly real with things we don’t understand; and, there is little so terrifying as our own ignorance.

Vodun, the African root of the variations of Voodoo that sprang from the diaspora – the slaves – and ‘transported’ which spread or were dragged to the Americas over the centuries. Haitian Vodou; Dominican Vudú; Cuban Vodú; Brazilian Vodum; and Louisiana Voodoo. Society, or at least western society, has grown to fear them all. They all have a common theme of worship of the earth, plants, and the sky, and a hierarchy of gods who preside over these spiritual domains. And, they all hold that the dead reside – mostly peacefully

– alongside the living. They are typically community-based religions, completely benign, and all about helping each other. They have little to nothing in common with the cannibalistic priests, curses, and voodoo-doll tortures that the media have planted in our minds, and that many associate with voodooists.

Witches have been both revered as the healers they mostly were, and burned at the stake for being in league with the devil, which they mostly were not. Wicca is a modern religion based on pagan and witchcraft traditions dating back not centuries as many ill-informed would imagine. It evolved in the 1950s and 1960s, led by a British civil servant. Again, it is a benign group whose spiritual views focus on the earth, moon, and nature in general. Yet even this group, with a modern theology of less than seventy years, can strike unease – even fear – into our thoughts.

Vampirism is typically considered more of a myth than a reality, but you would be surprised at the hold on our imagination the idea has of changing ourselves by consuming another. And for a small few, as I will explain, it can be more than pure imagination.

Cannibalism is a fact, with tribes known to practise it even today. Cannibals are typically motivated by consuming people they loved, to keep their spirit within themselves to prolong the relationship, or by consuming the energy of their enemy to gain power over other enemies and their own fears.

All of these religions, practices, groups and myths share themes of using aspects of nature to increase power in a supernatural or magical sense. Many mainstream religions echo it, too: This is my blood you drink; this is my body you eat.

In nearly all examples, these are benign belief systems whose followers' aim is to try to improve their version of society; and yet, they frighten us. Why? There are two reasons: We – people in general – are frightened of the unknown, which is a great survival instinct. Cavemen who wandered up to dinosaurs to find out what they were, quickly died out and shallowed the gene pool to make us descendants fearful of things until we are sure they are safe to play with. And the other reason is that over time, and without any real proof, we know in our hearts that although 99% of these aforementioned groups and religions are benign, well-meaning people, lurking among them, maybe less than 1%, there are real, terrifying, monsters. Of which I am living proof.

The Chord, Guance, your mystery attacker in Durham, and I have undoubtedly descended from men and women who, for thousands of years, have been the basis of the perceived evil in voodoo, vampires, and witch covens. These ancestors, much like us today, walked among the masses, hiding in plain sight. We are powerful in one sense, but could fall prey to a group of villagers with pitchforks, and can be defeated by a few clever people. Most of us are solitary beings and are too ashamed of what we have to do to survive, let alone the thought of using our abilities we have for personal gain. A very few – like the Chord – are sociopaths who relish taking life and abusing their abilities to satisfy their own goals, which typically amount to amassing greater power.

We Adepts, Boku-yōkai, Devil Priests – we have many names, and I will tell you what we call ourselves presently – are a separate species to humans. I don't know if we are the next evolution of man, or a throwback yet to die out. When I found out what I was I seriously contemplated suicide, but I didn't have that courage. Instead, like many of my ilk, I made a very personal decision that I would be the last of my line for I struggle to live with a curse all of my kind bear. As I will expand on in a moment, to survive, I must practise a form of cannibalism.

Modern vampire lore implies there are two types of vampires: The traditional evil vampires who hunt humans and suck their blood, for pleasure but also as a food source required to survive. And the second type is the 'moral' vampire who stay alive by feeding on lesser animals, or raiding blood banks, as killing humans is against their higher values. Like the latter, most of my species abhor violence and for many generations have sought peaceful ways to survive without impacting others. I don't pretend to understand what really makes us tick, but I've established that the ingredient we have required through thousands of generations is what we call human stem cells today. Until recently, they have only been obtainable from the womb.

My father was a moral man and would be a typical example of how most of my breed have survived. His parents were normal humans, but his uncle was one of my kind. This uncle ensured that, like him, my father trained in a profession that brought him into regular contact with a source of stem cells. My father was a doctor, specializing in childbirth. In his time, there were enough natural tragedies such as miscarriages or even abortions, that would supply umbilical cord blood, rich in stem cells for his needs. Those who could not be doctors might be priests, midwives, undertakers and, in earlier years, perhaps healers of a different type, such as witches and shamans. Taking advantage of others' natural misfortunes yes, to survive. A sad living indeed. One that made me decide to end my bloodline, as many have done with their lines over the centuries and so today, our numbers have dwindled to near extinction.

Yet at this eleventh hour for my species, stem cell research and science offers... I don't really know what. Not hope. Not yet. Confusion at least. Too late for me and my line, but perhaps a future for others less dependent on hoping for others to die.

Then there are the others in my species. Those who are predators first and foremost, a fact that would not change if they were human instead of my kind; they have no morals, no qualms. Many Adepts consider themselves superior to humans, as perhaps humans do to animals lower than themselves on the food chain. They don't wait for personal tragedy to strike; they often create the tragedy. Stories of human sacrifice; killing of the unborn. These Adepts actions taint our view of witchcraft, voodoo, and the like. They generate the fear of vampires and bogeymen behind which their ancestors have masked their real intent and painted my otherwise innocent brethren darkly. The Chord is one such group. Even today, when they don't need to kill, they often do. They are serial killers; gangsters; evil beings lurking in the shadows.

How do my powers work? I don't know it all. I've built on some of what my father showed me by studying recent advances in science. I know we, all human-like beings, are all linked together in ways we cannot see. My people can exploit those links overtly and can consciously push emotions through them. Either to help others, or in some cases, we essentially can weaponize our emotions and inflict them on humans.

Humans have a tiny sense of these links and connections and are subject to what comes across them rather than in control of the flow: The sixth sense; extrasensory perception; hunches; hairs on the back of the neck standing up if you are being watched. Fleeting, passive reception of stimuli over these linkages.

In me, these same sensations are a hundred times magnified. They are tangible. I feel them between people, animals, and all living things on the earth. Religions that are based around harnessing or witnessing the power of the earth or drawing on the energy around us are based upon these flows and are my vivid reality. I understand fully why human beliefs are so imbued with these concepts, even if you can only faintly feel them.

Even though my people have a much greater affinity to these pathways, our default physiology allows us to influence others only a little. In fact, the anatomy we are born with has these abilities dormant at birth and they don't manifest at all in our childhood.

During puberty, or sometimes in our 20's, our bodies mature to the point the additional bodily functions activate and if we do nothing, we die. Our bodies simply cannot sustain us past that point unaided. To survive we must supplement our bodies through diet, and as a byproduct these supplements amp up our abilities. We need an ongoing supply of human stem cells, in addition to what our bodies produce naturally. We must obtain the cells and treat them with a cocktail of minerals and herbs before consumption. Different mixtures will influence the strength and type of our extra-human abilities. With the right mix, if I am in close proximity to a human or Adept who is somewhat susceptible, I can broadcast emotions such as fear to them, and essentially hack their brains.

We can also go further and create circumstances where these small connections can be massively amplified thereby increasing our influence in both strength and distance. To do this I need to create a more efficient conduit to another person than typically exists naturally. I believe there are several types of conduit, but one of the most effective and easiest for me to use is to share something with my target that originates from a common source; a specific source with an affinity to optimize connections. Certain types of plants and minerals can be manipulated to create more conductive conduits for my mind-hacks.

I grow many plants in my greenhouses with the required qualities, and I eat what I grow. If I introduce another person to that same plant stock – orally as food, or via absorption through their skin, or as a smell as we did today at the picnic site as an airborne agent – my connection's efficiency multiplies greatly. The fact that we both absorbed the same plant gives me power over them. That is why my power was so much stronger than Guance's at my house. I have been eating and living in that environment for 40 years and am so entwined with the fabric of the place, and am unassailable there. The moment you were touched by the air from the greenhouse, I connected to you.

Once a conduit is formed, I can imagine fear, and you are terrified; I project ambivalence and lethargy, and I can almost put you to sleep. I can make you happy, too; there are quite positive uses for our power, as you saw with João. Most of my kind, if they use their powers at all, use them to help or cure.

With experience we can be subtle by carefully crafting what we project. If I project fear one way, you look for the source of fear. But sometimes people go to great lengths, often subconsciously, to avoid the things we fear. We prefer to ignore a source of anxiety for instance and hope what we fear just goes away. I can project emotions to trigger that feeling and walk through a room, and no one notices I am even there. I'm effectively invisible to anyone I've a strong connection with. I trick their brains into taking a shortcut; they look everywhere else than where I am, because I'm a threat they can't consciously acknowledge exists. To feel confident myself, yet project fear onto you is like rubbing your tummy and patting your head at the same time. It takes training and practise, but then like riding a bike, becomes second nature. My father taught me as I turned; transitioned from a child to an adult with power.

We call my kind the Nimbus, as post transition, when we see each other – and when a few humans with some latent ability observe us – we appear to have a halo, or a glow, like depicted in images of saints and angels. Although few Nimbus would ever claim to be either saints or angels.

In our early years we have no power, no need for supplemental stem cells, nor a nimbus. Other Nimbus see us begin to change and often this glow is the first sign we are not a normal human. Then as my father did with me, we are then advised of our reality. This phase is a time of great emotional risk, and many of us feel suicidal. Knowing you are becoming a monster destined to need to consume dead babies has driven many to end their lives early or to go insane. I was lucky in that my father could provide sustenance without harm to others through his country doctor persona – a job he loved, serving the community with great passion – until he died of old age. In my youth, he enrolled me in medical school, but I wasn't smart enough to become a doctor. I found a position in a laboratory where I could syphon off what I needed; and more recently, I've been able to acquire stem cells over the internet.

Like my father, I have devoted myself to helping the community in any way I can, such as caring for João's condition. I help cure addictions. I help people manage their symptoms of depression so they can tackle the causes of those symptoms. I feel such work is both the right thing in itself, but I know, deep down, it is partly the guilt of a millennia of wrongdoing by some in my species.

His story ended, and we sat in silence for a long while. Max broke the spell; I had forgotten we were on a conference call, being so drawn into the story.

"Our research suggested that entanglement of sub-atomic particles could play a part in what you call the conduit. One of the few commonly observed generators of entangled particles is in plants. Plants use photosynthesis to convert the sun's energy into glucose, consume carbon dioxide, and release oxygen. A bi-product of that is entangled pairs of particles. If you can get such particles to be shared between two people, changing one of the pairs could change the other."

We spent some time explaining the thoughts Naomi had shared with us, and the discovery that so many scientists have been killed in recent years, all who specialized in this field. Jim was visibly upset by the news, to the point that tears welled in his eyes and his nose began to run. We had been very careful not to mention Moy Lei, but then her voice came over the speaker.

"Mr Somersby. Is the transition to Nimbus coincident with significant weight loss?"

"Yes, it is. The body, especially the brain, begins to require energy in larger and larger quantities. Essentially, the brain starves the other systems and if not countered, can eventually kill. The more of us you meet, you will see we are a thin breed. Gaunt and pale. The tales of vampires again: pale, thin, blood sharers who can control those whose blood they have taken. You can't create a Nimbus by blood sharing, but you can take a person's mind that way. How did you know about the weight loss?" There was a long pause.

"I've lost 25 pounds in six months, despite eating everything I see. I have powers I don't understand. I look at my skin and it glows, but others can't see it. I'm terrified, sir, and I desperately need your help."

11: CORRECTING A WRONG

[MARCY] — Whether the helicopter would brave the storm that was brewing over the Scottish coast, threatening our short hop to Standoch, was a touch-and-go decision. Ethan talked personally to the two experienced pilots to ensure they felt no undue pressure to take the risk, yet they knew the urgency of our mission. Had the pilots balked due to the weather, I suspect Ethan would have flown us himself; but he also knew he was probably too tired and less experienced than this selected crew. We felt Guance could be hot on our heels, yet ahead of us was possibly another Boku-yōkai Adept. That said, Jim didn't sense either was actually the case, but at least at Standoch we felt we had a position we could defend and wanted to get there and rest with the gang. The final decision to risk it was made quickly, as conditions were worsening by the minute. The trip was very bouncy but, thankfully, short.

Julie Gonzalez had come through again for us with a new discovery: using footage from our cameras in the Azores, she had started a facial-recognition search across anything we had recorded, as well as any public feed she could tap into. We had video monitoring of all of our operational areas, including the loading bays we used for the logistics' effort to fit out Standoch. Several days earlier, John – Max's assistant who had been overcome by an Adept in the attack on Standoch – had been on the mainland overseeing the loadout of helicopters carrying supplies to the island. The recording of that period revealed Guance in several places, including touching the personal cases of several people, including John's. On closer inspection, we found he had laced their clothing with a fine powder. We didn't know what it was, but it was definitely plant based. Jim had quickly confirmed that with such an advantage, he would have been able to connect to John and convince him of the presence of someone who was not actually there. Just visualizing the imaginary person and projecting it with the right emotions would be enough. We realized that sounded very similar to how Jane Eldridge – Naomi's wife – could have been lured out into the street and to her death; likewise the deaths of many of the other scientists played out similarly. Knowing that after infiltrating our logistics Guance had proceeded south to attack us, coupled with a painstakingly detailed search of the island, we were now fairly convinced that the only Adept now at Standoch was Jim Somersby. That is, discounting Moy Lei, who Jim termed a fledgling Nimbus, not a fully-fledged Adept.

Gwen, Naomi, and Max met us as we touched down. Max was very manly and appropriately tough, but he held on to me in our 'hello' hug a little longer than he meant to, and I could tell he was worried for me. It was decided that we all needed some sleep. We had been travelling almost non-stop since St. Moritz, and Moy Lei and Naomi had been researching all of the possible triggers that activated Moi Lei's special abilities pretty much non-stop, too, with Gwen doing her best to be useful and keep Naomi healthy.

Moy Lei seemed thinner than when we last saw her, and I couldn't decide if that was the stress of the situation in general or related to her transition to becoming a Nimbus. Gwen had brought us all a beer from the stash she had acquired in London and we sat for a while, celebrating our reunion, and mourning our losses. Ethan felt so terribly sad for Ian's family, and took that death the most personally.

Jim inspected Moy Lei – almost giving her a mini-physical exam on the spot as he was so worried — and peppered her with questions about her health. Apparently, for a fledgling Nimbus this was an incredibly risky time – doubly so for Moy Lei, as she had no mentor. Jim shared that in his youth he had had the same struggle with peanuts and nearly died experimenting, as had the few other Nimbus he knew. The additional problem it had caused his uncle – Jim's mentor — was that when Jim experimented with peanuts to boost his powers, the exceptional amount of raw and uncontrolled energy he broadcast carelessly began to over saturate the airwaves (so to speak) for the mature Nimbus, preventing them from using their own powers.

After a few more fascinating revelations, Moy Lei led Jim off to an area to continue the discussion; I doubted they would sleep for a while yet, despite Ethan's insistence. Gwen put her arm around Naomi, who let herself be led off to the cabins to sleep. Ethan and I went with Max and had a quick call with Kelsie before we all stood down for the night, leaving the team to monitor developments and defences.

Six hours later, after some sleep, Ethan and I were about to set out for breakfast when he shared with me his thoughts on what we should propose to the group. He had been broody ever since Jim's astonishing revelation on the plane, and I know him well enough to let him think things through until he emerged from the process, rather than try to pry half-formed thoughts from him too early. But now, as he told me what he wanted to do, I agreed wholeheartedly with his idea and we set off for breakfast. Ethan diverted to talk to Moy Lei, as her consent to revealing at least part of her family background was necessary to his proposal.

Since we discovered Guance had tampered with John's luggage, Max had ordered in fresh clothing and food in sealed packages for everyone. We were all now dressed in unflattering green athletic wear and matching, warm-weather waterproofs. Moy Lei surprised us all by arriving with five bananas, having been informed by Jim that her body needed to increase its potassium intake dramatically. There were several other dietary adjustments required, which would have to wait for a future shipment from the mainland. Ethan asked for quiet and I settled back to see how the others would react to his suggestion. I love Ethan and am so proud of how he can always get to the truth of the big picture so clearly, despite complex emotions surrounding a subject. However, there was no guarantee his truth – no, I should say *our* truth – would be acceptable to the others.

"Jim, with respect, I want to start out by challenging you on your philosophy around letting your family line fizzle out. I know you are questioning it now because of the potential of a less controversial source of stem cells, but it feels like your base belief is that your people – your species, as you call them – are an inherent problem in themselves. Your position is that people with special powers are a danger to humanity because a few will misuse that power and others will suffer."

"I do feel like that, Ethan. It's a fact."

"Is it? If it is, it doesn't have to be. Here is what I think: In the past, ignorance and survival put Nimbus on a difficult path. Some took their own lives to avoid that hard path; others found ways to help society and minimize any burden; and a few took advantage of their circumstance. Some regular humans take advantage of their strength, or their ruthlessness, or their intellect, or race – or a hundred other things – and commit horrible acts. Unless you tell me otherwise, Hitler, Ted Bundy, and Charles Ponzi were not Nimbus — and look at the harm they caused. We don't condemn all smart, strong, or charming people because of the acts of a few. We look back in history with utter horror, as we know that witches were burned at the stake, drowned – whatever heinous method was applied – just because of who they were. People – humans and Nimbus – should be judged as individuals based on their actions, not their genetics. I accept that some of the Nimbuses acts to survive range from controversial to monstrous. Even stem cells from IVF procedures are controversial. But I refuse to condemn a species for attempting to survive. We don't kill all species of animals that could eat us. We've developed ways to coexist, and even protect those species from that ignorant layer of humans who want to kill just for sport, and those who would deplete a species even if hunting from necessity."

"I must say, Ethan, I'd never expect to hear that from a human" replied Jim. "especially one who my species has tried to kill and whose friend has been killed by one of my kind. Of course, I'm not opposed to the concept, but where are you going with this?"

"I see three problems: Number one, you need a less controversial way to survive; number two, if your abilities were more widely known then governments and other entities would attempt to weaponize them in some way; and three, one particular group of Nimbus, The Chord, want us humans all dead. I have a proposal to resolve the first two, but first we need to deal with the third; the more pressing issue of The Chord. I don't know how to tackle that third problem. But let's assume, for the sake of argument, we resolve that threat somehow.

"Earlier this year, we were threatened by a gang of human traffickers, and when we took them down and *we* were safe, the underlying issue remained: Humans were still in peril and needed help, which the authorities are not really set up to provide. Our answer was to set up a support group, led by Max's partner Gia, who are reaching out and helping people where others can't – or won't. I think we could do something similar for Nimbus.

"I can provide the resources to create a small private laboratory, which would study you and Moy Lei and any other willing participants we could locate. The objective would be solely to come up with a less controversial survival method. Something like an abundant, synthetic replacement for human stem cells. Science seems to be on a path to a breakthrough; in fact, it is so close that The Chord has been systematically killing researchers in this area for years to prevent that knowledge from being developed. I can provide the money for the research and for protection. The fact we will do this in private, and not share this information with governments or people who might want to capitalize on your talents, should reduce the risk of weaponizing your species."

"That would cost hundreds of millions, Ethan. Why would you offer that?"

"Because I can, for God's sake. I have the money, but not much of a personal stake. I – or should I say, Marcy and I – were planning to be the silent partners; we were hoping that you, Moy Lei, and Naomi would be the leaders of the research group and take on the challenge of solving the problems, while we fund it. What would you all say?" There was silence for a short while, which Jim broke with a laugh.

"Holy shit, Ethan. I would love to." The others nodded with growing enthusiasm. The only person who didn't seem as enthusiastic was Gwen. I thought I knew why and spoke up.

"In our building in Vancouver, we could set up what you need in no time. Vancouver has a great medical research industry and has companies in the stem- cell field already. How would that suit, at least to begin with?"

Everyone agreed. Gwen subtly patted my hand and smiled. Our secret! Cocky lesbian Yoda has a soft spot for Naomi, I'd correctly deduced. I'm getting the hang of this detective stuff.

"You know," began Jim, thoughtfully and suddenly serious, "there is a story among the Nimbus that resonates with your kind offer. It's a legend of hope for my kind. More a moral lesson than reality, if I'm honest. But what you are offering would rival its impact on both our peoples. It concerns the Sheriff of York, back in the sixteenth century, about halfway through the reign of Queen Elizabeth I. What today we would call a serial killer had been preying on pregnant women in the middle of England. Mostly in the Doncaster area. There was a small village called Brownwick, and the name The Brownwick Devil haunted the area for decades.

"Nathen Braithwell was the Sherriff of York, and he was also a Nimbus. The Brownwick Devil had struck in York one night, and a fellow who was the uncle of one of the victims had survived the slaughter as he had hidden in an old priest's hole when the killer struck. He told his story to a guard, and of course everyone thought he was crazy. Except Braithwell, who knew better; he recognized the modus operandi of an evil Nimbus sating his needs. He listened to all of the stories from the night and inspected the scene of the crime. It struck him that the coach driver who had ferried the victims down from Doncaster might have additional information. Soon after dawn, he took the guard down to an inn called The Barley Boy to interview the man. As they entered the premises, they found the coach driver was in fact the Nimbus, and was about to kill the barkeep. It was only that Braithwell was a Nimbus himself that saved the humans that morning.

"Braithwell realized that it was probably common for Nimbus to prey on humans, and he created a fellowship known as the Knights of Nimbus. Their mission was to investigate bloody events which had a supernatural fingerprint wherever they occur and, if Nimbus were behind them, act to correct their wrongs. Braithwell's actions attracted three other Nimbus, and together with the help of a dozen mercenaries, they dealt with many serial killers over their 20 years of service to humanity. Their actions have taken on a symbolism not unlike some of the Christian faith's parables such as The Good Samaritan.

"It ended when they confronted a killer in Bath, near Bristol in England. If it were just the killer – human or Nimbus — they would have been successful; but the sociopath wasn't alone. Four other Nimbus were with him as part of a group. This group slaughtered Braithwell and all of his knights in a single evening. This group named themselves The Chord. And we still fight them today."

"So, now all we need to do is kill a handful of superhuman Adepts who have preyed on humans for nearly 400 years, and want to kill us," said Max, bringing us all back to our more immediate reality with a thud.

"Actually, I've had a bit of a thought about that," said Moy Lei. As she and Ethan had discussed, she painfully revealed to Jim and the others the details she knew about her mother's profession, and how we had been caught in the web and forced into finding Moy Lei. We expected Jim to be upset, but I guess he had seen so much life and death from angles we couldn't imagine that he just sympathized with Moy Lei.

We kicked around Moy Lei and Ethan's various thoughts and slowly a plan emerged. The plan was initially centred around Ethan taking another huge risk, throwing himself into the lion's den. But as I pointed out, it was really more of a den of lionesses, and he would have to let me take his place if we were going to be successful. It was high risk, and I watched him struggle. Max didn't help by vehemently voicing his objections to me putting myself into harm's way. On the one hand, Ethan had an overriding need to protect me; on the other, he had to respect me, and not treat me as his inferior. He knew that in all ways I was better trained and he needed to let me go. I could see it eating him up, but my man did the right thing, as I hope I could do if our situation had been reversed. We decided we would launch the mission. Yes, it was high risk, but so was sitting here on a rock in the ocean.

12: BLUE TO THE SKY

[CHIYOME] — For the past two weeks, I have been losing my mind, with irrational fears, jumping at shadows, and an uncharacteristic inability to act. I've become an emotional wreck overnight. My personal physician — a man I have known since childhood — has visited me twice but has been unable to divine the cause. I can barely function, let alone leave the estate or run the Kanbo. It is inexcusable behaviour on my part, and unforgivable that I cannot help to protect Moy Lei due to these sudden personal weaknesses; but here I am. My undertaking to Moy Lei and Ethan to investigate our archives remained unfulfilled, as that had required me to travel and I just dared not leave the estate. I should have contacted them and explained, but even that seems too much to achieve.

I have cut my interaction with the Jonin down to the minimum of once weekly and have bluffed my way through the last two short meetings, quickly passing routine business. However, tomorrow is full moon and the Jonin will meet in person for a whole day, which is much more intense than our weekly encrypted-skype connections. I fear my condition will be discovered, and I will be exposed as the weakling I have somehow become.

I sit meditating – seeking comfort – perched on a small bridge spanning the corner of our koi pond at my estate in California, high on a hill, just to the south of Saratoga. We are not overlooked by a higher point, and an 18-foot wall encircles the property, which has stood for nearly 70 years as a replica of a Japanese garden favoured by Tokugawa Yoshimune. He was the eighth shōgun of the Tokugawa shōgunate of Japan, ruling from 1716 until his abdication in 1745. It is said Yoshimune spent time meditating in his garden during his most troubling times, and my estate normally provides me with such peace. But lately, it feels hostile and unsettled.

Protected by Kame's staff the estate is physically secure, from all but a large government force. If such a force descended, there is nothing here but people and computer terminals; our data could incriminate us, but that is hidden in the dark web. There is nothing here to find that would tie us to a crime. But we are rarely, if ever, on a government radar. A physical threat could be from a disgruntled client, or someone related to a target, attempting to retaliate. Kame's precautions are more than adequate to defeat such a threat as no one like that would ever get close, and there is nowhere higher within rifle range that a sniper might set up. Today, I know that the imminent threat to my wellbeing comes from Tanuki, Kame, Tatsu, Choho and Kitsune – who are arriving tomorrow. We will start our day with a pleasant breakfast before things unravel. Probably fatally.

My pathetic self-reflection and pity are interrupted by a soft whining, and I turn my head sharply to snap at the offender, annoyed at the interruption and fearful again that my apparent breakdown might be discovered. What I at first thought was a hummingbird turns out to be a tiny helicopter – which I deduce is a drone – that settles four feet from me on the bridge. Its rotors stop and abruptly there is silence. A piece of paper is tied to the side of the drone by a red ribbon, and I can read one word on the side: Bearpaw – Moy Lei's secret code. I picked up the drone, pulled off the ribbon and note, and set the drone back onto the bridge. It immediately starts up and shoots high onto the air, gone in a breath. Silence returned. I unwrap the note, eager to hear of my daughter.

Dear Haha;

I have proof that a Boku-yōkai Adept has infiltrated the Kanbo. Your uncharacteristic lack of contact suggests they are aware of my discovery and are influencing your mind. As far-fetched as that may sound, I have personal experience that Adepts can do such things, and any unusual emotions you are experiencing should be taken as proof. You should assume they can observe you without your knowledge, even if you have had your location swept for surveillance devices. I have been surveilling the estate from a high altitude, which is why I picked this moment to deliver this note. From here, I can see two people in your compound, which it appears no one else can see. They are invisible, thanks to their great power. I am familiar with one of them, as he recently killed one of Ethan's men. They are both Boku-yōkai Adepts, and I believe they work for another; I suspect that third person, who runs their coven, is Jonin.

Tomorrow is full moon, and I will arrive to take my place in the Kanbo. I will renounce Setsudan sa reta shimai, disconnected sister, and take the Ceremony of Allegiance. Tradition dictates this renunciation must be made before, and accepted by, the full council of Jonin on the day of the full moon, hence tomorrow. I will arrive by helicopter tomorrow at 10 am, from the north. Per tradition, I will arrive with a 'second,' and that person will be Marcy. She does not know that our tradition holds that once I take my pledge, I must take a life to prove my commitment, and that 'the second' is traditionally sacrificed. She believes she is coming for moral support. It is a shame that I must sacrifice such a strong woman, but needs must prevail; and, after all, she is an outsider.

Ethan will pilot the helicopter. He will drop us both then depart. I will come and take my place in our family business. Then, from within – together – you and I will rid the Kanbo of this Boku-yōkai cancer that has penetrated our ranks. Frankly, it is not the life either of us wanted for me, but having barely survived two attempts on my life in the past two weeks, it is the only course I see that offers any hope.

And, of course, I must save you, as you are in the gravest danger.

Delay the announcement of my arrival until 9:55 am.

Love Moy Lei

I read the note several times over, the news of our infiltration shocking, and the news of Moy Lei's course of action, terrifying. The note was made of rice paper, and therefore edible. It took me several minutes, but I disposed of her note while I sat and contemplated the next 24 hours with renewed dread.

*

At 8 am, the Jonin began to arrive by helicopter and by road. By 8:30, our greetings were complete, we selected what breakfast we desired from a small buffet in the summer room, and then took our places on the main patio. The patio was set in the centre of a large, square garden and was laid out with six floor-cushions arranged in a circle around a low maple table. I took my place on the single slightly raised cushion — as was appropriate to my rank as sensei — and picked a piece of banana off my plate. No one would eat until I started, and so this was the signal to begin.

I covertly scanned the council of Jonin, using everything I had learned over my five decades of concealing my feelings. Of the two supposed intruders, I saw no trace, and no sign that any of the five in front of me were anything other than they seemed. We have men in our organization, but most of our key roles are occupied by females; all five women here looked relaxed and at ease, dressed in traditional Japanese robes, makeup, and hairstyles. In the pleasant morning sun, in this carefully-crafted garden, it looked like time had stopped 300 years ago. The food was served on traditional wooden plates, and we ate with our fingers or chopsticks.

Tanuki, 'the raccoon dog,' was to my immediate left. In her lime kimono with her hair pulled back, it was difficult to see she was nearly 60 years of age.

She looked more like a 50-year-old yoga teacher, jovial and laughing lightly, her eyes happy rather than the stone killer eyes one would expect of someone who leads the two hundred trained assassins she kept busy across the Americas.

Kitsune sat next to her. She is our youngest, partly as we are now so reliant on technology. Her communications organization is a state-of-the-art marvel which I doubt many people over forty truly understand. Her skin is marble white, eyes painted larger than life like an Anime characters, but that is just today. In her role as head of a technology giant just down the road in Silicon Valley she would normally wear t-shirt, jeans and a hoodie, possibly costing two thousand dollars for the outfit. Her hair long and swept forward today and jet black to set off the yellow robes she wore, but by tonight, it would be back to a ponytail and a lighter shade.

Kame is our oldest council member at 62. She wore a spectacular silk kimono, depicting a blossoming maple tree winding its way around her body. The base colour of the robe blue, resembling the sky on a sunny day. She is also the spryest of us, as delicate as a dragonfly. If she resembles me, it is because we are in fact related; she is my cousin. Kame sits on the board of several companies, which like the one she owns and is their President and CEO, are mostly in the security and protection sector. She is quiet today; focused on her breakfast and the meeting agenda. There were many moments during the night when I considered contacting her as she is trusted family as well as head of Kanbo security. Preparing her for Moy Lei's sudden reappearance by helicopter — which would get the guards overly excited — would be smart and avoid any accidents. Only Moy's warning about being observed stopped me. I would not put Kame at risk. I must trust her guards are professional and would hold fire until I gave a command.

Choho is especially animated, always the centre of conversation. She laughed now, throwing her head back as she did so, and as she did, I noticed her eyes skip around the perimeter of the garden. My senses told me she was hiding how alert she really was. She was nervous about something. Unusually unsettled. She wasn't overweight, but she was the heaviest at the table and had a sheen on her forehead, feeling the California sun's power as it got a grip on the day and sank through her lilac kimono.

Tatsu the dragon sat on my right. Serious looking and quiet as usual; always sitting back observing, but when she spoke, we listened. Although the tallest of us, she somehow managed to be overlooked and slip into the background. But she missed nothing. We relied on her ability to think long term and strategically. Her quiet and thoughtful contributions elevated our venture to the level of an international business, as opposed to it being a secret society. Without her skill, we would not continue to outgrow the contenders from cartels and mafia. We might be swallowed up by one of them, rather than remain aloof, and an organization to be outsourced to and feared, not seen as an acquisition to run or to asset-strip.

The terrors that had plagued me recently had eased, and I felt a little more in control of myself. I joined the conversation for the next hour. It is important to renew our bond before venturing into the day's business, and so this hour of reunion is a standing agenda item. At 9.25, the staff politely removed our breakfast, topped up coffee and other drinks for the table, then quietly withdrew, leaving the garden empty except for the council and four guards. The guards were dressed traditionally, complete with a katana – a long sword – and a tanto – a dagger – which were sheathed and secured in the cloth bands at their waists. This being 2018, they each also carried a CZ 805 assault rifle over a shoulder.

Over the next 15 minutes, the four guards went through the familiar process of scanning the garden, our meeting area, and anywhere we could be surveilled from, using state-of-the-art detection equipment. Our conversation slowly diminished, and we gradually became more formal as we readied ourselves emotionally and mentally for the meeting. We had a packed agenda with some hard decisions to negotiate.

I watched the group. Only Kame seemed distracted as she fussed over her guards like a mother, proud but closely checking they were perfect. At the same time, she scanned the perimeter, and I hoped she would not see signs of Moy Lei's surveillance high above us or hear the approaching helicopter, which must be inbound by now. Her attention was biased to the north, but I could see nothing.

At 9:55 am, the guards had finished, and each moved to a wall — north, south, east and west of us — where they took up a position facing outwards, away from our meeting.

I brought the meeting to order. I ran through the tabled agenda, and asked everyone individually if they proposed any changes or wanted to add other business. Once all had their say, with my heart in my mouth I added an item of other business of my own.

"As you all know, Moy Lei — Setsudan sa reta shimai — has been missing for many weeks. I have news of her. She has been in retreat, considering her future, and has reached a decision. In a few minutes she will join us, arriving by helicopter. Our first order of business will be to preside over her Ceremony of Allegiance. She is bringing a second – an outsider – but that status will not be an issue for long, for obvious reasons. I am proud to have my daughter join us, at last, and ask that one of you will find her a role among the Chunin where she can learn our profession." As I spoke, the noise of a helicopter grew louder in the distance, and the guards began to fidget, heads turning. I clapped my hands twice to get their attention.

"We are expecting two guests. Have them brought here immediately!"

The Jonin all looked at each other. Surprised and excited.

"You have been patient Chiyome-san. We are so happy for you. It will be an honour for us all to welcome Moy Lei sama to the fold," applauded Kame. The others nodded.

A helicopter appeared in the north; it lifted its nose and dropped its tail as it slowed and lowered out of sight where our helipad was placed, but then reappeared quickly and banked off to return the way it had come. In a few moments, two figures entered the garden through the north gate, accompanied by four guards, one of who was carrying a small bag, which she handed over to one of the four inner guards. My breath caught as I saw her: Moy Lei was dressed in a simple white kimono with a blue sash at the waist, and she kept a formal stance, eyes on the floor. She had lost so much weight since we had last seen each other but looked healthy otherwise. Marcy wore a respectful, formal, grey business suit and modest flat boots; her hair was slicked back with product into a tight ponytail. Both were searched for what would be the second and possibly the third time since landing, before being escorted towards the table.

I longed to break tradition by running over and pulling my daughter close to me. Both motherly and protective instincts were vigorous within me. I felt such pride as she marched into danger with no sign of fear that I could detect. Marcy, too, showed great courage and composure, and it crossed my mind if she should be saved – perhaps converted to work for us. But no; she dedicated her life to convict the likes of us and there would be no corrupting her so, sadly, she would meet the fate my daughter had laid out. A waste, but inevitable now.

We all rose into a formal line of welcome as they approached. Marcy stood back while Moy Lei made her way along the line, starting with Choho, exchanging ceremonial bows and a word of two of greeting. She gave Kame an extra deep bow of respect, which I attributed to her being a family member. As she reached me, we bowed and I stepped forward, put my hands on her shoulders, and kissed her cheek.

"Are you sure, my brave one?" I whispered.

"I am, Haha-sama. Let it begin."

I sent the nearest guard to fetch Yasside, a ceremonial katana made by Gorō Nyūdō Masamune, Japan's most prominent maker of samurai swords from the Edo period. While that happened, another guard emptied the bag Moy Lei had brought with her onto the table – normal protocol – so we could ensure that unexpected visitors didn't bring weapons or anything inappropriate to the meeting. There was a bottle of an energy drink and a few personal items, including two of Moy Lei's EpiPen's, which she carried because of her peanut allergy. The guards inspected everything and ran each item through their anti-surveillance protocol. I noticed that despite what should be a happy – if formal – occasion, tension had grown in the air and everyone was fidgety and showing signs of stress and unease. My own terrors had resurfaced and grown steadily since the sound of the helicopter had penetrated into the garden. I wasn't sure if this unease was caused by the unusual situation of our agenda being disrupted in this way, or if the Boku-yōkai Adepts were behind it, perhaps realizing Moy Lei was joining us. It was becoming stifling and hard to maintain a normal outward face. I could see others in the group also looked anxious and on edge.

The sword arrived and a small table with a mustard-yellow, felt, cushion-topper was placed in front of Moy Lei. Yasside was settled reverentially on top, handle towards the initiate. Marcy stepped forward, standing a yard to the left and behind Moy Lei, in the appointed place, to witness the ceremony. The Jonin and I gathered on the opposite side of the sword in a semi-circle. All that was left was for Moy Lei to say the words, and each Jonin to utter the word of acceptance, and then I would say the words of confirmation. Then the ceremony would conclude with Moy Lei taking the sword and slaying her second. A second who follows our ways would usually volunteer to be slain, as they would see this as an honour and perhaps gain a boon for their family. They would kneel and bow their head, and the end would be swift. Marcy would put up a fight, of course, but it would be an unarmed woman against a woman with a long sword. Where Moy Lei had not had much experience, the length of the weapon and the lack of places Marcy could run would ensure Moy Lei's advantage. Again, I felt resentment that she would be sacrificed after she and Ethan had help me with much honour.

"I guess we are ready?" questioned Moy Lei, her voice tight and pinched with anxiety. She pulled herself to her full height and prepared herself. She started to speak, but gave a little cough, her throat dry. She stopped, turned, and picked up her energy drink to quench her thirst and loosen her vocal cords for the important words she was about to say – and possibly to hydrate fully, ahead of the battle she would soon make with her second. She took several large gulps, glancing at Marcy as she did so, presumably battling the guilt she must be feeling; worrying, or perhaps probing her psyche to determine if she has it in her to take this step into her new, dark world. Taking a life. Accepting the forbidden sin into your soul.

As she returned the bottle to the table, she abruptly began to breathe quickly and paled, except around her eyes and nostrils, which had turned an angry red. She hunched over and fell to one knee, her skin now turning pink and water running from her eyes, nose, and mouth. I recognized the symptoms: she was having an anaphylactic event. Had someone poisoned her with peanuts?

Then all hell broke loose.

I was hit with a wave of terror, as if the devil were visiting us. Kame fell forward, her hands on her temples, her eyes wide. Then as suddenly as it had come on, the wave of pressure lifted, and it felt like a swift summer storm had blown through and cleared the air. Then two men abruptly materialized out of thin air.

[ETHAN] – At 9:55 am, we activated the tiny communication packs on our belts and our wireless earpieces sprang to life. We had been listening to the commentary from Kelsie ever since. From the vantage point of her drone, which circled overhead at 4000 feet, she relayed the drama unfolding just yards away in a tense, real time, play-by-play account. We had deliberately kept any electronic device, which might give us away in an anti-surveillance sweep, turned off until five minutes ahead of Moy Lei and Marcy's arrival time as a precaution to avoid discovery. At 4 am this morning, Gia, Jim, and I had parachuted into the compound. Jim had used his powers to keep us invisible to human observers, both during our descent and the short, tense walk from our landing point to the maintenance shed, in which we now crouched, adjacent to the assumed meeting spot. Various Darcy-borne, electronic countermeasures coupled with a night-black, tactical, armored outfit helped hide us from electronic surveillance. We had not looked outside since our arrival as we didn't want to lay eyes on an Adept, and thereby make them aware of our presence.

Over the past three days, we had seeded the area around the estate with pods that took turns, depending on wind direction, at spraying a mist containing extracts from Jim's greenhouse plants in São Miguel. This had given Jim some ability to strengthen his connection to the residents of the estate. We would need any and every advantage possible for what we were about to attempt. We were sure the Boku-yōkai Adepts here would already have seeded the grounds strongly in their own fashion.

Both Gia and I had some parachuting experience, which we had supplemented with four sets of practice night-jumps, in similar terrain, two nights ago. Jim had no experience and no time to learn, so Darcy and Max had rigged a remote-controlled jumpsuit and Max had piloted him in, at which point disaster nearly struck. Just 20 feet from the ground after an uneventful descent and approach, the signal to Jim's suit was momentarily lost. We had planned for this, and the suit was rigged to auto-flare at 12 feet from the ground, but the rough landing damaged Jim's right knee. He was in immense pain, but he refused drugs as we needed his mind at full strength to shield us from detection. The last six hours had been very hard for him and he was nearing the end of his strength. Max had more combat experience than everyone in our team combined and had argued hard for a place in the infiltration team. I wanted him to provide overhead cover for the team with his sniper skills. After piloting Jim in by remote control, Max had jumped into the back of a specially modified helicopter that would move in and hover roughly 1200 yards from the meeting spot at the last minute. Lying prone in the rear, with the door open, he had a passible shooting platform to snipe from when the time came.

All three of us were familiar with the area outside of our hiding spot since we had studied aerial photographs, which we had also brought with us in paper form as a reference map. Kelsie had rapidly explained how that area was now set up and being used when we had first tuned in, just before 10 am. Chiyome and her team were on a raised patio roughly 40 feet to the south, and between them and us stood two other Adepts — one of who was Guance — who appeared to be invisible to people in the garden. Kelsie relayed that Moy Lei had signaled to us by making a larger-than-usual bow of formal greeting, that the devil-priest in Chiyome's inner circle was a thin, Asian woman in a sky-blue kimono and present in the main group of women.

Kelsie advised that Moy Lei had just drunk from her energy bottle, which was the signal for Max to move into position and for us to emerge and attack. However, a very frustrated Max countered on the radio that turbulent, high winds had sprung up, and that there was no way to accurately aim and shoot safely into the compound from that range. We were on our own, and his voice was torn with concern for us, especially for Gia.

Moy Lei's energy drink was laced with a dose of peanut oil designed to trigger an anaphylactic shock and, in doing so, cause her to radiate her mind-blocking force that would hopefully interfere with the Boku-yōkai's ability to be invisible and control those around them. Unfortunately, it would impact Jim, too. But the time for stealth was now over, and we had a very short window to capitalize on the situation and our element of surprise before Moy Lei passed out from her symptoms. We had to move quickly if we were to save her, as she could die from such a high dose. I led Gia to the shed door, cracked it open, and we spotted the two Adepts just ahead of us, just as Jim halted his efforts to mask our presence and collapsed in an exhausted heap.

In whispers, I instructed Gia to go for the Adept who was not Guance at the south side. Guance and I had a reckoning over Ian Po's murder; he was mine and I wished he could have known how very, very short his time was now. Part of me wished he would suffer more. I took three steps out of the shed, dropped to one knee, levelled my silenced Ultimate Ruger rifle, set the sight on the back of his head, and squeezed the trigger. I was unashamedly pleased with the result.

The guard nearest the two Adepts had reacted very well; he closed the gap on the intruders and drew his long sword. He didn't flinch as my bullet exploded the head of one of the Adepts. As he approached the remaining target, however, I felt a wave of terror begin to rise within me and knew instinctively that the short window provided by Moy Lei's 'peanut bomb' – as we had come to call it – was ending. She was passing out and her blocking energy was fading. The guard hesitated and lowered his sword just as Gia, running flat out, reached the pair. Her first strike was a straight-finger jab to the Adept's throat, crushing his windpipe. Whatever happened next, he would live only as long as he could hold that last breath. But he didn't have even that long. Gia pivoted behind him, dropped him to his knees with a kick to the back of his legs, embraced his head, and with a jerk and a loud crack, snapped his neck cleanly. To avoid any misunderstanding with the guard, she continued in a fluid motion with a roundhouse kick to the side of the guard's head, and he dropped unconscious at her feet.

[CHIYOME] – The two intruders appeared near the guard by the east wall, standing dumbly and looking shocked at their sudden exposure, and they seemed very distressed by some unseen force. The nearest guard reacted instantly and professionally, unsheathing his sword and advancing quickly. But he hesitated as he neared. As I watched the guard struggle against whatever distracted him, one of the intruder's heads exploded. As the intruder fell, I saw Ethan Booker in a shooter's crouch behind him, intent over his gunsights with an expression of unrestrained anger on his face. A second later, the other intruder — and my guard — was taken down 'martial arts' style by a lean woman dressed in loose-fitting, black, tactical, paramilitary clothing.

As we watched that drama unfold, the feeling of terror returned and overwhelmed us. All except for Marcy who, although also appearing to be on the verge of a panic attack, stepped forward, reached down, took the EpiPen, checked she had the blue end to the sky, and drove the other end into Moy Lei's thigh. She took the other EpiPen and tried to stab it into Kame's buttock but was only partially successful as Kame struck at her with her elbow. Marcy went to her knees and spewed a strange, green, thick paste out of her mouth. As she did so she pointed directly at Kame, looked directly at me, and spoke urgently, yet respectfully.

"Chiyome! That woman is the Boku-Yōkai Adept. Those two men are also Adepts, and Moy Lei's temporary interference with their powers is already waning. If Kame recovers, we are all dead."

I had no real understanding of what was occurring, but I knew one thing: my daughter had marched into this lioness's den and risked all to save us.

I held one hand up to still the guards who were bearing down to kill Marcy, Ethan, and the mystery martial artist. But even without my signal, the three remaining guards and the other members of the Jonin had stopped their motion and were either entering a trance-like state or, in some cases, quivering on the ground in fear of some unseen monster. Kame stood animated, and with everyone else down and somehow in her thrall, I saw her raise her head confidently and begin to laugh. I looked to Ethan for help, but he too had dropped his gun and his expression was vacant.

Kame took her time walking over to the nearest guard, relieved him of his gun, and used it to shoot him through his heart. She then sauntered over and stood in front of me, speaking casually as she walked.

"Well, cousin. This is truly a shame. What a waste. It took me years to build this perfect façade for my true power-base and, believe it or not, I am fond of both you and Moy Lei sama. For base humans, you were lovely, and I will miss you both so much. In fact, I will honour you by killing you first, so you do not have to watch the death of your young daughter."

She slowly raised the gun and took aim, but then hesitated as if fighting off a bad dream or memory.

"You...will...not...," gasped Moy Lei from the spot where she lay. She was glaring intently at Kame, her eyes ablaze, locked in some fierce battle of wills with my cousin, which I was unable to see or interfere with. Moy Lei's left hand had grasped the energy drink and, with great effort, she inched it towards her lips. I intuited it must be the source of the peanuts and feared another sip would kill her. I looked at Kame, who seemed to be mentally trying to stop Moy Lei and, at the same time, shift her gun to aim towards my daughter. I fought whatever had me in its grip with renewed vigour, but to no effect. I was helpless and watched on in horror. Kame seemed to double down on her efforts and, although Moy Lei maintained her stare, the bottle slipped from her grasp as Kame seemed to once again take the upper hand in this back-and-forth battle of minds.

Kame almost had the gun aligned with Moy Lei's chest when she froze and gasped "NO!" Her head snapped to her left at some new threat and I followed her gaze. An elderly black man stood next to Ethan, with his arms raised and an equally intense stare levelled at Kame. The new intruder, Kame, and Moy Lei stood locked in this invisible battle for I don't know how long. It could only have been seconds, but it seemed longer. My head pulsed, and I was on the verge of passing out. Slowly, very slowly, Kame seemed to get an edge over the other two. The old man was sweating and had dropped one hand to his chest; he breathed heavily, straining at the effort. Moy Lei's eyes were beginning to droop, and she looked as if she might pass out at any second. An unnatural, golem-like grin began to form on Kame's face as she forced her hands to once more point the gun in Moy Lei's direction. She only needed to pull the trigger and it would all be over.

Facing me, Kame jerked suddenly, looked me in the eye, and then stared down at her own chest. I could see at first a trickle and then a river of blood spurt from just beneath her sternum, rapidly spreading its stain down her kimono. Yasside, the samurai ceremonial sword, emerged from her chest, razor point gliding out through the bloody fabric, forced through her from back through to front. I looked past Kame to where Marcy had risen to her knees, her lips clamped hard together in a ferocious effort, a raging growl ripping from her throat as she ran Kame through with the ancient katana. All of the mental pressure, terror, and stress evaporated in a heartbeat.

There was a long moment of silence before the gates to the garden were flung open and guards flooded the yard. They grabbed Marcy, Ethan, and the two strangers and whisked Moy Lei quickly away for medical help.

EPILOGUE

[ETHAN] — The guards held us for 20 minutes; then, without any explanation, marched us to the helipad. There was no sign of Chiyome and Moy Lei. Ten minutes later, our helicopter approached, touched down only as long as it took for us to board, then lifted off and spirited us away.

As soon as we were clear of the area, we turned south and put 100 miles between us and the estate, flying at low level and full speed. We debriefed on events, but mostly Marcy and I leaned together and held each other. Shooting someone as despicable as Guance is one thing; running another person through with a sword is quite another and would haunt Marcy forever. She shook as the adrenaline receded and shock crept in, and I provided strength and a safe place while she dealt with it, at least for today.

It was Moy Lei who had provided the key to our plan — the peanut bomb — when talking to Jim at Standoch. We had experimented and essentially created the biological equivalent of an EMP — an electro-magnetic pulse. An EMP occurs when a nuclear weapon is set off, and the electro-magnetic wave kills all electronics within a wide radius. Moy Lei's reaction to the overdose of the peanut oil mixed in with her energy drink had temporarily disrupted the Chord's Adepts from using their powers. We had struck during that brief window of time.

Our other secret weapon had ensured Marcy had been relatively unaffected by the mental attack from the three Adepts; we inhibited their connection to her. We assumed there would be some airborne substance at work at the site to amplify the powers of the Adepts. We later divined that the peaches and apples from the trees within the estate were the catalyst. Kame was in fact famous for her quaint hobby of making soap, perfumes, scents, jams, and anything else she could come up with to spread the entangled particles far and wide. All three Nimbus had consumed their fill to ensure the connections to anyone in the vicinity. Their hold was so complete that Guance and his companion — the last remaining members of The Chord led by Kame — were practically invisible. Assuming that such a tactic would be in play, we had at last come up with a potential defence and with limited testing, we took the chance. Someone had to stay close enough to Moy Lei to administer the EpiPen and save her life. Marcy's body was painted entirely in a transparent chemical preventing air contact. She wore non-prescription contact lens, had gel made of the same coating covering her hair, and for that short time, only her airways were a concern. Marcy had her mouth stuffed with a green, bread paste to prevent oral ingestion and was therefore forced to breathe through her nose. Her nostrils were plugged with microfilters that removed most particles from the air. She was grossly uncomfortable, could not speak until she spat out the paste, and had struggled all the way through the short encounter. But to anyone looking at her, it appeared that she was just totally stressed out. Which of course she was. This elaborate countermeasure had saved us all in the end.

For the following week, we hid out in a cabin near Paso Robles – a wine region North of Los Angeles – until we heard from Moy Lei by email. She relayed her mother's commitment that there would be no repercussions, and that she was still keen to start working with Jim and Naomi on a management strategy for the Nimbus' physiology. Much relieved, we arranged see her in Vancouver in a few weeks.

That night, we returned to Vancouver and found that Gwen had disappeared into her suite with Naomi as her 'guest,' and they had yet to emerge, except to walk Elvis. We took over the latter duty on arrival and were soon face-slathered by an enthusiastic hound.

Jim returned to the Azores to arrange for an extended absence and to check on his flock. He planned to return at the same time as Moy Lei. Max and Gia had already resumed their work tracing and helping the victims of human trafficking and the sex trade. Every day they delayed meant another lost soul might elude their rescue efforts, so they worked tirelessly.

Marcy and I have been to a lot of funerals this week, the hardest of all being Ian's. His family was distraught, and it was, of course, so unfair. If your partner is in the Forces, perhaps you are partly prepared, but Ian's wife and kids had no such opportunity. It was little comfort, but Marcy and I named the new company we formed to research Nimbus physiology, "The Po Institute," in his honour. Many people made a sacrifice, but we personally felt his to have been the biggest. Our feeling paled compared to the loss his family suffered.

*

We spent a week recovering and getting back into shape. It had been a long time since we had a regular exercise regime, and we spent hours in the dojo. We also introduced Elvis to the Grouse Grind, other trails on the mountains of North Vancouver, and went on paddle-boarding forays up the Indian Arm of the Burrard Inlet.

This morning, Marcy had asked to meet me in Gastown, a shopping and restaurant area just to the north of our building in Yaletown. Gastown was named after John Deighton, aka "Gassy Jack." The nickname came from his talkative nature. Deighton had been a sailor from Hull, England, and had travelled the world. He was a veteran of several goldrushes in California and

New Caledonia, and the latter became a colony of British Columbia. He is most famous for the bars he owned in New Westminster in the 1860s and in the area which is now Gastown. The neighbourhood is gradually gentrifying and is begrudgingly shared between Vancouver's least fortunate and most fortunate. I met Marcy there at 10 am, and we worked in a soup kitchen together for an hour and a half before visiting a pub in the small square next to Gassy Jack's statue.

We ordered drinks, which arrived quickly, and we then gave the server our food order, which took a little longer to appear. But we didn't care; we were lost in conversation like two relaxed young lovers should be. As our plates were set down, a woman at a far table knocked her glass on the floor with a loud crash, and all heads turned to watch. When we refocused on our table, a small, cherry red, varnished lacquer box had appeared from nowhere. It must have been left by our server. I suspected that the noisy glass-smashing was a decoy and glanced around just in time to see Chiyome, dressed as a restaurant server, step off the sidewalk into the back of a waiting car. She smiled our way, closed the door, and the car sped off.

Marcy took the box, removed the delicate ribbons that held it closed, and flipped open the lid. Inside there was a simple note.

The act of being close enough to assassinate you both, but instead leaving you this note, is designed to demonstrate my personal assurance, and that of the Kanbo, that you have nothing to fear from us. For your brave acts you have our gratitude, forever. I appreciate you may never take me up on it, but you both have a lifetime boon you may ask of us at any time, which I, or my successors, will gladly honour. For my daughter's life, I can never repay or thank you sufficiently – Mochizuki Chiyome.

This encounter put me on edge, but Marcy laughed it off and was quite insistent I have a couple of glasses of wine with her. She led the conversation away from events of today and the past weeks, and we talked about the future at length. After brunch, and time to digest our food, we both had a bit of buzz and were in a bright mood. We felt relieved now, despite the intrusion earlier.

Marcy suddenly looked at her watch and jumped up with a start.

"We better get moving if you are going to make your appointment. Come on, lazybones."

"I have an appointment? What did I forget?"

"I'll tell you as we walk!" She opened her purse and dropped cash on the table — enough to cover our cheque — and pulled me out onto the street.

"Where are we going?" I asked, pulling on my jacket.

"Just here," she replied, with an evil grin, pointing to a doorway next to the bar we had just rushed out of; I was confused. She pulled two envelopes out of her bag, one addressed to me and the other to a Janet Jenkins.

"I got to realizing a couple of things this week," she explained, with a coy smile. "Firstly, your house is one big mancave. You were a bachelor there for too long, and it needs a woman's touch. So I've decided it needs some new artwork. Something more to my taste."

"OK. Are we going to a gallery?"

"Um, not quite." She bit her lip and smiled cheekily.

"The other thing I realized is that we just solved the case of the missing woman, followed by the case of the Nimbus. The castle in Durham covered the missing woman, but you still owe me, Booker. Time to pay. Up you go! And make me proud!" she commanded. With that, she walked – no, she skipped – away laughing. I had a bad feeling.

I scratched my head and pulled open the envelope with my name on it.

My Beloved Slave,
Please proceed up the stairs and give the other envelope to Janet Jenkins. Janet and I crossed paths through my previous employer, and she runs a quality photography establishment. She is expecting you, and you are to pass on the envelope. It contains a variety of photographs I arranged for her to take of a new talent in the Vancouver 'modeling' world. You. Watching you work out all week reminded me what a fantastic bod you have, honey, and I think it might look good on our wall. We will have to see how it comes out. The list inside her envelope contains a series of progressively more revealing suggestions for pictures she should provide to me – and only to me. I also gave her full licence to do what she thinks might look good. You have the easy part; you just have to follow her instructions, without question, and look your best. Who knows how far she will take it?
Lovingly yours – Phoenix

I looked up at the staircase and read the name of the establishment. "Jenkin's Boudoir Photography."

Oh, crap!

End

BOOK THREE – THE NUDEST DETECTIVE

As I publish The Nuder Detective – book two in The Nude Detective series – The Nudest Detective – book three – is firmly under construction. The outline is complete and spans three centuries. Moy Lei, Gia, Naomi, Jim, Max, Kelsie and Darcy return, and will all need to step up if Ethan and Marcy are going to survive the thrilling conclusion to the trilogy.

The target release date for book three is December 2019.

Check www.melissajaneparker.com and subscribe for the latest news about Ethan and Marcy's adventures

ACKNOWLEDGEMENTS

My fantastic partner and fun collaborator, who believed in my writing ability – perhaps before I did – and who helped me maintain my drive and discipline (no pun intended). The only personal fan club I could ever need.

Anita Kuehnel, whose unrivalled editing skills (and matching tact), combined with some invaluable story suggestions, helped me make a better book.

Cappy, a thoughtful test reader who provided many perceptive and valuable insights.

The women, men, and recently acknowledged variations — in our new non-binary world — who have battled for equity and recognition for their gender, race, age, orientation, and/or kink.

The many brave people who have researched – often at significant professional and personal risk – the psychology, physiology, culture, history, and evolution of BDSM and similar topics. Fascinating stuff. Thanks to their efforts, and freely shared findings, I was able to reach a more educated viewpoint than would have been possible in previous decades.

I encourage anyone with an interest in BDSM to do their own research and form their own opinion. Whether you end up with a conservative or liberal viewpoint at the end of that journey, at least it will be based on the new data, which didn't exist before this century, instead of the dogma from the 1900s and before.

The inventors of the internet. A fascinating part of my journey was realizing how the internet allows us to amass data to *combat stigma,* and provides the ability to connect and find out that *we are not alone.* A dramatic acceleration to social change. If we are ever to reach fairness and equity in our lifetime, the internet is invaluable to our quest.